GALLOWS DOME

BOOKS BY NOLAN KNIGHT

The Neon Lights Are Veins
Gallows Dome

Collection
Beneath the Black Palms

NOLAN KNIGHT

GALLOWS DOME

Crimson Gate Books

Cover design by JT Lindroos

ISBN-13: 978-1-971751-27-6

For T & C

Leave the road
Follow the path

I closed my eyes
so I could see the way
waiting for the world's end
it happens every day
hand of glory
—The Flesh Eaters, "Hand of Glory"

And the dawn
don't rescue me
no more
—The Band, "It Makes No Difference"

PROLOGUE

With the sun his god, Repo Helm knew better than to curse a giant star for California's dead soil. Arid farmland had brought prosperity, for him at least—albeit fleeting. His pistachio ostrich boots kicked through pits in what used to be a healthy apple grove. He was meeting with the orchard's owner to discuss why their business had spoiled worse than his harvest. A lone acre ripe with Pink Ladies glistened under moonlight up ahead, its crisp scent churning Repo's guts. After all these years, the prospect of violence still made him hungry.

He wiped sweat from his goatee and brow, adjusting a weary trucker's cap. A picnic table sat at the heart of the lush grove. Standing before it was the owner, Willis, a tall drink of water in a bone Stetson. As Repo approached, Willis met him with an outstretched palm. Shaking the man's hand, he noticed a large boy holding a rifle, beyond.

"My grandson," said Willis. "Caught him out here taking aim at railroad signs back that way."

Repo nodded to the boy, looked to be in his late teens, a linebacker. The kid leaned the rifle on the table at his grandpa's request.

"Hope it didn't take you long to drive down, Mr. Helm."

"Easy coast from Greenfield to San Miguel, but you know that."

"This time a day, I suppose. Six car pile-up yesterday. Pregnant gal lost her baby. 'Nother fella lost an arm."

"We all have our stories."

"Indeed, Mr. Helm." He pointed to the boy. "Ours began here, four generations ago. One of the most bountiful farmlands in California for a spell. Now look at her..." He removed his cap, head wagging. "All them politics behind water rights—damn drought—what have you...Trying to teach the boy here that no one can ballpark what the future holds anymore. Not much reward for hard work these days either. Family business has been forced to adapt to unforeseen elements."

Repo pierced through the man's banter with an empty gaze.

"You've come down 'cause our relationship has hit an impasse, correct?"

He didn't flinch.

"That's a shame, really. Thought we had us a good thing going—you supply the goods, me an' my boys deliver."

Repo inched closer. "Where's the money?"

Willis nodded to his grandson; the kid pulled a briefcase from under the picnic table and slid it over.

"Do I need to open it, or you gonna tell me?"

"It's all there."

"What took you so long?"

"Some a the product never made it to its final destination. Had to track it down like a wounded elk."

"Funny." Repo leaned in. "That's not what I heard."

"Oh really? Do tell."

"I hear you got a problem with my new endeavor. Feel conflicted working for me all the sudden—was about to pinch and cut loose, then got cold feet."

Willis smiled, exposing missing molars. "I never once saw you as a boss, Mr. Helm. Always thought us moving your dope as bein' independent contractors. Equals, really."

"Ain't nothing equal here between us." Repo turned to the boy. "Don't you reach for that fuckin' rifle."

From behind a patch of trees emerged a slim black figure, pistol in hand; the shadow stealthily approached, out of sight to Willis and the boy. Repo had told his elder cohort, X, to survey the grounds as an added precaution and there he was, right on time, as always. His right hand. These days, good help was hard to find.

Repo's shoulders eased. He plucked an apple off a tree, admiring its shine. "What's on your mind, Willis?"

"It true what they say—about this Gallows Dome?"

"Depends. What they say?"

"Say you preaching a one-way ticket to the end of days? Using some of this drug money to hold an ungodly ceremony—that you plan on starting a hedonistic church?"

"You heard wrong, Willis. I've had my go of religion. Didn't take. And The Dome ain't gonna pose a threat for anyone in these parts."

"How you figure?"

"The Dome ain't a problem—it's a *solution.*"

Willis spat, grumbling.

"I'm confused, old man. You already forget about the Great Recession? Haven't I helped you keep this farm's title in your name? Have I slighted you by supplying a means to feed your family?"

"My brood are a God-fearing bunch, Mr. Helm. And because of this...this nonsense, a line must be drawn somewhere."

"How 'bout right here?" Repo carved his boot into soil. "*God-fearing,* you say?" He huffed. "All this time, I pegged you for a *me-fearing* bunch. For such heavenly creatures, never once did you have a problem transporting dope to city folk—now, why's that?"

Willis shrugged. "He *is* mysterious, I'll attest to that—has a plan for us all. One day you'll meet Him too. Face the wrath for what you're about to sow. And my family won't have the burden of playing any part in it."

"That your final answer?"

"We just can't knowingly support blasphemy, Mr. Helm. You

understand?"

"And you thought by stealing my money, that that would somehow prevent Gallows Dome from moving forward?" He smirked.

"Not at all. Like I told you, there was a hiccup, some of the product never made it—"

"*Shhh.*"

"Excuse me?"

Repo bounced the apple from the crook of his elbow, back to his palm. X was now ten feet behind the boy, his wraparound sunglasses glinting moon rays, pistol leveled at the back of the kid's skull.

Repo bit into the apple. "All this talk about your righteous family...Let me tell you a bit about mine. My pops was a sleight-of-hand man. Not a magician by any means, but a thief. A good one too. Would steal cars, fence goods, run numbers. My old man knew how to spark a dollar, and let's just say, I inherited the curse."

"And now here we are."

"Yessir." Repo unbuttoned a loop on his shirt, scratching his chest. "When I say sleight-of-hand, I mean he was a master of *the touch.* Example: One time he brought home a live lamb. No bullshit. Some farmers—much like yourself—couldn't pay off a small debt, so he took one of their herd. My baby brother, Darcy, and I thought it was fuckin' great, right? Our own little pet. But Pa made it known that it wouldn't be anything but food for us, and we understood. So, we grabbed some sprigs of lettuce and took it out back. Pa told us—and I'll never forget this—'Calmer the beast when killed, the better it tastes.' Now, we didn't know if that was true or not, being just city boys. But one thing's for certain—a clean cut through the throat is necessary—lets the lamb bleed out real quick. After being told this, Darcy damn near fainted; he's never been one for the sight of blood—the two of us worlds apart. See, I embraced what was about to happen, felt a calm wash over." He held the apple before the old man's dumb grin.

Willis' eyes bounced from the fruit to Repo.

"My pop held that lettuce—just like this. Soon as the lamb went for a nibble." His hand shot past Willis' jugular.

X fired the pistol; the boy's head burst before he crumpled to dirt.

Willis went to turn his head toward the shot but couldn't. His eyes bulged, fixed on the small blade in Repo's fist. The burn of hot blood oozed down his chest. He grabbed his neck, gurgling, clawing at the bench for help but never reaching the rifle.

Repo sliced a sliver of apple and tossed it in his mouth. *Tastes good, don't it?*

X walked over, firing one final round that exploded Willis' heart.

Repo outstretched the apple to X.

"No, thanks. Already ate 'bout a dozen."

"How long you been out here?"

"Too damn long."

Repo wiped the blade before sliding it back under his shirt and into its sheath, dangling on a steel cord around his neck.

X grabbed the briefcase.

Willis' lifeless stare beamed back, frozen for eternity.

They strolled out the grove.

X cleaned his sunglasses, leaning against the trunk of Repo's two-tone Seville, the middle finger of his right hand lopped to a nub.

"How can you see through those things on a night like this?"

X slid the shades on. "Decades of practice."

"Someone on their way to clean this mess?"

"P-Stone just texted. He'll be here in ten."

"Should be here already."

"What can I say? The dude be slippin' lately."

"Where you parked?"

"Half mile that way, over them railroad tracks."

"Lemme give you a ride."

X slid inside the Caddy; Repo tossed the briefcase in the back seat. As they drove out the orchard, Repo said, "Listen, I want you to take this car and head to Los Angeles. Have to grab one last thing needs priming for the ceremony."

"Now?"

"After you drop this cash off with my wife. She's done her homework and will fill you in on everything regarding this L.A. situation. There's a girl. Need her delivered to the ranch."

"This girl know I'm comin' for her?"

"No."

X sparked a cigarette, marinating. "Alive, right?"

"Yeah—and intact."

"Not a problem."

"X."

A "Yeah" burst through a haze of smoke.

"We need her *intact*."

"X-man got you, Mr. Helm. Don't even trip."

Repo pulled the Caddy beside X's rust bucket Buick. X-man handed over his car keys, got out and slid into the Seville's driver seat. The warm leather toasted his hide like a glove.

Repo bent to the window. "Call us when you have the girl. We'll secure everything from there on out—have her transported to the ranch."

"Sounds good."

"Play it cool. Keep your nose clean."

"Hey, come on now."

They shared a laugh.

"Where *you* headed?"

"Supposed to meet up with my brother soon, talk business. He's making sure The Dome will be in full force, legally speaking."

"Tell Darcy I said hey."

"Will do. Travel safe now."

X-man watched his boss jump railroad ties, melting into darkness, a wayward phantom.

PART ONE
LOST HIGHWAYS

1.

The storm's flurry wasn't to blame for Los Angeles County Fire and Rescue calling a halt to their search for Tess Madadhi, a Santa Clarita teen believed to have been swept into a current of mud and debris—victim of a severe flash flood. Rescuers had been busy for over forty-eight hours when the girl's mother, Lena, paused from biting her cuticles beneath a sheriff's canopy and was whisked into the rear of an unmarked sedan. The driver and copilot were in plain clothes, badges hanging over hearts; their eyes darted to the rearview before turning their stone faces to her.

Lena gripped a headrest, her chestnut hair dripping wet. "Did you...find? Is she—she's not—she can't be?" Shock had zapped all strength, leaving her words floating. Before anything was said to her, Lena went lax, weeping through raindrops about her cheekbones.

But young Tess hadn't been found alive or presumed dead—at least not yet.

Something had surfaced, shifting all focus on the girl's disappearance. Lena was told she would be taken to headquarters.

The entire ride down, she replayed the past two days, trancing on the car's windshield wipers or out her rear window—the moon, a smoker's fingernail. She'd risen early on Monday, having to do some further prep before her midday lecture at CalArts. Soon as the toaster sprung, she bolted outside, foregoing a customary kiss to her only child, not wanting to wake her. They had been a duo since birth, teammates against the world. This lost kiss was now a writhing worm in the soils of her brain. How was she to know the day could take such a turn?

The nightmare began when a new professor interrupted her class:

"Pardon me, Ms. Madadhi. I need a word."

She excused herself from the classroom. "What's up, Stacey? Lock yourself out of the office again?"

The woman's face remained frozen, flush.

"Well, what the hell is it?"

"There are some gentlemen outside—police officers. They're asking to speak with you?"

"Me?" Her brain pinballed every terrible thing she'd ever done. "About what?"

Stacey started to tremble. "About your daughter."

Whenever rain came to Los Angeles, it was met by ten million skeptics. With the state still locked in severe drought, this untimely storm held up to expectations, gushing more than barren foothills could handle. Flash flood warnings were put into place, but only after sludge began to slide. The largest section impacting the Santa Clarita Valley ran directly adjacent to Tess' middle school. Normally, when a student was truant, the office waited until third period to notify the child's parent or guardian, as mental lapses for doctor's appointments and such were often the case. With the sudden flooding being so severe, and young Tess never arriving to her first class, they attempted to contact Lena. Lena's phone was shut off for the start of her class. When she didn't pick up and faculty at Tess' school felt something was awry, proper authorities were notified, fearing a worst-case scenario.

***

As the sedan pulled into the precinct's parking lot, Lena began to shake, knowing damn well the amount of time that had passed and that she was now entering a *worst-case* kingdom. The detectives gave her a blanket and sat her in a cold room with jaundiced walls, one reserved for shackled thugs. She continued to shiver as the black cop wheeled in an ancient television. The second one smelled of *tres flores*, short and obese, he placed coffee before her, its creamy hue matching her skin tone.

Lena pushed the cup aside. "Can someone just *please* tell me what the fuck is going on?"

Tres flores: "We caught something on tape you need to see."

"What is it?"

"While out canvassing with Tess' picture on her normal route to school, an ARCO clerk recognized her. Said she'd purchased an energy drink earlier that day. Sheriff's department confiscated all surveillance video. A disturbance was captured upon review."

"Show me." Lena peered into the static-laced tube, searching for clarity as if, at any moment, she would catch the blip of an apparition.

"Clerk said that ownership recently set up a hidden camera on the roof after thieves had tampered with a cage of propane tanks. Now watch here; it happens at the 8:18 mark."

Tess entered an external frame positioned at the rear of the gas station. There, she was approached from behind by a lithe, swarthy male, clad in a dark ballcap and hoodie. Cops said he was either black or Hispanic, but they couldn't be sure. Lena wringed her hands as Tess fidgeted with her soft drink on the screen, oblivious of the predator. Lena screamed the moment this monster removed a blurry item from his pocket, raised it quickly and plunged it into her daughter's neck.

Tess slowly crumbled on the screen.

Lena collapsed to the floor, never witnessing the entirety of her darling's abduction.

***

She blacked out during the news presser, lulled by empty eyes of reporters, flash bulbs like fireworks in the skull. The lead detective took over once Lena's silence hit crescendo, gently nudging her into the arms of a fellow female officer. The embrace of a stranger had Lena wishing she had someone else for comfort. But no one was left, she an only child herself with both parents below ground. No boyfriends or lovers since before Tess. After that weekend binge in Vegas, she never heard from Tess' father again—the name he gave her a blatant lie.

Was this an aftershock to all those sinful years?

Hours upon hours spent kneeling at Reconciliation...Father Calhoun assured her that she'd been absolved, her tears for mercy enough for Him to cleanse. But how could past transgressions melt away with a simple nod? Her love and devotion to Tess was only a means to salvation. Calhoun triumphed her "raising an angel" at nearly one Mass per month; but a glimmer in his eye always told Lena he really meant "bastard."

There was no true forgiveness in this world.

A human being was not capable.

Her repent was null and void now. Tess' kidnapping *was* an act of God: a declaration of war, a test of her mettle.

Now, she must walk through the fire.

Days turned into weeks. National news sensationalized the tragedy, utilizing the audacity of the act for a bump in their ratings; however, no new evidence came from it. A reward put up for information leading to Tess' whereabouts and the arrest of her kidnapper teetered on fifty grand. But the calls to detectives became fewer and fewer. Lena began calling them for updates, as if they wouldn't have phoned when something broke. Fresh cases were profiled on L.A. newscasts: homicides, hit-and-runs...No person owned the spotlight. Tess had received her spell; now that beam swung to the next tragedy.

Neighbors attempted to console Lena with food those lingering weeks. Seemed like every time the doorbell chirped, there was a new face holding a foil-wrapped platter of commiseration.

"Hi there. Lena, is it? Howdy, we're you're neighbors at 501 over there—"

"Where?"

The stout woman slowly turned, pointing directly across the street.

"Oh, yeah. You moved in when?"

"About two years ago."

"That's right. Nice to finally meet you."

"Yes, well. Thought a little Frito casserole was in order, considering the circumstances. I mean, we get the paper and...well...this might cheer you up through these hard times."

Lena took the warm plate. "I appreciate your concern. Thanks for...this."

"Frito casserole. My own recipe."

Lena lingered on the woman's chipped fingernails.

"Well, then. I won't disturb you any longer, Lena..."

Soon as the door closed, every forced meal made its way into the garbage. One of Lena's greatest achievements was purchasing a home for her and Tess, a simple two-bedroom with rugged views. She'd always seen the beauty in Canyon Country. Had she known they'd still be living among strangers, she never would've left Downtown Los Angeles. But her career advancement urged the move. The commute to CalArts now was nothing compared to traversing the city. Schools for Tess were better too. Could hike through Vasquez Rocks or be at Castaic Lake in no time. The city would always be there. This was their sanctuary from that never-ending hustle. Going into town for modern art exhibits or to catch a Dodgers game was only a short drive away. Daycations. The best of both worlds...so Lena thought.

When she told her employer it would just be a sabbatical, she knew better. She'd return to work once her life was back intact: a floating question mark without any answer. Finding Tess was her only priority, good or bad, alive or dead. With police efforts on their pilot light, she had no other option but to take up the case herself.

Tess' scent lingered in her bedroom, albeit much less than the first night Lena slept on her girl's bed. Photos and trinkets lined every wall; typical teenage keepsakes: cute clothes, toy animals—baby-faced boys. Tess loved to draw, puppy sketches mostly. Yorkies were her favorite, many in fine-line strewn atop her desk. A picture taken at church of the two of them was framed on a dresser; Lena blew a kiss at it each morning, admiring the last photo of her kid. Tess' features were fleshing into adulthood: no more baby fat, an olive complexion. With hazel eyes below a short mocha bob, she was easing gracefully into those loathsome high school years. Granted, Tess was a good child, Lena left nothing to chance—emptying every drawer, backpack and notebook, attempting to find a magic key behind her vanishing. Police had dubbed the abduction "a random act of violence." Regardless, Lena dug into Tess' cell. Facebook/Twitter/Instagram/Snapchat. Emails and texts. Tess' password was always her favorite My Little Pony: *Rarity*. The most startling thing Lena came across wasn't a picture or message, but a glib comment beneath a photo of some shirtless dunce from school named Garret Jenkins; Tess had typed, TASTES YUMMY. LOL.

Lena rose from the bed, yawning in her pee-jays as if it wasn't already dinner time. With her investigation headquarters being at home, most days began to pass her by. She went into the kitchen to uncork a cabernet.

The detectives were Bo Martin and Ivan Banuelos. Lena was on a first name basis with both these days, although she could sense everyone was tired of her droopy face popping into the precinct, unannounced:

"Miss, detectives Martin and Banuelos are not in the office at this time."

Lena's elbows crowded the secretary's desk. "I just saw their unmarked car in the parking lot."

"Miss, all of the unmarked sedans generally look alike."

"They all got a dent on the rear left fender?"

The woman sighed.

"Seriously, I need to speak with them!"

"They are on lunch."

"Oh, great. Where? The usual spot—Big Wangs in Stevenson Ranch?"

"Miss...*please*..."

After a legion of texts and a few more precinct visits, eventually Banuelos answered and swung by Lena's home to bring her up to speed on Tess' file. This wasn't protocol, but more an act of kindness. Lena saw it as a sign of cultural solidarity—Ivan somehow convinced she was of Mexican descent. Well, she never claimed she wasn't. But she didn't care why he let her peruse the file, taking notes and pictures; although, she would've done *anything* that he asked for the opportunity. Hell, most of the skeletons that lurked in her past made chubby little Ivan look like a goddamn Adonis.

Before he could start in on the case, Ivan had to take a work-related phone call in Lena's backyard; she watched as he gazed upon monstrous clouds in a painfully blue sky, wondering what new crime had stained which happy family. She splashed the file's contents atop the dinner table. Its bulk contained either facts she'd memorized or false leads that never panned out. Pages of scribbled notes featuring crossed-out detective jargon remained intact for fear of retreading. There was a crisp manila that held video screenshots of the abductor—same video she'd seen at the station that night. She was thumbing through them when Ivan came back inside.

"Those are the best profiles of the bunch. We've been canvassing with them, but so far, no dice. Caught something we hadn't seen in the initial viewing of the tape though." He leaned over her shoulder.

That cheap floral pomade in his slicked hair forced her to stop breathing.

His finger pointed to the culprit's fist. "Right there, see it?"

"See what?"

"Guess I should say, what *don't* you see?"

Lena squinted at the image, locking onto the man's right middle finger. *It was missing.* "Is there a way to—"

"We've already run it through our database—obtained a federal sweep as well. *Nada.*"

"Can I have one of these?"

"Yeah, sure."

She placed the photo aside and scavenged, hoisting up what appeared to be a laundry list printed onto a canary sheet: Snicker's wrapper, glazed donut (partial), Flyin' P coffee cup, Winston cigarette butts (2)..."And this?"

Ivan plopped onto her purple sofa, exhaling in fatigue. "Trash can."

Lena's eyes went back to that photo; there was a waste bin in the foreground of the camera's view. She held it up. "This one?"

"Yeah. A list of its contents. Only a few items. Was a long shot but figured, why not? Maybe this perp was huddled back there, smoking cigs, wolfing donuts—lying in wait for a victim. Could've disposed something with DNA on it. A long shot but..."

"No dice."

"Yeah."

She reread the list, recognizing an image on the coffee mug of a bombardier pig dropping a missile with the letter P. Flyin' Ps were big rig service stations throughout the state. Three summers ago, they'd held a contest for an artist to design their new logo— this logo; Lena had heard about it on the radio and urged her students to submit.

"What about this cup?"

"What about it?"

"Have you canvassed Flyin' P truck stations in California?"

"Me personally? No."

"Well, anyone then? This could be something major right here. Do other departments know about this clue?"

Ivan rose and placed a hand on her shoulder. "Lena, we're trying our best, okay? Have faith. Something can pop up any minute and break this thing."

She deflated, gently cupping his hand, finger grazing his wedding band.

He left her alone with the file for another ten minutes before wrangling it with a rubber band and gunning his unmarked toward oblivion.

She hadn't seen black hairs on her legs this long since the fifth grade, a time she thought herself part-spider. She reminisced giving Tess her first shaving tutorial, a few years back. As she demonstrated razor strokes, images of her girl in diapers clawed the heart.

Those days at the zoo, gazing at giraffes.

Walks on Venice Beach, our toes seeped into shoreline.

That was *then.*

These days, showers were meant for crying—the only time of day she allowed herself to breakdown; the crux of her efforts demanded deep focus and resiliency—a well of strength for Tess. The laptop on her prickly knees beamed a website for missing Los Angeles persons. She monitored it daily for new cases, hoping to see one that could put a fresh twist on her daughter's abduction. But most were either older citizens suffering from dementia or prostitutes/runaways that would surface by week's end (some in jail, others at the morgue). There hadn't been a decent lead from the Facebook page she'd set up to profile the case; however, she refused to let hope diminish. After all, she could feel Tess' heartbeat with each thump of her own.

In between meals of mac 'n' cheese or French bread pizza, she'd relax by watching a true crime show about others who'd disappeared, aptly titled, *Thin Air*. Most of the cases remained unsolved, the occasional episode ending in murder. The constant downer was not what drew her to the show. Commiseration with other damned parents also wasn't essential. The spectrum of temperaments within every case caused concern; she'd focused on the universal unraveling of police procedures during those first crucial hours, re-enforcing her notion that the sheriff's department had done right by Tess—and they had. Most missing person cases started with the investigation of the victim's days leading up to their disappearance, their actions and words often establishing a motive behind an absconding. Lena took this fact and ran with it, contacting every friend, teacher and acquaintance that Tess had been in touch with those days prior. Closing in on one month's time, she'd received all the answers she'd been searching for.

Again, there was nothing suspicious.

A random act of violence...

The calendar on Lena's phone lit her oily face: Tomorrow it would be six weeks. Her finances were dwindling. She'd already downgraded her Audi to an Accord, cashing in at CarMax. Would put up the house too, when it came to it. The only real items she needed beside food and alcohol these days were new clothes— some Walmart cheapies. Her wardrobe was still nice, only it didn't fit anymore: She'd dropped just under thirty pounds, weighing lighter than her college years. Had to make it a point to go shopping when she got a sec.

Creepy piano chords sparked a new *Thin Air*.

Lena rushed to pour another cran-vodka, leaping over trash and laundry into the kitchen.

***

It was an L.A. episode—one not featuring Hollywood for once. Another girl lost, this one from Long Beach. Her name was Rochelle Anne Quell, sixteen, dirty blonde hair with a beach bunny build. Pictures of her were angelic, hairdo and clothes quite dated. She'd vanished nearly a decade ago—January 15, 2009. The narrative began with some poorly trained actors; the lead hardly resembled the *real* Rochelle. These were the most trying parts of every episode, tepid reenactments, poorly lit, shot by hack directors. The lead detective in Rochelle's case had since retired, a gaudy Hawaiian shirt covering his inner death for the camera. He began with the girls' family dynamic, an only child torn between divorced parents. The father came on the screen. He was seated on a sailboat named *Bessie Mae*. Lena recognized some structures in the shot's background: Shoreline Village, used to take Tess there to ride the carousel. Without the disappearance of his daughter, anyone could tell the man had lived a full life: leathery skin, a long, ashen beard. He was a salty dog, arms bleeding blue tattoos (all kitchen work). The growl in his voice was intimidating, but whenever he said *Rochelle*, the tone fell into a gentle zone. Lena zombied the flat screen, chomping cuticles in between hearty swigs of sweet juice.

There was another torn parent in town, one who'd experienced her same hell...

She grabbed the laptop, eyes bouncing back to the screen before Googling the name, Perry Quell.

2.

Perry Quell was digging dregs out a corned beef hash tin onto a hot plate when the television called his name. He licked his fingers, knowing damn well what was on, searching for the remote control. The hull of his boat was cluttered with old mail, paperwork and news articles; he swiftly moved piles to see where the clicker had fallen. The tube called out again, this time, *Rochelle.* He turned to catch the image of his girl. *Thin Air.* He'd been interviewed for her episode five years ago. *Shit, there hadn't been an easy day since '09.* The sailboat rocked gently from his jostling. He waited for her picture to fade off the screen before unplugging the TV at its source.

His dinner was burned, so he added extra hot sauce, eating on the deck, cracking another tallboy. Stars shimmered high above The Queen Mary, just outside Shoreline Marina—one of the few places in Los Angeles County they could still be seen. He'd been in this slip going on twenty-three years. It was peaceful, although he had to march the dock at night to take a shit. Used to captain the *Bessie Mae* out for fishing trips off Catalina—twilight harbor cruises even, but ever since Rochelle, well, Perry hadn't taken her anywhere but for maintenance.

What was the point?

To enjoy this life?

He'd do that soon as Rochelle came back.

A dragonfly buzzed overhead. He swiped hash from his moustache, listening to seals cry in the distance.

Fresh sunrays pierced vintage neon signs as Perry walked from a Belmont Heights bus stop, down Broadway, heading to work. The 36 36 Club was a drinker's establishment that opened at 6 a.m. sharp, seven days a week. Many of the night birds frequenting the bar scoffed at the untimely start, and Perry was always first to tell these co-eds (or worse) that morning hours weren't for *them*. Weren't for drunkards either. Most early birds had just gotten off overnight shifts at the docks: crane operators, welders, stevedores. Working men and women who'd put in their solid twelve and needed to unwind before bedtime. Most of the other patrons he'd known since Wilson High. To love this city was to respect it, and the people about Long Beach made that downright easy. Snot-nosed brats from CSULB were the least of his concerns.

A bell chimed as he walked into Loma Liquor; he headed past a small Vietnamese clerk glued to a newscast on a tiny screen beside the register, grabbed a pack of Ding Dongs and swiped a *Press Telegram*.

"Morning, Sammy. What's the shitstorm today?"

"Fuckin' Lakers, man."

"Ain't worth the stress. Look at you—like someone pissed on your boots."

"Story of my life."

"I hear that. Gonna need a handle of Tito's, a tall Bulleit and the usual Patrón."

"Going dry over there, or what?"

"Not on rotgut. Been cutting back on premiums for the day-timers. They never buy the shit, but it looks good on the top shelf. Now's time to replenish."

Sammy rose from his stool, eyeing the wall of liquor at his back.

"Toss me a pack of Reds while you're at it." He perused the

paper's front page, eyes skipping atrocities. "'Nother shooting in Cambodia Town yesterday."

"I heard."

"Kids these days…"

"No respect for human life." Sammy stamped a pack of cigs on the counter and grabbed a stepladder to gather the order.

The bell chimed.

Perry looked up from his paper to see a young man entering in baggy jeans and a crisp white shirt, four sizes too big. He took in the sight as if the boy were a two-headed freak. The boy sidled him at the counter, demanding "papers" from Sammy. No hello. No good morning. Sammy eyed Perry, letting him know this one was trouble. The kid reached for his wallet, somewhere near the back of his knee. Perry shook his head, a *pfft* expelling from his lips.

The boy turned. "Say what?"

Perry smiled at the engagement, wanting nothing more than to destroy. "Was just admiring your costume, son. That shirt. My daughter had a dress just like it."

The kid puffed out his chest. "Fuck you say?"

"You heard me. Now, pay the man."

The boy scoffed, grabbing the Zig Zags, turning to leave.

Perry said, "Hell you think you're goin'?"

"Shut your cunt mouth, grandpa."

Perry lunged, grabbing the kid by the neck and wrist, cranking the arm behind the boy's back. When the dunce began to squirm, he slammed his bald head onto the counter, smooshing his face atop lottery ticket glass. "Sammy, 'member last time I broke that guy's arm in here? The sound it made?"

Sammy laughed, "Like snapped celery. Music to the ears."

The kid's eyes grew large.

Perry cranked the arm, drawing a whimper. "You're gonna pay the man with either cash or bone, it's your choice."

"Cash."

Perry torqued. "Speak up."

"Cash, man! Cash!"

Perry let go, retrieving the sports section as the boy tossed bills at Sammy.

The bell chimed on the kid's exit.

Sammy placed Perry's order on the counter.

"Thanks. You put it on the bar's tab?"

"Sure thing."

Perry scooped the booze.

"Hey, Perr'?"

"Yeah."

"What if that kid had pulled a gun?"

"Then I'd finally get put out my misery."

Sammy went to chuckle, then saw truth in his pal's eyes.

"See you later, Sam."

The bell chimed.

Perry placed the bag of booze beside an ashtray at the club's chrome front door, flaring his second smoke of the day. The spectrum of neon about the building went from a crackling hum to nothing in an instant. Dottie must've killed them; had beat him down here, like most days. She was a big gal with purple hair, always nosing in on his business, a sweetheart half the time. In high school, she'd given him a blow job at a beach bonfire—beneath a lifeguard tower. *Summer nights.* Inhaling his lifeforce, voices resonated inside. He cracked the door with a toe to absorb an earful.

Dottie: "I'm just saying, when he gets here, don't bring it up."

Male voice: "So, you saw it?"

Earle.

"Yeah, I mean, I came across it. How could I *not* watch it again?"

"So sad. Rochelle. Sometimes we forget, you know?"

"You, maybe. Me, never. Can be a good thing though. Perry don't wanna be treated with kid gloves."

"Not what I'm saying, Dottie. Maybe you don't bust his balls in here so much."

"*Me!* Whataboutchoo, motherfucker? *'Where's my drink, Perry? Pouring awfully light this mornin', Perr'!'*"

"Fuck off."

"Fuck *you!*...Can you believe how much he's aged since then?"

"We ain't a pair a lookers anymore, but hell—I barely recognized him—"

Perry barged in, sunlight brightening the joint.

Dottie and Earle shielded themselves like vampires.

"Who, Earle?"

"What's that, boss?"

"Who can't you recognize no more?"

Dottie: "Mornin', Perry. Coors delivery should be here in a few."

"Hold up, Dot." He slid the booze onto the aged wood bar. "Answer me, Earle."

The pepper-haired duffer put his hands up in surrender, nearly knocking over his Bud.

Perry panned at the two of them. "Say it to my face, assholes!"

Dottie's voice cracked, "Last night's *Thin*—"

"Yeah, I saw it. Who fuckin' cares anymore, huh?"

Earle said, "What'ya mean? We all do."

"Yeah? Cops sure as hell don't." He swiped his Ding Dongs from out the bag and headed through pool tables to flip on the juke.

Dottie leered at Earle.

Earle hoisted his brew. "Way to go, Dot."

By midmorning, the joint had filled out with its crew of frequent ghosts. The scent off every union worker, a clash between sea grime and tobacco, tinged the nose hairs. Perry dunked filthy glasses into their bath, trying to enjoy the tune out the juke, its singer howling about a cold night for alligators; but he couldn't, not with Clark, Ollie and Earle yammering at their stools about the pussification of America.

Clark and Ollie were neighborhood regulars, vets turned bikers turned too damn old. They looked at Perry as if he were still a kid, now in his sixties. He let Dottie serve them, not wanting to get caught in the quicksand of their pointless conversations. Drying off with a mildewy rag, he squeezed past Dottie to refill the garnish tray. Hildy and her sister Mona were sucked into *The Price Is Right*; most mornings they babysat bloodys till every ice cube was toast, watching their favorite shows while dishing gossip. With two drinks max, they could never be counted on for tips. He reached for a monster jar of maraschino cherries.

Hildy slid her glass before him. "'Nother go, Perr'."

He dumped the tall glass' contents and refilled ice. "How you doing there, Mona?"

She blinked at her drink; a lone olive bobbed in clear liquid. "Still workin', hun."

He gave a heavy pour of vodka topped by a splash of mix, tossing in pickled green beans, just the way Hildy liked it. "Here you go, madam."

"Say, Perry. My granddaughter is trying out for a modeling gig on this here show."

"No shit? She's gonna be a Barker's Beaut, huh?"

Mona: "Drew Carey hosts these days, Perry…so, like, they don't call 'em girls that no more."

Hildy: "Don't listen to her, Perr'. She dunno what the hell she's talking about."

"And you do?"

"I know they call 'em Drew's Beauts, you fuckin' 'tard!"

"*Bitch*, is that so?"

Perry zoned out of the sisters' row, gazing at clacking pool balls, rehashing a moment he'd had with Rochelle. She'd planned on being a model too—not the New York type, but one featured on surfboard ads and bikini displays. She gave him a time about not being able to have pictures taken until she turned eighteen.

He wouldn't allow it, and she was feisty like her mother, Anne. One time the girl threw a fork at his face and got grounded for a month, back when they all lived under the same roof. The thought of her pouty face brought a smile. That day of her disappearance, she was two years shy of attempting her dream.

Anne received the phone call in the middle of the night. At the time, she lived in a house off 4th with her new husband, Bill, a civil servant who provided a financial and emotional blanket. Perry could still hear the knocks from his neighbor in slip Q-08, notifying that some folks were shouting his name at the dock's gate. Soon as he saw his ex's eyes, he knew something terrible had struck their baby.

Rochelle had gone behind their backs, but there wasn't time to get angry. She'd answered an ad in the back of an *L.A. Weekly*—some company that provided cheap headshots to actors and models. Her friends told police that after school that day she'd hopped on the Metro Blue Line, planning to hit transfers up into the San Fernando Valley. The ride alone would've taken her well over two hours from Long Beach, so none of her pals would accompany her. But Rochelle was determined, leaving her cell phone in a school locker as not to be traced. Owners of the company (a pair of young newlyweds) were legit; however, it turned out that Rochelle had lied to them about her age. Investigators didn't have to probe any further since Rochelle never made it to the appointment.

Metro cameras in Downtown caught glimpses of her at the 7th Street Red Line station, taking the subway up into the valley and exiting two stops short of her destination. There were no eyewitnesses on hand, and her whereabouts after leaving the station were a dead end. After months of false leads, Perry hired a private detective by the name of Joe Delancey. He'd been recommended by a detective on the case. Joe specialized in missing persons. Perry was ready for answers, although he couldn't fathom the depths to which Delancey would delve over a period of eighteen months, expensing most of Perry's life savings.

Anne and Bill had come to terms, no longer willing to toss money into an empty gorge. Anne wanted her baby back but claimed God had told her in a dream that Rochelle was dead. Perry never shared in Anne's superstitions, refusing to ever give up. Upon termination, Delancey handed over the entirety of his findings, interviews and leads, all of which now cluttered the hull of the *Bessie Mae*.

The *Thin Air* episode was prompted from a breakthrough made by Perry with Delancey's info. Joe figured that if Rochelle had gotten off at the wrong stop, there was a strong possibility she realized her error on the streets, well past the line's exit point at Lankershim and Chandler. Any normal adult would've retreated back into the subway to locate a map; however, most teens relied on adults for directions. Without her phone, Rochelle could've entered a nearby establishment looking for help.

At the time of her disappearance, there were only a handful of places she could've gone, one being a greasy spoon off Lankershim. A coworker disclosed to Joe that he'd seen a girl enter that day asking for directions who matched Rochelle's description. One customer, a heavyset truck driver who'd illegally parked his ivory rig along the boulevard, offered to show her the way. The employee couldn't discern whether the truck was a Mack, Peterbilt or other, but did recall the lug nuts being spikes. The restaurant's video didn't capture the pair upon their exit, and no further sightings of Rochelle were made. Perry handed over the information to newly assigned cold case detectives; however, white big rigs turned out to be the norm, nationwide. When nothing came from a police sketch of the driver, Perry took up where Joe had left off, borrowing a chopper from a friend and heading to truck stops outside Los Angeles. Armed with his daughter's photograph and a wish, he hammered every pit stop he came across for six months, fishing for leads on his white whale. With the amount of trucker hangouts in California alone, it was only a matter of time till he became a dog chasing its tail. This outlaw approach to justice was profiled in the *Times* with a headline that read, *LOST HIGHWAY*, a play on a popular cult film screening at a nearby revival theater when Rochelle disappeared. This headline caught the eye of a Hollywood producer in conjunction with *Thin Air*. After nothing materialized from his nomadic journey on the open road, Perry agreed to do the episode, hoping that someone out there would come forward with new information and help erase his torment.

But no one did.

And at this point in life, he was starting to believe no one ever would.

His shift ended at three o'clock, soon as all trash cans had been emptied and floors swept for the night crew. He stopped back in Loma Liquor for his daily tallboys, settling on sardines and crackers for supper. Instead of taking the bus back to the marina, he always walked along the beach, absorbing all the beauty he could handle for one day. It was a nice three-mile stroll, gazing upon empty cargo ships and island oil derricks outside a waveless shore. Runners and roller skaters returned his greeting nods, the final thread he had to the normal world. And he'd give *anything* to get back to that place, that naivety to horror—all innocence left to lose. He panned for lifeguards on patrol before cracking his first brew of the night.

Perry made it to the marina at half past five. Shoreline Village was bustling in the distance with mean happy hours in effect. He rummaged his pockets for the key to Gangway Q, a flat disc shaped like a dog tag; not the easiest thing to use. Just as he inserted the key, a gentle voice came from behind. He spun sharply. Wasn't every day a random voice called out to him.

The woman was rail thin, clothes a bit saggy about the breasts and hips. If his father's ideal woman was shaped like a Cadillac, this gal could've been a helicopter. And she didn't look homeless either, dark hair and makeup done nicely. If she wasn't carrying a manila folder, he would've thought one of those clowns on Gangway R had felt sorry for him and sent over a prostie.

She approached, her Vans sneakers squeaking warm gravel. "You're Perry Quell…right?"

"Yeah. What's this about?"

"Rochelle."

Aw, Christ. Another TV vigilante. Must've seen the episode last night and tracked him down, like the others.

"Do you have a minute to talk? My name is Lena Madadhi." She shot out a hand.

He stared at it for a beat before extending his own.

"I'm in a similar situation…"

"How's that?" He saw the glaze in her eyes, a familiar gloss he met in the mirror most mornings.

The hurt.

"My daughter, Tess…she was abduct—"

Without any words, he opened the dock gate and ushered her toward the *Bessie Mae*.

3.

The hull was too cluttered with boxes for them to sit comfortably; Perry flipped over a seagull-stained deck cushion, brushing its backside before inviting Lena to sit. The sun had fallen to its lowest point, turning the sky into rainbow sherbet. He climbed into the hull for a glass after she'd accepted a beer. He cracked a tallboy and poured half into a trophy pint that read *Yankee Doodles/9 Ball Billiard Champ/1986*. When he returned to the deck, she had a stapled document in her fist. He handed her the brew in exchange for her pages.

"That's a summarized version of events involving my daughter's case. After seeing the *Thin Air* episode last night...I had to come find you."

He perused the text. "Well, you ain't the first."

"You've had other parents with missing children reach out?"

He met her stare. "Not exactly. Internet bloodhounds, mostly. Everyone wants to help after they see a show like that—problem is, in my experience, they usually just want to take part in your misery. Like the thought of feeling something foreign to their own lives. Something terrible. They never realize it can crush 'em too."

"Well, I'm not here to bother—"

"I didn't mean you, lady. Just that, occasionally, I get visitors. That's all."

"Oh."

"Says here your girl went missing for two days before the pigs realized she was abducted?" He scanned some more. "Caught on video."

"Yes." She took a gulp off the pint.

"Hate to break it to you, but even if they started searching five minutes after the girl—"

"*Tess.*"

"After Tess was kidnapped, I'd be amazed if they were able to figure out a damn thing. All cops are alike, you see? *Heroes?* No. Civil servants—ones who take orders to wipe their own ass." He kept reading. "Now, you can say, 'But these were sheriff's deputies not boys in blue,' then I'd have to say, 'Pig's a pig no matter how slow you roast it.'"

Lena was afraid to break his tirade, thankful enough that he was reading her text. She didn't blame him; anyone would have the same perspective if they'd gone through the man's situation. Hell, she was well on her way.

"So, what exactly brought you down here, Lena? My girl went missing in '09. Yours, some weeks back. I miss something?"

"Show mentioned a private detective you worked with before you went out on the road—a Joe Delancey."

"Yeah."

"I'm trying to locate him to help find my daughter. There's no contact info for him online. I recognized this marina during your interview and came down—"

"Haven't seen Joe in years. There are plenty of other PIs in Los Angeles, you know?"

"How many of them would've gone as far as he did, searching for Rochelle?"

"Got a point there."

"Joe is who I want on my daughter's case. Do you have his contact info?"

"Used to." He drained his beer and burped. "Not sure if it's still relevant. Joe's a rambler. A runaway bloodhound if he gets a case that tickles him. Could be anywhere these days. Always changing his phone—don't have his email. See those down there?"

She gazed into the hull. "What's that?"

"*That* is everything. Boxes filled with Delancey's notes, findings. Look through 'em. Stay for long as you like. Whatever contact I have for him will be in there."

"Can I look now?"

"Knock yourself out. Getting dark, but there's a bulb down there you can light." He pulled the tin of sardines out his pocket. "Got dinner for two."

She grinned. "Thanks, Perry."

"Least I can do. Lord knows, all I wanted was for someone to help *me* when life slipped into the gutter. And pigs ain't *ever* good for that."

Lena insisted on ordering pizza in return for Perry giving her access to Delancey's documents. At first, he rejected the offer, only complying once she tossed hot wings into the deal. They ate from out the pizza box, Perry asking if she'd like a wing every few minutes.

"How long you been living in Long Beach, Perry?"

"Born and raised. Father worked the docks. Ma always held waitress gigs in Downtown. They're both gone now."

"Siblings?"

"Nope."

"Then we got another thing in common. That glass you're drinking out of...my father used to shoot pool at Yankee Doodles when I was a kid. Took me there a few times."

Perry recalled the haunt. "The heck you do to deserve that?"

"Funny. I was thinking the same thing."

"A stickman, huh?"

"He loved any kind of action, really. Born to hustle."

"What's his name?"

"You wouldn't know him—he's much older. At least, for your

sake, I hope you don't."

"Well, I never met anyone named Madadhi before tonight, if that makes you feel better."

"That's my mom's maiden name. She grew up in Lakewood. Me too for a second, till we moved to Echo Park—back when it was a war zone."

"Why'd she go an' do something like that?"

"A man."

"Say no more." Perry watched her take tiny bites off a slice, knowing damn well she couldn't have an appetite. His heart sank a little.

Their chat lasted a good hour, sprinkled with various topics: kids, work, Los Angeles. Perry marveled at her being an accomplished painter, as if she were some exotic fish. All the years of hard work that it took Lena to attain the feat was lost on him, as if she were born with a gift and that was that. Regardless, from the warm conversation, Lena realized one thing:

"To be honest with you, Perry—after catching you on television—I was kinda scared to come down here."

"Yeah, why's that? 'Cause I look like boat trash?"

She smiled, consciously realizing it was her first time in months.

"You're not scared anymore, I hope?"

Lena wagged her head. "Your hardened shell has a marshmallow center."

"I've been called worse." He held out the last buffalo wing.

She took it.

Joe Delancey's notes were barely legible, although meticulous to a fault. Every minute detail had been scribbled down—an entire box dedicated to the subway platform where Rochelle was last seen on surveillance. Lena's head began to ache; the thought of combing through all these documents just to locate a phone number or address consumed her. She reclined across manila folders in momentary defeat.

Perry was dockside, sharing a joint with a grimy neighbor, the two of them giggling like children, their raspy howls ending in coughing fits. She climbed to the deck, moon sparkling across the sleepy marina. The neighbor took notice of her.

"Friend wants you."

Perry's brow scrunched at the thought. *Friend?* "What is it, Lena?"

"There's no way I can sift through these in one sitting."

"And?"

"I have an idea."

Perry gave a look to his neighbor that sent the man back to his fishing boat. He turned to face her. "Never been big on *ideas*."

"Hear me out. Show said you two would meet up for briefings every few months at his office to compare notes from the road. If I paid you, could you take me to this office tomorrow—and, say, if he's there—introduce me, tell him about my kid—"

"Listen, I gotta go an' see a man about a dog tomorrow..."

"Come on, Perry. No bullshit. How much?"

He thought for a moment. "Ain't gotta pay me, but it's a long shot. We'd meet at a spot in Harbor City." He climbed aboard, grabbed a pen and paper and began scribbling a crude map. The way he eyed the paper screamed that he needed glasses.

"Could you please come—introduce me."

"Can't introduce yourself, huh?"

"I just imagine he's a busy guy. Can't afford to be given a raincheck. Every second that passes is a lost opportunity to find Tess."

Perry tranced on the water, knowing what he wanted to say and that Rochelle would never allow it. "I got work till three."

"I'll pick you up."

He nodded, reaching for the last tall can. "Split this?"

"No, I'll be on my way."

"Thanks for supper."

"Thanks for the hospitality." She leaned in for a hug, startling

Perry, a dog struck by a garden hose. He didn't return the gesture, so she squeezed both arms into his rib cage.

4.

Repo Helm's mean-green boots crunched down the hallway of a bed and breakfast he'd been holed up the past few days, guiding him to a heavenly scent of sausage and waffles. The Gosby House Inn, Pacific Grove. Normally when traveling, he'd stay at roadside dives or a Courtyard Marriott; however, this old canary Victorian sat directly across from another residence, one that had been converted into office space—inhabited by the law practice of his kid brother, Darcy. They were supposed to have had this meeting weeks ago, but after much hemming and hawing, today was the day.

For the grand occasion, he had ironed a cowboy button-up, cinched on a bolo and ditched his cap for combed hair. It'd been years since last seeing Darcy face-to-face, the occasional awkward phone calls their only real discourse. Repo splashed sausage links onto a plate, foregoing a questionable quiche, settling on blueberry coffee cake. He cleaned his fingers, looking out the window at the office, waiting for signs of life inside. A woman's soft voice called to him; he turned to see a pair of older couples—retirees, most likely—seated at the dining room table; they were huddled around a coffeepot, inviting him to sit and mingle. The number of antique trinkets, ghost pictures and dead-eyed dolls in the room had him on edge, but he obliged, forcing a smile and pulling a chair.

A rotund man with a crooked moustache leaned over to him, hand out. "Bob and Joanne Gunderson from Ukiah and that there's Meredith and Walt Ketchum—they're up from Morro Bay."

Repo nodded as Joanne poured coffee into his mug. He introduced himself as Stan Laurel from Goleta, here on holiday.

Walt: "No shit, like the actor—the comedian?"

Meredith: "Which one was he, dear?"

Joanne: "The skinny one, right?"

Bob took over, launching into a story about the Keystone Cops, to which Walt retorted a ditty about Abbott and Costello that lead to an uproar of laughter; Repo munched pork, eyes locked out the window on that office, ready for someone to walk up and open shop. The crowd guffawed.

Bob asked, "You surf down there in Goleta, Stan?"

Repo's teeth clenched coffee cake.

The hell you at, Darcy?

Pink neon bathed Darcy's face as he hoisted his first whiskey of the morning. The butterflies in his stomach were killed in an instant, a comforting glow returned to the brain. He checked the wall clock: thirty minutes fast. Had time for another round.

Sunlight screamed him into the living as he exited Segovia's Tavern. He gunned his purple Porsche up the Monterey peninsula to Lover's Point, cutting south into Pacific Grove. The streets were speckled with tourists and sleepy locals. Here, time crawled and birds chirped; there wasn't a single race for rats. And far as he knew, these days he was the last rat in town. Made business easier too, the type of clients he kept: upper-tier thugs needing help establishing shell businesses to launder filthy green. He pulled into his parking slot, wondering what the hell his big brother looked like these days, if he'd gone bald—earned a belly bigger than his. He climbed steps past a wooden sign that read *Jackson Helm, Esq.* Inside, the look on his secretary's face told him all he needed to know.

Repo was behind his desk, ogling picture frames, testing the edge of an ivory letter opener. Darcy stood in the doorway with a devilish smirk. They froze on each other for a beat, gazing like a pair of stray dogs before a lone bone.

"Where'd your hair run off to, Darcy?"

"Fuck you, old man. And it's Jackson these days."

"Saw that when I came up—your cute associate hadn't a clue who I was looking for."

"Know I always hated that goddamn name. Time for a change."

"Any name in the world, and you pick Dad's…"

"So what? I lack imagination—got a fine ring to it. Folks that never met the bastard find it comforting, I'm told."

They embraced with a handshake and shoulder pat.

"Well, just don't expect me to call you it."

"Of course not."

"Don't tell Mom either."

"Last I checked, the bitch was still dead."

"How could I forget?"

They shared a laugh and sat at a conference table by the window, a childhood of horrors at their backs—beatings and violence their birthright. Today began a new era, the documents strewn before them forecasting a lavish future.

Their glasses clinked (whiskey neat for Darcy; ice water for Repo). They toasted Gallows Dome's finalization as a legitimate entity. Darcy rocked back in his desk chair, grinning as Repo flipped through the paperwork again, making sure everything sang.

"You stop drinking entirely, or what?"

"Been off the sauce for years." He fingered his skull. "Need this old bean firing at capacity these days."

Darcy took a hefty swig and crunched ice. "Lemme ask you somethin'. Why a church? When it comes to money laundering, most my clients request auto shops or laundromats."

"Told you. Ain't a church."

"I know, I know. That's the way I drew it up though—nonprofit, tax exempt."

"So?"

"I'm just curious is all. Seems a lot of work for a front. Could be simpler."

"How?"

"You remember Jimmy Disco—ran whores off the Boardwalk in Santa Cruz?"

"Unfortunately."

"I just set him up with a strip joint outside Salinas. Guy sits in the bar, sippin' coffee, watching asses bounce as cash swims through, daily. Fucking mindless."

"You think dealin' with a dozen strippers nightly is the easy money?"

"Just sayin'. Starting your own chur—I mean denomination, sect, what-have-you—that's heavy lifting."

"Unlike Disco, I enjoy using my mind."

"That so?"

"How you decide on this racket anyway? When I put you through law school, always envisioned your clients being fake-titty divorcées."

"Hey, you got your people, I got mine. Never ask about your business, do I?"

"Don't wanna know 'bout mine."

"True. So, when you get this idea? The Dome."

"Dope's been haulin' a good amount the past year, needed to set up something to cover my ass. But I'd be lyin' if I said I hadn't been humoring the idea most my life. Ever since that time Pa gave us a tip on that church—one in L.A. with that Day of the Dead fiesta. 'Member that?"

"Of course. Broke into some donation boxes, hauled the best score of our young adult lives."

"Exactly. That day's stuck with me through the years, a thorn in my brain. Plenty folks praying for better lives, right? Ready to depart with their hard-earned green. Well, maybe if I presented an enticing doctrine to those searching for it..."

"Just funny, is all."

"People?"

"*You.* Never figured faith ever being on your mind."

"I had faith when the Dodgers won in '88—same when Pa said we'd score big from that damn church."

"Not what I'm sayin'."

"Spiritually, it's been on my mind too. Faith is a slippery beast, but hell...so am I. Plenty of folks out there praying for good— gotta be a bunch that're on the hunt for bad. So far, reception to the sermons has come across well, building a decent fellowship. Shit, the state of current affairs has many folks angry, wanting an escape. Figure, I'm onto something bigger."

"That's all good, transitioning into your shell, but you gotta remember The Dome's primary intent. You want it to be a ghost in this world, filtering cash first and foremost—preaching comes second."

"Of course. *Buuut*...if things keep going the way they going, might have a legitimate enterprise on our hands—first time ever."

"Hold up. *You* might have a legit enterprise. My ass has done its job and will remain seated right here. What can I say? I enjoy seeing you every nine years."

"If you say so."

"You're fixin' to be the next Benny Hinn, huh?"

"Nope. The *first* Repo Helm."

"And you're ready to leave the dope game?"

"Who said anything about leaving? Plan to punch the gas on both."

"Shit, long as I get paid, and you avoid a cage—those are my only concerns."

"Have I ever steered you wrong?"

They leered at each other.

Repo tossed over the documents. "Walk me through these one

more time."

Darcy killed his glass and leaned over. "IRS makes rules about religious organizations intentionally vague, right, to respect the religious liberties in the Constitution..."

The Gosby House cocktail hour was in full swing upon Repo's return. Bob and Walt were in the cups while Joanne and Meredith watched grandkid vids on their phones in the den. Repo declined their sloppy invites several times over, shaking hand after hand as if he were a used car salesman. Soon as the key punched into his room's door, it couldn't swing open fast enough.

Although Darcy had come through with the documentation and legalese, there was still plenty of work to be done before the Gallows Dome ceremony. First on the list was finalizing his next sermon to record and distribute. He closed the lace curtains, killing the view of the courtyard patio and its lush foliage. The teddy bear placed over the fireplace got shoved into the closet. From out his suitcase, he removed a legal pad, some colored pens and a dense book: *Clandestine Teachings of All Ages*. The ruby reading glasses he slid on would never find their way to his nose outside of being in complete seclusion. He flipped through dog-eared pages, highlighted and scribbled with notes; it was an encyclopedia of mankind's ancient occult and esoteric traditions. With chapters like *Ancient Mysteries & Secret Societies* and *Atlantis & the Gods of Antiquity*, he would pull concepts and symbols to help warp his own credo, the ideal Gallows Dome doctrine being a mashup of tried-and-true principles that could cloud fellowship minds, yet keep them thirsty for more. He flipped to a chapter titled *Ceremonial Sorcery & Magick* and began reading for hours.

...Idolatry was therefore introduced to the masses, urging the worship of select images which, initially, the wise had devised solely as symbols for study and reflection. However, throughout the

ages, false interpretations were given to these emblems and figures of the Mysteries; hyperbolic theologies were then created to confuse the minds of devotees. Those devout, deprived of their right to understanding of ancient knowledge, became forever lost in ignorance, the humble slaves to these spiritual imposters.

Repo sat back in reflection. Hadn't checked on their Savior in weeks, The Dome's future idol. Every major congregation had one. Theirs would be a trinity, something familiar to the zeitgeist. He, a father to the world's destruction. His wife, Gallows Dome's foreboding prophet, a ghost from times past—the seer of all ages. Then the girl. She would be their daughter—a Savior to be sacrificed during the ceremony for all the fellowship to see. Her death would be a symbol for the devout to cherish, an offering to usher the end of days. *Time had come to serve a taste of what's in store to those listening.* Bait on a hook into a barrel of angry fish. He pulled two phones from his suitcase: a prepaid and his personal. He dialed the burner.

X-man munched popcorn as he exited the Vista Theatre, its emerald neon popping with the last hint of sunshine about to kiss Los Feliz. From under the marquee, he turned up Hillhurst, wiping salt off his fingertips, ready to drive to Sweeney Todd's Barber Shop and get his fade on when his cell buzzed. He tossed the snack and checked the screen from out his track pants. A jumble of digits meant two possibilities: either the boss man or someone trying to sell shit.

"X-man here."

Repo spoke softly. "How's the girl?"

"Oh, she be cool. Got us a room at the Harvard House, low-key, in the back. Been feeding her dope since day one, got her strapped to the bed, let her shower every few days. Paid for months in advance, so no maids or nothin'. Nobody 'cept the stars saw me carry her inside that first night too. Been wonderin' when the hell you'd call me back. What's the word?"

"Keep her pumped and safe. Nothing else can happen to her yet. About to move her to the ranch. Have you spoken with my wife?"

A loud burst of car horns tore through the intersection.

"Say dat again?"

"Trench! Have you spoken with her?"

"Not since I left that cash, like you asked—way back when."

"She'll be calling you then. Soon."

More cars honked.

"Where the hell are you, X?"

"Just got out the movies."

"The girl's by herself?"

"Not really."

"What you mean?"

"Got me one of them baby monitors—camera feeds to my phone. She asleep right now. Prolly wake in a hour or two, ready for another dose."

"Huh. See anything good?"

"What?"

"The movie."

"*Sheeit!* Only thing Hollywood's good for nowadays is a guaranteed nap and some stale ass popcorn." He approached the Seville, parked in a metered slot, admiring its beauty while listening to further instructions. "You got it, Mr. Helm. Don't even trip. X-man's on the bitch. Talk soon."

The call went dead. X slid inside the ride, fired it up, cranking the stereo, singing along: *Diamond in the back, sunroof top, diggin' the scene with a gangsta lean...*

5.

There were no tears in the shower today. Lena carefully groomed her body with a zest she'd not felt in a long time. She slept through the night, waking up eager to slay the day. Her wardrobe was still an issue, but there was no time to go shopping. Perry was off at three, and she wanted to arrive early at his bar, order a couple cocktails to ease the nerves she knew she'd have when meeting Joe Delancey.

The outfit she threw together was casual yet strong. To her surprise, a pair of marbled stretch Levi's she'd bought Tess this X-mas (but were too big) fit nicely. Tattered motorcycle boots, a frayed charcoal pocket tee and her favorite leather jacket rounded out the ensemble. She printed out a fresh case summary and slid it into an accordion with Tess' copied police docs.

Delancey would listen.

Delancey would help.

She repeated this mantra the entire drive down to Long Beach.

There was a parking spot in a residential neighborhood across from the bar. The 36 36 Club's neon was nostalgic—straight out the Atom Age. She entered its chrome front door, removed her sunglasses and was met by the stares of two fogies playing a quiet game of pool. A thick woman with violet hair—some bizarro

Betty Page—smiled behind the wood bar. Lena grabbed a stool before a television, the juke starting to spin one of her all-time faves.

Oh, baby don't it feel like heaven right now…

"What can I getcha, doll?"

"Take a Cape Cod, please."

"Kinda vodka?"

"Well's fine."

"Ain't fine, but it'll work, right?"

Lena returned the woman's warm grin. She wanted to ask for Perry—needing to know if he made it to work today—but refrained, not wanting to draw any more attention to herself. A remote control was placed next to the drink before her.

"Put on anything you like, hun."

"Thanks."

The women's bathroom door slammed open; Perry emerged with a mop and bucket. The sight of Lena didn't surprise him. He nodded in greeting, fumbling the items into a rear closet. Coming behind the bar, he nudged past the barkeep, saying, "Excuse me, Dot," before scooping nuts into a paper tray and sliding it before Lena.

She tossed a peanut into her mouth. "Nice place."

"Yeah? Well, I only cleaned the shitter since you were coming."

Dottie chimed, "Bullshit, Romeo."

His eyes rolled. "Dottie, this' my friend, Lena—Lena, this lady cracks my whip."

"Nice to meet you, Dottie."

Dot reciprocated the gesture. "How you two know each other?"

Lena: "We're doing business—"

Perry choked, "Boat stuff—she wants a slip on Gangway R. Told her I'd talk to some folks. She's paying me a shit ton more than *this* dump."

Dottie smiled, not believing a word out the two, but not caring enough to pry either. "Well, then. I'll leave ya to your *business*." She grabbed her pack of Camels and headed outside.

Lena sipped the drink, a grimace climbing her face.

Perry poured her more cranberry, staring at Clark and Ollie playing pool. "What, fuckers?"

The men grumbled into their Budweisers, attention returning to their game.

Lena's Accord whined up the crest of the Vincent Thomas Bridge; Downtown skyscrapers were a speck north; Port of Los Angeles bustled below. After Perry explained the greatness of Dodgers baseball for a good ten minutes, Lena found a window to ask about Delancey.

"What's he like, you say?" Perry stared at monster cranes unloading shipped cargo. "He's a good man. A bit intense, but that's what I like most about him. Could tell he had passion for his profession—a rarity these days. But that became a double-sided coin."

"How so?"

"Liked to embed himself wherever the case took him. A chameleon, can work his way into any crowd. When I was out there searching for Rochelle, so was he—different truck stops, months at a time. Let's just say that in the heat of a case, Joe's urge to solve it can cloud his better judgment at times."

"Example?"

"Puts himself in harm's way following leads—often oblivious to danger till it bites him in the rear. Been stabbed on a case. Robbed plenty of times. But that's Joe—why he's a fine sleuth, I guess. A curious cat with hopefully more than one life left. I swear, he'd get so juiced on a tip, he'd explore it to the bitter end, regardless the cost—and we were funding him, naturally—me and the ex-wife."

"He quit on you?"

"Quit? Man never heard the word. No, we just—or *I* at that

point—couldn't afford to keep him on. But he's a goddamn soldier. Made copies of every document he had and handed 'em over to me—said he planned on tackling the case alone, least till another paying gig came along. I'd hear from him every few months, usually a letter with a strange return address. Never any real news, just him letting me know he hadn't lost hope." Perry paused, reflecting on that hope. "Been years though."

"Well, I can't wait to shake his hand."

Perry met her giddy gaze in silence.

Lena let out an awkward cough as she veered onto the 110 Freeway. "Where do I get off?"

"PCH. This was his makeshift office—The Palm Motel. Joe inherited the place when his aunt died—used part of the manager's quarters for business."

"Oh."

"Just head toward the beach, and I'll point her out. Mind if I smoke?"

She hesitated before remembering this was no longer her beloved Audi. "Smoke away."

Perry cracked the window and sparked a Red.

This stretch of Pacific Coast Highway bled through Harbor City, lined by motorcycle shops and questionable motels. Lena admired a small tattoo parlor, followed by blinking bulbs about a topless joint. Daylight had children of the night still indoors, bus stops and parking lots peppered with carts of the deranged. Even the streetlights were on the nod—drooping hunchbacks outside The Palm Motel.

A frayed American flag greeted them at half-mast; they entered the narrow driveway before some single-story bungalows—except for an upstairs unit located above the front check-in. NIGHT WINDOW buzzed in blood red over a lone bell. Perry exited the car; Lena trailed, crushing a swell of nerves by rifling through her purse. There was only one other car in the lot, a spearmint

Bonneville with all four tires slashed. Perry leaned at the night window and slapped the bell. Rustling could be heard inside, an auburn-haired twentysomething approached the screen; she was decked in exercise gear, slender, her T-shirt declaring a creed on inner strength.

Perry barked, "Hi there. Lookin' for Joe—he 'round?"

The girl grabbed a towel from off a chair and swabbed her neck. "Who's asking?"

"Name's Perry Quell—we're old business associates. This here's my pal, Lena—"

"I remember you."

"You do?" Perry eyed the girl more intensely. "Becca?"

She smiled, nodding.

"Jesus, you're all—"

"Skinny."

"Was gonna say, grown up. Can't believe I didn't recognize you."

"Had my underbite fixed."

"No shit? Well, you're a sight for the ages."

She shook her head no.

"Where's your dad?"

Her smile fell. "Your guess' better than mine."

"How so?"

She pointed to a door; Perry and Lena walked over as Becca unlatched it, inviting them inside.

Becca paused a Zumba video on her small flat screen, offering them glasses of iced tea before going into the kitchen. Her manager's suite was clean and cozy; its living room held commanding views of Bill's Liquors across the street. Perry and Lena sat on a floral print couch, one with wood arm accents from the '70s. Becca handed over their drinks and sat on a blue exercise ball before them.

"Haven't seen Dad in months. Went hunting on a case up near Fresno. I'm in charge of the Palm for now, finances, et cetera.

Was calling in every so often, but it's been a good six weeks since I last heard his voice—told me it might happen. Said he was on the trail of something juicy."

Perry said, "Reason we came by is to ask for his services. Lena's daughter, Tess, has gone missing. You're telling me he's out on another case?"

"All I know is he's in the field, rubbing his nose through something that stinks—couldn't tell you what." Her stare shifted to Lena. "I'm sorry 'bout your girl."

Perry: "Lemme ask you this, Becca. He still hammering away on Rochelle's case?"

"I remember he kept on for a while, not sure how much further he got." The front desk's phone began to ring. "Excuse me a moment." She rushed to answer.

Lena turned to Perry with hungry eyes. He patted her knee.

The phone slammed. Becca approached, shaking her head. "Bill collectors. Hey, if you wanna dig through Rochelle's files, go right ahead. I can let you into his office."

Perry said, "Thanks, but I already got 'em."

"Well, if he's come up with anything new, could be there—might give you an idea on where the hell to find him."

Lena said, "Sure, we'd love to take a peek."

Becca went for her key ring.

Perry waited for the women to hit the outdoor stairway before making his ascent. The motel's roof was crumbly, in desperate need of replacement. Plump termites fluttered about the eaves. Cars sped down PCH, canceling the jangle of Becca's keys. The door popped, expelling a musty odor similar to an old library. Boxes and file cabinets surrounded a splintered oak desk whose top held layers of paperwork. Becca opened a window. Lena held in a sneeze as sunlight danced about the room.

Becca pointed. "Whatever cases he was working last will be on that desk. Cabinets and other shit may look in order but—

Perry, you know Joe—chaos abounds."

Lena lifted the lid to a box with *California* scribbled in Sharpie; it was jammed with crumpled notes and receipts, many of which the ink had vanished from like one of those trick pens. She picked out a torn piece of legal pad filled with handwritten phone numbers, none of which had any claim to whom they belonged.

Becca went for the door. "He's a pack rat, I know, but this is the best I can help you two. Stay as long as you like. Know where to find me."

Perry shuffled papers atop Joe's desk, a labyrinth of information. He sat on the desk chair and got to it; Lena pulled up a crate to sit and help out.

Forty minutes had passed. They were able to pile the documents into three towers, the largest being old race forms from Hollywood Park, a track closed years ago. A handful pertained to Rochelle, according to Perry—nothing new, a truck stop in the Central Valley that he'd cased in 2011. The rest of the paperwork belonged to another job, one that predated Rochelle's. Joe had taped newspaper clippings to legal pad sheets, handwritten notes everywhere. They referenced a missing foster child near Fresno; Perry had never heard of the girl, a rarity considering the extensive amount of time and energy he'd spent analyzing cold cases and missing teens. The newspaper clipping summarized a runaway female by the name of Somerset Boyd, a fifteen-year-old from Clovis who'd possibly fled foster parents by train, hopping down to Los Angeles. There was nothing in the text or Delancey's notes to suggest that a missing person's report had been filed on the girl, although Perry couldn't believe that one hadn't been made for a minor (unless nobody cared to find her). Lena rifled through some of Joe's notes on the girl—ones legible.

"Perry, look at this."

He took the page from her fingers. Joe had logged a list of sightings of the girl in the Greater Los Angeles area in 2005, many of which had been crossed out: Olvera Street, Sam's

Hofbrau...There was one address unscrawled, alongside it the name Miggy Rojas and the word STAMPS.

"What you think it means, Perry?"

He grabbed documents on the Central Valley truck stop, analyzing its whereabouts, outlying Clovis. "Could be Joe thought this gal fled using this truck stop we checked back then. Maybe she didn't jump no train, hitched a ride down with a trucker. Who knows?"

"Let's ask Becca."

Becca's head gave a Labrador's tilt at the documents. "All I remember about this Somerset Boyd was that Joe had planned on visiting the stop to ask about her. Know this wasn't a new job that came in either—I handle all the calls."

Perry said, "Me and Joe searched the place, way back when."

Becca's eyes shot to Perry's. "Then I'd say there's a good chance my pops is still working your case."

Lena butted in. "What about this Miggy...and the stamps?"

"No clue. Postage stamps, maybe?" She read the address. "Had to be something good, my dad ain't one to investigate if it didn't cut to the bone. I'm sure he went there. Ain't too far away either, Crenshaw and Washington."

Perry gave Becca a hug. "Thanks, dear. If Joe calls, can you give him my number?"

"Sure thing." She grabbed a pen and paper.

Lena approached, arms out.

"Hope everything works out for both of you—deep in my heart, I know it will."

In the car, Lena could sense Perry was fighting with this new mystery in his head, a fire rekindled from dark embers deep within. She couldn't tell if he was happy or sad, starting the engine instead of asking his thoughts. They shared silence.

"Where to, Perry?"

"You know where."

***

The drive to Mid-City couldn't have taken any longer, dusk settling behind black palms as they sat trapped along the 405 north. Lena exited at La Cienega, assuring Perry she knew the way. His familiarity with county infrastructure wasn't that great these days as he rarely left Long Beach, avoiding the city all together. Regardless, Perry was a lifer just like her, and once baptized *Angeleno*, you were part of the soup. They talked how persistently influx L.A. had been over their decades, always morphing into something odd just when they'd thought they'd figured it out. Build/Destroy/Gentrify/Repeat. Love it or hate it, there was a tragic beauty to its progression: a resilience to never be held in place.

At the southwest corner of Crenshaw and Washington sat a rundown strip center, anchored by a *carnecería*, the scent of street meat steaming out its doors. Perry glanced back at the address scribbled by Delancey and said, "This is the place." Lena waited for a Prius to move out the lot before pulling in. They exited the vehicle, Lena's stomach grumbling at the moon.

There were seven units in the center, four of which were vacant. Aside from a check cashing place and the Mexican market, a third business caught their attention: 9 Muses, a stationery store that had seen better days. A bell jingled upon their entry. Paper stocks, pens and other assorted goods peppered displays, hardly filled with product. No one seemed to be on duty. Lena and Perry split up, nosing about. The flush of a toilet could be heard; a stout man emerged from the back room, barely five-five and balding, his glasses and attire could've pegged him for a lowly professor.

He wiped wet hands on the seat of his trousers. "May I help you?"

Perry sidled up to the counter. "You guys sell postage stamps here?"

"No, just rubber stamps—for businesses or personal use." He

pointed to a side wall filled with ink pads and wood toggled impressions.

Lena approached the wall.

The man took her eagerness for interest, pulling out a book from behind the register. "Miss, it's all custom work—personalized for any need—company logos…"

Perry noticed the man's glasses were broken, electrical tape at the arms. How lucrative did this business think it could be nowadays? "Your name Miggy Rojas?"

"No, sir. Paul Alessandri."

"Did a Miggy ever work here?"

"I haven't a clue. Maybe before my brother and I purchased the business, ten…twelve years ago."

"Huh. I was told to swing by here and ask for Miggy." He gave a stare implying the man was lying.

The man didn't waver. "That's strange. You came in asking for postage stamps." He stepped back from the counter. "If you two are planning to rob me, I'll show you there's only loose change in the register."

Lena approached the counter, conjuring a lie. "No, mister, we're just following a story…for the *Times*."

"About what?"

Perry: "A girl named Somerset Boyd. Got a lead about some Miggy and this place."

"I assure you I don't have any knowledge of either individual."

Perry nodded.

The man came from around the counter. "If you'll excuse me, it's time for me to start closing up." He unlocked the metal gate before the windows. "If you're actually interested in our rubber stamps, please feel free to browse while I get things in order."

Perry stormed out.

Lena walked to the door. "Sorry to disturb you…Paul, was it?"

"Yes."

"Well, *Paul*—a lead is a lead. On the bright side, if I ever need a stamp, now I know where to go. *9 Muses*. I like that. Greek mythology, right?"

"I believe so, but we didn't name the business."

"If I can remember correctly, they were inspirational goddesses for art, science and literature."

"Sounds about right."

"You make these stamps by hand?"

"Yes ma'am. A dying art."

"Isn't it all?" She smiled, bell jingling as they exchanged good nights.

Perry was sucking down a Marlboro at the car when she walked up.

"I'm sure this place means something, but only Delancey can tell us—and he sure as hell ain't here."

Perry huffed. "What now?"

She chirped the car alarm. "I'm hitting the road to find Joe Delancey."

The entire ride home, Perry mouthed off on the harsh realm of the road, a reality he couldn't see the petite and righteous Lena being able to survive. Lena let him talk (as usual), a crooked grin on her face; this old man didn't have a clue who she once was, in a past life.

Perry lit a second Red with the butt of his first. "And what about funds, Lena? From the sound of this car, you've already spent a shitload. An endeavor this extreme must be approached like a black hole—one that'll cripple you financially—take it from me."

"If I run low, I'll sell my house. Without Tess, I can't live there anymore. I'm going to ride this to the end, Perry. No more waiting around for the police or anyone. I'm going to find her. Just hoped you of all people would understand."

"Oh, in spades, my dear. Thing is, you can't fathom the inferno you're walking into."

"I've seen the worst of humanity. My twenties were a hell ride that I'm not about to bore you with."

"The road will take its toll, and the price is different for all who enter that void. All I'm sayin' is when you lurk inside a sordid place, what is seen cannot be unseen." He exhaled a plume, trancing on neon lights in the night. "You'll become galvanized to the world. Numb. To survive, morality must take a hike. Everything you know as good," he thumped his heart, "inside here...will be altered."

Lena reflected, having lost all faith in religion, simply going through routine acts of penance like some lost sheep, praying for Tess, not herself. "There's nothing good about me, Perry. Stick around long enough, you'll see."

He watched her knuckles squeeze the wheel.

"So?"

"What?"

"Are you coming with me or not?"

INTERLUDE
A RANCH, A WOMAN
& MIGGY ROJAS

The cabin's stone chimney billowed clouds into a newborn day, sun piercing caps of rolling hills, tips of Monterey pines. At the porch sat a woman with hard features and caramel braids—her jaw slack on the left side, once cracked and never properly set; a shell worn well beyond its twenty-eight years. She sipped warm black tea, listening to birds awaken across the sprawling ranch, surrounded by dense California Valley oak woodlands. Greenfield, California. This time of year, the roughly three hundred acres was cast in golds and greens. Morning chill reminded her of ice skating as a child, brought with it an excitement to innocence. But that was long ago, the cold no longer a frivolous comfort through long Fresno winters. She'd learned to love it out here—had to. Place she was before this ranch had sunshine but was much colder. Had frozen many a young girl over the years, but not her. She was a survivor—least till today. She took a long sip and closed her eyes, recalling friends lost, dreams dashed, reminding herself she was a unicorn—that something in the universe loved her...

Something besides Repo Helm.

Sure, they had shared happy times, at first. Nowadays, she hardly saw her husband. He never called but to discuss business or check in on her whereabouts. A flatlined marriage in a few years' time, and she knew it. She'd grown cold to this life, the constant uncertainties—death around every corner. A change was warranted, welcomed. She rose and walked past one of her husband's armed guards manning a semi-automatic rifle at the porch steps. There were six of them in constant rotation, all fairly young, ex-military—she could never keep track of their names.

They surveyed the grounds, day and night, protecting the small fortune Repo'd amassed through criminal enterprise; each lived in a shack at the far end of the property (where she preferred them).

She said, "You can head home now."

"Following orders, ma'am."

"Well, now you got a new one."

"How 'bout I stand over there, ma'am?"

"It's not necessary."

The kid slung the weapon over his shoulder and headed twenty yards into the field and re-posted.

Trench sighed, closed the front door behind her and went into her bedroom. There were stacks of cash strewn atop the bed. Tithings had begun pouring in for Gallows Dome, roughly eighty thousand that she'd counted so far. This was her new detail, managing crates of mail delivered to a PO Box; the latest sat on the floor. She tore open another envelope, this one harboring forty dollars. *Repo had something going, alright.* After all, The Dome was nothing more than an empty promise to overeager participants so far—folks dissatisfied with the current state of this world. Who knew if it would become anything more than a front for laundering money? She drank in the sight of cold hard cash: Repo's instinct was correct.

And now *her* plan was set in motion.

She swiped ten thousand from off the bed, balled it in a rubber band and slid it into a shoebox in her closet. Her husband may be eager to charge into this new endeavor, but she'd had enough. If she played her cards right, Gallows Dome could work to her benefit, providing an escape, allowing for a new life somewhere else. *Paradise abroad.* Feeling the money at her fingertips, she could finally taste the freedom of a crimeless world—one with a new identity to provide a decent second act, one she always thought she never deserved.

Soon, she thought.

The throttle of an engine broke through morning chirps

outside. She went to a window. A large Ford truck was kicking dirt through a cut road down the meadow. First, there was plenty of work to be done to attain this new goal. She locked the door to the bedroom and grabbed a shotgun.

The rusty Ford glugged down gentle hills, its two inhabitants in desperate need of showers. The driver was burly, his bald head nearly thumping the roof with every dip; his name was Preston but all the brothers called him P-Stone. Beside him sat a short-stack with a handlebar moustache, quietly taking in the scenery as they approached the wood cabin.

P-Stone killed a Waylon tune on the radio, needing to address the situation at hand. "Miggy, we gotta be on our best behavior now. Trench is nice most times but remember, she's Repo's old lady—don't do nothin' set her off."

"What am I gonna do, huh?"

"I dunno, man...use the commode and piss on the lid. Say something stupid. Just mind your Ps and Qs. This ain't some lot lizard here. This' the boss' wife."

"But she *was* a lizard...once upon a time—I mean, you said so."

"That's long ago. And don't bring it up neither. That type a shit'll get us both fucked." He checked on their haul in the rearview, three metal canisters chained in place.

Miggy twisted to eye the cargo, getting the picture P-Stone was painting. "I'll be a good boy. Promise."

P-Stone sparked a Backwoods cigar.

Miggy admired dense scars about Stone's right forearm, adolescent gifts from punching out car windows to steal. "I hear Trench's supposed to be some kinda...what you call it—*psychic* or somethin', huh?"

A plume of smoke filled the cab. "You listen to that tape I gave ya?"

"Yeah."

"Then you know the gal sees things—High Priestess of *Gallows Dome.*"

Miggy stewed, contemplating Gallows Dome, the little he understood of the pair's underground gathering. Knew better than to pry for more info too, not having been invited to become a member yet. He thought of something else to harp on. "Tell me somethin', why does everyone call her *Trench?*" He pistoned a fist, insinuating a fuck machine.

P-Stone bit the cigar. "Ask Repo yourself...before he kills you."

Miggy laughed.

The Ford came to a stop, and both men smiled at the young lady wearing an olive flannel, white knuckles clenching her shotgun.

Trench inspected the canisters as P-Stone dropped the tailgate. Miggy stood back, careful not to get mud on the walking cast covering his left foot, even though it was already soiled in filth. P-Stone helped the woman into the bed of the truck; she hadn't even asked about Miggy yet.

Trench ran her fingers atop one canister's lid, dimpled with drilled holes. "Repo said there would be one of these. The others are to be fed?"

P-Stone stammered. "Far as I know—the one you're touching is in rough shape. Been holed up for a spell, strung out. And, I didn't talk to your husband. When I picked her up, X-man told me this was 'what the doctor ordered.'"

Trench said, "That damn doctor better be me."

"You are."

"And the feeders? What did they do to end up here?"

"Something untoward, I suppose. Been on ice, but should be thawed by now. One's that apple farmer."

"The other?"

"Think his grandson."

She nodded, taking a gander at Miggy, then focusing on a barn down the way. With the shotgun, she tapped the canister with holes. "Take this one into the barn. Unload the rest at the hog pen—mix it with some greens and bread. There's a bale over there. They ain't eaten in a few days—should slop it up fine." Her attention returned to the new guy. "Who's gimpy?"

Miggy went to speak, but saw P-Stone's eyes bulge.

"That's Miggy Rojas. Repo brought him into the fold, few weeks back. Helping bring goods up from TJ."

"I heard about you." She sized up the short fucker. "Rojas, huh? You don't look like no wetback."

Miggy blurted, "That's 'cause I ain't."

P-Stone's face went flush.

Trench adjusted her weapon.

Miggy's gold tooth glistened. "My daddy was."

The woman gave a quick snort; P-Stone forced a hoot.

Trench jumped off the truck and headed toward the cabin. "Coffee, Miggy?"

"Love some."

"Preston can partake when he's done. With that bum foot, you're about useless, now ain't you?"

"Just came along to keep my pal company."

"Aw. Hear that, Preston? Looks like you got yourself a new butt boy."

P-Stone held a frozen grin, angry words bouncing inside his skull as he watched Miggy open the door for Trench and walk inside the cabin.

Miggy gawked the cabin's interior: empty log walls, sharp wood furniture. He sat at a rustic table in the dining room while Trench poured coffee.

"How you take it, gimpy?"

"Black."

"Like your tramps?"

"Like my soul."

She smiled, sliding the mug before him. "Repo's got you diggin' down in Mexico, then I'm sure you have something for *me.*"

He reached into his denim vest and pulled out two large baggies containing a slew of painkillers, all laced with fentanyl. He watched her eyes come alive as he took a hearty swig, studying every square inch of her face. He was itching to ask her about these *visions* but refrained. "Ranch is nice. Been here long?"

"Since my wedding day. Got hitched just east of that berm." She pointed out the window.

Miggy craned to see, only to catch P-Stone at the sty full of boars, crowbarring a canister, pouring its contents into the trough—a pile of crimson-glazed human flesh.

"How's my husband these days?"

The question juxtaposed with the visual caught him off guard. "Fine, I suppose. Ain't seen him in a few weeks."

She lit a cigarette. "Welcome to the club."

There was something wild in the way she looked through him that made him turn away. Like she knew all his secrets. "You grow anything on this land?"

"Few pot plants, hybrids, but that's only a hobby—along with a vegetable garden out back."

"Must be peaceful, having this place to yourself."

"Not always. Sometimes assholes show up, like today."

"Sorry if we disturbed you. I—"

"Not you." She jutted her crooked chin at P-Stone. "Look at him, making a mess over there. I swear...he's worse than a child these days."

They watched as P-Stone fumbled with a shovel, spreading out the poor bastard's remains.

"All part of the trade, I guess." She rose and went back into the kitchen, grabbing another coffee mug.

Miggy studied the woman's numbness to the situation, years of mayhem and violence having rotted her through. P-Stone entered the cabin, hands pink from scrubbing off gore. Smelled like that orange stuff used by mechanics.

Trench approached with Preston's coffee. "I'd offer you boys something to eat, but by the looks of it, neither you like pussy." She coughed a raspy note.

The men followed with forced chuckles—all three of them awkward as teens in a sci-fi book club, twitchy, avoiding eye contact, pretending all was right in their parallel universe.

The Ford took off up the pass, kicking dirt and gravel; Trench didn't bother to wave them off, anxious to inspect the precious cargo in the barn. The boars were grunting, beyond primal in their pen; the taste of blood always sent them into frenzy. She entered the barn, flashes of sunlight slicing every which way. The lone canister was upright, specks of dust floating about creating an aura. She placed her shotgun on a butcher's block in the corner, grabbing a ladle from out a workbench drawer and scooping well water from its bin. She approached the canister, dumping cold water into its porous lid. A muffled noise resonated inside; the metal began to shake. She walked out to the sty and retrieved the crowbar, stench in the air like a slap to the face.

Cracking the lid would be a surprise, as she'd never done such a thing before. If the person inside wasn't properly hogtied, they could explode upwards soon as she broke the seal, sending the lid into her septum, crushing her nose...or worse. She popped the top and kept her distance, shotgun at the ready. Slowly, she peered inside, hand cannon leveled.

A teenage girl in torn clothing: cropped brown hair, liquid hazel eyes. Zip ties fused her wrists to her ankles, duct tape across her lips. She was barely conscious, mumbling, snot bubbles bursting out the nose.

Trench kicked the canister on its side and marveled at the odd girl—the one from her dreams, a vessel destined to be molded into a Savior.

PART TWO
WHITE LINE FEVER

6.

Joe Delancey *was* Miggy Rojas.

Rojas: Joe's latest persona, his cover to permeate the darkness—a world he was becoming anesthetized to. Luckily, not nearly as comfortable as Trench in her ranch house; call the woman whatever she wanted, Delancey knew Somerset Boyd the moment he saw her. *Another piece to the puzzle slapped into place, and not a day too soon.* This never-ending job had turned into a beast that had consumed him. But he didn't care; every day might bring him a little closer to learning what happened to Rochelle Anne Quell.

Dusk fell as P-Stone dropped him back at his motel in Los Banos, a two-meal town in the center of the state. The Speckled Hen Inn was located just off the region's central drag (Highway 33), a two-story complex reminiscent of a motor lodge found in Palm Springs, not the middle of nowhere. The bastard palm trees at its perimeter were as out of place as a Mercedes in a tractor farm, but that subtle touch provided an added comfort to the joint's bed bugs and blood stains—reminded him of his motel in Harbor City. *Should give Becca a call.* He slowly climbed the stairs, walking cast on his leg giving hearty thumps. At the door to room ten, he craned down to see P-Stone's truck make its way past the algae-green swimming pool, chains clanking, kicking up dirt as it charged onto the highway. He exhaled a deep sigh, letting the Miggy demon take an overnight breather while Delancey got back to work—that was, soon as he could block images of pigs chowing body parts from the brain.

A frozen burrito exploded in the microwave as Joe took off the cast and massaged his left foot. It wasn't broken or sprained, the walking boot a cheap find at a thrift store when he was buying clothes to become Miggy. He figured a slight vulnerability could be utilized to his advantage—maybe he'd get overlooked as being any type of threat among the underground world of nomads. And like everywhere else he'd navigated through life, he relied on his mouth to lead the way—and it did. The plan was simple: Once a lead presented itself, establish Miggy among the trucker world, this time attack the investigation as an active player—someone questionable with something to offer, not some average schmo. And as luck would have it, a lead finally came—only via another case, one providing a direct link to Trench (aka Somerset Boyd), one person that might have an answer to Rochelle's whereabouts.

Nearly a year after Perry Quell had relieved him of his services, he'd taken a job for a client desperately trying to find a foster child that'd skipped town the moment they turned eighteen. With Joe's stifled income stream, along with being tired of taking cheating hubby/wife gigs, he accepted the case. The way he saw it, he'd rather milk the guy out of a few weeks' per diem instead of blurting out the obvious: "The child never loved you, pal." It was during this investigation that he delved into records of runaway foster children that he stumbled across a familiar face: the girl known as Trench.

Back when he'd first investigated the disappearance of Rochelle Quell, he'd befriended a lot lizard named Devon. She was nineteen and white with the curves of a potato. He'd give her a buck here and there for information; she mainly provided names of dealers, sharks, fences or pimps. Toward the end of his stay, the girl was helping to ask around about Rochelle. The trail of this world was overwhelming when seen on a map, but, as he soon found out through Devon, *everything* was connected—from the movies playing in truck stop lounge rooms to backdoor drug distribution, statewide.

One rainy September afternoon, he found Devon seated on the hood of his El Camino, parked at a Motel 6 near Fowler. Even with rain beating down, he knew she'd been crying. Didn't look beaten or traumatized, just blue. She'd recently lost her pimp, a Mexican named Mario, taken out with a shiv during a bad crap shoot. She hadn't cried a tear over him either, excited to get out the life, trying to scrounge all she could by polishing rims on eighteen-wheelers, hoping to hitchhike back to Albuquerque. Over a lunch of prepackaged hero subs, she divulged the following:

"Think I might have a bead on her, dude—was in the game room of that Cali Gold stop up near Madera. I'm shooting nine-ball, minding my own when this gal approaches me—real stealth like. Honey blonde, about five-five. She slaps a quarter on the table and asks if I'm runnin'. First, I got confused, thinking this ho be just another liz trying to poach my pool table. Then she asks again, and I know what she's gettin' at. I tell her to mind her own fuckin' binness, but she don't budge. Says a dude name Repo Helm wants to talk with me. See, word's out that all Mario's stable are orphans now, and this Repo cluck wants to swoop us all up. I don't tell her that I'm off the clock permanently, but humor her a bit—let her play some eight-ball. I buy her a cream soda an' we get to yappin' 'bout this an' that: where she's from originally (Clovis), how good Repo is to her and other nonsense. I plan it that before I'm fixin' to bail, I ask her 'bout the others—you know, if this Repo Helm is King Lord like she says he is, how many girls he runnin'— what kinda bills he stackin'. She starts rattlin' off names: Shasta, Carly, Baby K...Then she says Ro and stops, dead cold. I start to pry, make up some story about how I had a bestie named Rochelle, but ain't seen her in a blue moon. I start to describe Rochelle, and the girl clams up on me—looks odd like I dun broke wind. I ask if Ro's

here, an' she says no—that Ro won't be comin' 'round no more. I look her in the eye and know exactly what she be gettin' at, right? Then I see him. Ain't that big, maybe five-seven with a grizzled goatee, green ostrich boots. He's leering at me like I'm some deer that's already taken an arrow. So, I flip him the bird an' roll on— but I got a hunch he knows somethin', and so I come find you. Sitting outside earlier, just got me to thinkin'—how my luck's played out these past years. I know many a liz that didn't make it out the lot, and here I go—ready to fly blind. Guess it just got the best of me and I got all weepy...Oh! This gal I spoke to...they call her Trench. Don't ask me why, but you could imagine—and I don't know her real name. I grabbed a pic of her with my cell. Here look...I'm fixin' to hop a Greyhound tomorrow, so hope it'll help..."

Delancey stood on the toilet and unscrewed an air vent below a crease of the water-stained ceiling, pondering the odds if Devon ever made it home, knowing they were stacked against her. With no loved ones to welcome her with open arms, the girl might as well have been dead—better than a lonely ghost forced through life's misery, alone. He reached inside and pulled out a leather carrier bag and a compact firearm—a Saturday night special. The satchel held files and composition notebooks. He opened the first notebook labeled *S. Boyd*, flipped to the final page and scribbled, *Boyd is Trench*, beside her mug shot he'd found on that other job.

This was a watershed moment.

A link that could prove paramount with the case.

Or lead to another dead end.

When he first came back out undercover, he actually believed that it could all go smoothly: infiltrate the scene as Miggy, get to Trench, ask her about "Ro" being Rochelle, take it from there. But then the drug angle got him deep with Repo, sucked into the fold. He fronted a large haul, promising another that would complete their transaction; Repo felt safe since he had nothing to lose— payment upon final delivery, that and the pills were primo. This quickly became a whole 'nother headache—one that led him to hear about Gallows Dome—a story P-Stone divulged one drunken night last week; when he heard it, he didn't believe it. A story about Trench that was so strange, it replayed in his melon like a never-ending film reel—one that he would give anything to shut off.

One of the first things he learned on the road was the right way to dine at a truck stop buffet. If a warm tray of food was full, pull from the middle; if half gone, only eat from the rear portion. Never touch any shellfish or pink chicken. Simple germ rules, ones that could help you avoid the shits or the plague. A trucker's livelihood never depended on their hygiene, common knowledge to anyone who'd used a truck stop bathroom once. It was at one of these lovely restaurants that P-Stone, hammered on Thunderbird, casually told a story over a plate of green eggs and ham (he pulled from the front).

"So, Repo says you can ride along this time."

Miggy: "No shit?"

"He liked your product and wants you 'round some more. Leavin' it up to me to get you acquainted with some a the boys. How soon can you move the second batch of those meds up north?"

"How much he want again?"

"Whatever you got."

"I'll make some calls. Gonna have to go down there personally though. See when my connect can handle it."

"Hey, you said, 'Tell Repo anytime, anyplace.'"

"Yeah. Anytime. Anyplace. But first I gotta put the wheels in motion, my man. Can't just bounce into TJ with hefty demands, right? Repo has protocol with all his shit. I got mine. Don't worry. It'll play. I promised two shipments to start and always deliver to my clients."

"Anyway, said you can come with me next drop."

"To the ranch, right? When?"

"Few days. 'Nuff time for you to make some a those calls."

"He gonna be there?"

"Nah, just his old lady. Wants her to get a bead on you—make sure he's making the right choice bringing you in."

"She gonna interrogate me or somethin'? Ask me about where I went to high school...when I popped my cherry?"

"Hardy har, fuck-o. It's custom. Not every day Repo brings someone new aboard. And give her a taste of the supply."

"A taste?"

"Whatever you got left a what you gave Repo."

"No problemo."

"Good."

"Good."

"What's she like anyway? I heard things but nothing solid."

"—"

"Come on, Stone. I wanna make a good impression. Give me a leg up. What's in store when I meet your High Priestess?"

"She's ageless, you know?"

"Ageless? Like...she's got a good complexion or what?"

"Ageless as in immortal."

"—"

"Sees visions, the girl. I dunno what of—maybe space aliens or some shit. But she has a gift, and Repo's got the wheels in motion, making a fortune too—you feel me?"

"I don't."

"You don't see it?"

"I'm lost."

"Guy builds himself an empire slinging lot lizards, then abruptly closes up shop—gets into moving dope and starts his own fellowship on the side."

"So?"

"Repo is a wise man. Found himself a prophet and set out to capitalize."

"And Trench is supposed to be this prophet?"

"Don't mock the unknown, Mig—your ignorance makes you the fool."

"There a mass every Sunday or secret handshake? I'm genu-

inely intrigued."

"There's a ritual coming up, first of its kind. Gonna sacrifice a Savior, usher in the end of days—do what we will."

"Sacrifice? Like...kill?"

"Don't ask questions you may fear the answer."

Miggy called his bluff. "Well, can I come?"

"Nah."

Miggy tried to take a bite of his biscuit, but it was a brick. "And why Gallows Dome—the hell kinda name is that?"

Stone wagged his head. "The Dome is this toxic world we live in. Gallows are what we intend for it."

"Intend?"

"With the Gallows our god—death to the world as we know it."

"And here, I thought this was all some shitty cult or fleece or somethin'? You're serious about this."

Pork shot from P-Stone's mouth. "Ain't no fleece, motherfucker! Gallows Dome is the truth to ALL mysteries. Trench is the light— the serpent, reincarnate. Her soul has transcended the ages— witnessed the world's cataclysmic events. She was there during the Great Sphynx's creation—practiced the Eleusinian Mysteries—spat in the face of Jesus—laughed at the fall of Rome. And now..."

"Now what?"

"America."

Dead silence.

Stone returned to his food.

"Must've sucked being reincarnated as an average truck stop whore. Shit, look at my dumb life—I musta been Genghis Khan."

P-Stone grabbed Miggy by the collar and pulled him close, sneering.

"Easy, man—easy! Just fuckin' around."

He flung Miggy back to his chair. "Ain't funny, Rojas. There's a reason for all things. I truly believe this."

"I'm not doubting your beliefs, man. To each his own when it comes to spirituality, I always say. Just pretty heavy is all."

"The Savior will come to save us, regardless of doubters like

you. The sooner you recognize that, the faster you'll advance."

"Whatever you say, son. Sign me up too though. I wanna party with you guys till the end zone dance."

"Can't."

"Why not?"

"Ain't worthy yet."

"How so?"

Stone scoffed.

"When then?"

"When they say—if they say."

"They?"

"Repo an' Trench." His eyes began to swim. He reached into his jacket and removed a cassette tape, clean of any markings. "Listen to this, then tell me your thoughts. The Dome ain't for everyone— but everyone ain't gonna be saved either. If you're evolved and on board, I'll put in a good word—see what happens."

Joe rewound the cassette in an old yellow Walkman, copper earphones on his head. He'd listened to the thing twenty times. Might as well have been a concert flyer, given to select truckers as an invite into the fellowship. P-Stone said Repo wanted to fish for followers over CB, but then thought better—that being the same way lizards hollered at johns. Didn't need everyone knowing just yet—only the likeminded could start an uprising. The tape deck clicked dead. He pressed play and cracked a beer to wash down his burrito as the raspy voice of Repo Helm began to play.

Hear me, brothers and sisters! Your call to Gallows Dome is a testament to your strength—a primal birthright bestowed by a legacy of...brutality. Let's not forget that we were bred from savages, warriors whose rampage through the ages has blessed our survival for centuries—a timeline far greater than what archeologists have determined thus far. Through Gallows Dome, we are immortal. Now's our time to assault a new era—one dictated by a chosen few, bound by blood—in honor of our forefathers. Embrace Gallows Dome, brothers and sisters. Through the powers of our High Priestess and the coming of our Savior, let us do whatever *we* will…

As the tape spun, Delancey fell into dreamland, his body bruised and mind exhausted. Hopefully he could sleep through the night. Lord knows what tomorrow would bring, but one thing was certain: There was no way he could get anymore pills from anywhere—especially down in Mexico, like he was expected by Repo Helm.

When Joe concocted the scheme to embed himself among Repo's men as a runner, it was mostly out of impulse—drugs, the one criminal item he knew he could probably get his hands on, albeit not easily. He struggled with the act at first, but only briefly, justifying it by telling himself someone else would be supplying Repo dope if not him; his involvement wasn't going to *really* help anything happen that already wasn't going to take place anyway. And it would be finite. He'd bring a comped package to Repo to entice him into doing business, promise a second shipment to keep him on the line, stall, then skip town soon as he obtained the information that he'd come out here for.

He had to follow this *Ro* lead!

And all he needed to do was land some clean dope.

But there was a hitch: He didn't have the money to front a large amount of prescription meds (the current rage often relayed by Devon). Furthermore, he didn't have any connection on how to procure such things other than greasing a quack doctor or hoping to cop in Downtown off San Julien and 5th. However, what he did have was an ear to the street, and when being a private dick in Los Angeles, there was always a current of dirt flowing your way. One such nugget fell into his lap the week before his departure.

It came as no surprise every time a headline blared rampant corruption within Los Angeles County law enforcement. On the morning in question, Becca had brought coffee and the *Times* up to his office, knowing he'd worked overnight. The slap of the paper woke him, cheek smashed on his desk. Front page boasted of a raid on one of the more prominent biker gangs within Southern California. As he read through the lists of weapons and narcotics that were confiscated from those arrested, one name kept jumping throughout, and it didn't belong to a one percenter: Sergeant Mel Brown. Brown was the mouthpiece of the article, relaying info on the force's raid findings. To Joe, the name might as well have been in neon; it was commonplace within PI circles—the man known for skimming evidence rooms, working both sides of the coin. And with the amount of meth, coke and pills freshly seized (per Brown's own words), there was now a good chance where Joe could score—for free.

Brown was the proud owner of two homes within the county: his main residence housed his wife and three daughters in Redondo Beach; the second, his primary stash/gash pad, was located in Highland Park. Joe knew of the place, paid by another ranking officer to place it under surveillance back in the mid-aughts, hoping to catch Brown in the act and shoot photos that would take him down. Needless to say, nothing transpired from the job, other than Joe's usual fee. And with no other options presenting themselves for the drugs he needed to proclaim himself a "heavy" on the road, Joe fired up the El Co and headed to Highland Park.

Brown's second house was located off Avenue 56, a single-story craftsman draped in iron bars under the Highland Theatre's shadow. Joe parked the El Co down the block; as he approached on foot, he slid on a Day-Glo DWP windbreaker and hard hat: No one in L.A. ever questioned the harbingers of water and power (*although they should*).

There were no visible security cameras at the home's exterior, a tip he'd remembered from being out here on the Brown case years ago. By the looks of it, no one was home. He rang the doorbell to be sure, recalling the style of lock he'd picked last time, sliding on open-knuckle driver's gloves. When there came no answer, he gently massaged a tension wrench into the slot, checking for any witnesses before advancing the pick; a trick he'd performed on a thousand such occasions. If a security alarm were to go off, he'd call it a day; however, Brown being a cheap bastard, Joe bet on the security being exactly the same.

And he won.

The living room was dusty, zero outside light bleeding in. The smell of fresh marijuana jolted the senses. Bindles of the plant were stuffed into garbage bags throughout every bedroom; they were far too bulky for him to walk out with, let alone take with him in his travels throughout the state. There had to be something more manageable he could steal here.

Rummaging through kitchen drawers, he came across a fully loaded Saturday night special (the one still in his possession). He kept searching. After twenty-plus minutes, he struck paydirt. In the freezer of a busted pink refrigerator sat eight large bricks of crude prescription painkillers. He loaded them into a backpack that he'd stashed under his windbreaker and carefully returned the house to the way he'd found it. This would hopefully be the last break-in required for him to taste success on the road. Somebody upstairs had a shine for him. With these pills never going to be reported as missing, and nothing to tie him as being the culprit, playing a criminal in real life began with some relish. Then again, Joe never bet against himself, always liking his chances when the stakes were high.

The following morning, Joe became Miggy, jumped into the El Camino and went roaring north with a boatload of meds; a single act with dire consequences that, as of his current situation with Repo, could kill him well before ever finding out about Rochelle Anne Quell. And with all he'd witnessed (and participated in) so far, a single prayer just might not be enough for that someone upstairs to still have a shine for him.

7.

Tiny triangular flags on streamers, thousands in spectral hues, flapped violently above their heads, screaming as to notify every salesman that Lena and Perry had just walked onto the used RV lot. Perry had already assumed a combative stance, fists clenched, knowing damn well that anyone who approached him with so much as a fucking "hello" planned on taking him for a sap. Just a few hours previous, Lena had accepted a whopping eleven thousand dollars for her used Accord (four thousand under Blue Book) at the very same CarMax she'd surrendered her new Audi a few weeks before. The order her life was moving in twisted her stomach. She eyed the flyer in hand, torn from the innards of an *RV Trader*:

> 1994 Rexhall Aerbus 30' with a Chevy 454. Queen bed. Spacious bathroom. Corner shower, toilet and vanity. Kitchen has a 3-burner stove, oven, microwave, large door fridge and L-shaped counter top facing the living area's plush recliner chairs. Well equipped with dual roof A/C units, furnace and high-capacity water heater. 5000 KW generator to give you all the power needed to PAR-TAY! All yours for only $7,995!!! Call Curley's RV Sales. 1-888…

She tilted her face to catch sunrays; Perry's hard voice met with that of a pudgy employee in front of a line of C Class specials. The flags roared through her eardrums. She squinted to watch them dance, tethered in place, high above luxury buses—stuck to something firm, like she once was: a home, a job, a family. She focused on one that was busted, a green mess about to snap from its cord; they'd be one in the same, soon as the RV was purchased—lost to the wind with no direction home...

Here we go.

The powder-blue beast coughed to start, trembling like a codger slipping into a warm bath. The salesmen waved them off; Lena watched from the shotgun captain's chair, wondering just how long this beast had been sleeping on their lot. The smell reminded her of a bowling alley her father took her to as a child: sour booze with a hint of sweet tobacco. Perry cranked it into gear, a grey plume exploding out the rear as they rumbled back to Long Beach.

"Not bad, Lena."

She smiled, flipping on the radio, finding out it didn't work.

Their plan for this first stop was to rent a room at the motel Perry and Delancey had frequented the last time they cased the truck stop; after, they would establish themselves among other guests and locals. Perry had addressed the pitfalls of prolonged motel living and the RV would help soften the blow for lodging; if forced to hunt for an extended period, it would also save them funds. If Delancey wasn't there, and they had no idea where they were headed, the motor home could utilize campgrounds or Walmart parking lots for overnights. Another plus of hauling an RV was the ease of slipping into this new nomadic culture, especially with one as rough around the edges as "Dreamboat," a name adopted for the beast before Lena even signed the papers. She'd packed her bags, reassembled her folder on Tess' case, and pulled out cash this morning; only thing left to do before leaving tomorrow was for Perry to tell Dottie that he needed some time off.

"Fuck no, Perr'!"

"Here's where you an' I differ, Dot. I ain't *askin'* for permission."

"Think that highly of your job, now, d'you?"

"Hell, I thought coming down here and telling you was *me* being *nice.*"

"What'd been *nice* was if your inconsiderate ass would've made it to your shift this mornin'. Left me hangin' with all the roustabouts."

"Hey, more tips on ya. You're welcome."

Lena was playing pool with Earle in the rear, not looking up from her shot while the two settled their differences. She'd always been decent at smashing a break, one thing she'd learned as a kid—even before riding a bike. It's funny how the mind worked; here she could recall her father's exact words on the right angle when smashing a cue but could barely remember the restaurant her mother worked at that same year. *Trauma heightened memory.*

Perry shouted from the chrome front door, "Lena. Let's get on."

Earle watched as she ran the table, slack jaw, in between glances at her ass; the man was glad they hadn't played for drinks. The juke paused to rotate CDs. She sunk the eight, handed the stick to Earle, slammed her Cape Cod and hustled out the door.

Perry loaded a large gym duffel with clothes in the hull of the *Bessie Mae*; gearing up for another stint on the road felt like he was in a time warp—some cyclical hell that he was forced to relive until graced with a grave. He gazed out at Lena, tossing breadcrumbs to some filthy seagulls on the dock. He didn't have to guess what was running through her mind. Even with a slight smile at the hungry birds, her eyes refused to comply; *the hurt* was strangling her. If only he could make it stop, but he knew better. He slid a matte black revolver from out a kitchen drawer, checked its contents, wrapped it in a washcloth and placed it inside the duffel.

Now, where did he place those bullets?

Dreamboat glugged up through canyons on Interstate 5, Tejon Pass in the windshield, onward to the Grapevine. Among them in the slow lane, eighteen-wheelers charged past as minivans zoomed on their left. Lena put down her phone, having lost reception while reading the *Times*. In every direction, the hills were a barren gold, atypical for this time of year; usually a slight snow runoff would've returned brush to being lush. But winter hadn't happened in a few years, other than the deluge of rain at the time of Tess' disappearance. That seemed like a lifetime ago. She gazed out at a few grazing cattle, thinking that a simple tossed cigarette or smoking vehicle could potentially create their barbeque hellfire. She yawned and stood gingerly, walking to the rear commode as if on a pirate's plank.

Perry toyed with the CB, testing all forty channels with random, *Hey nows*, adopting *Dream Team* as their handle. He got a few call backs, easing the mind. The CB would come in handy at every stop. Even though the radio was busted, its tape deck appeared to work, spouting a David Allan Coe cassette he'd found in the glove box. Planned on buying a few more at the Grapevine's Petro stop up ahead, knowing damn well what he wanted for a soundtrack on this expedition (G'n'R or Crüe). Taking Lena's age into consideration, he hoped she wasn't some rap head or nu metal nut. On second thought, instead of rolling the dice and asking her, he'd just grab something artsy—a band she probably never knew existed. One thing he remembered about the road, most truck stop music sections were surprisingly eclectic.

"Not far from Central Valley, Lena—be there by lunch."

The RV crawled along the slow lane. A broke down vehicle at the highway's shoulder caught her eye—a man held a baby in his arms, waiting for a tow truck. Was a girl, wearing a pink onesie over a soiled diaper. Her father was stone-faced, scabs about his neck and nose. She stared till Perry noticed.

"That blown radiator is the least of their worries."

"Hope they're okay."

"Hope?" He scoffed. "You look at a family like that and want to think there's hope—a future of happiness. But that's not guaranteed, as we both know."

"It's always a possibility."

"Ideally...but that ain't *reality*. Reality says the marks on his head are prolly from meth—that the baby's diaper is full a shit 'cause he don't have another to swap it. Reality says that we're embarking on a lost cause, and that's how we need to treat this thing. If we come across Joe, we come across him—if we don't, we don't. But we gotta keep our heads straight, toe the line— realize nothing magical is gonna spring up to solve either our problems. Out here...hope is for the hopeless."

"Hope's all I have left."

Perry shook his head. "You don't get it yet, but you will." He fired up the beast and stoked the engine. That address scribbled by Delancey, out near Clovis, was now humming their names.

The sights and smells of Highway 99 were stark and pungent, mostly dairy farms and pro-life billboards. As they drove through Selma ("*Raisin Capital of the World*"), Lena fixed chicken salad sandwiches in the rear; Perry grumbled over the CB, creating banter with other recreational vehicles, an activity utilized to mask the disappointment with his navigation skills that had come to light. When they'd left the Petro Center a few hours ago, outside Clovis was their destination; however, soon as Lena put the address into her map app ("just to be sure"), turned out the Cali Gold truck stop they were after was actually past Fresno, just before Madera—a good twenty-five miles northwest of Perry's recollection. An argument over technology versus the refined human mind ensued, resulting in Lena making lunch earlier than intended. Regardless, they were back on track and making excellent time.

As they pulled off the Golden State Highway and shot west, their destination could be seen in the distance, half mile ahead; its dingy grounds held a half dozen Freightliners festering below a large tarnished sign that blared a gold nugget below Barbary Coast font. Perry held for a beat at a stop sign before making a right, instead of heading straight for the Cali Gold.

There was a desolate strip along the western side of the highway, a motel row—many of the structures boarded up, fenced in barbed wire. Their signage reflected the neon boom of years past with gaudy artwork that when vibrant, enticed road weary travelers the same way electric zappers caught mosquitos. But that was long ago for most of the motels. A few remained open, although one couldn't tell by looking in their parking lots. Deadened tropical foliage welcomed them before an inn that pulsed with activity, its parking lot peppered with vehicles and soiled mattresses. A hefty neon sat at its heart, the top of it, stained in rust patina, held tubes spelling VILLA; beneath them, a lithe female in a swim cap swan-dived into the words MOTOR LODGE. Lena snapped a picture of it with her cell, then took in the rest of the joint, horseshoe-shaped with a two-story barroom at its northern flank. Perry pulled Dreamboat in before the main office. Hand-drawn poster board across its barred windows pro-claimed, *Under New Management* and *Truckers Get Special Rate*. He surveyed the lot, searching for Delancey's Harley Davidson.

"His bike ain't here—don't mean he didn't drive something

else, undercover. We stayed here 'cause it's the last decent place near the Cali Gold—a straight shot to the highway in case things got dicey. Let's grab that room. Start snoopin' around."

She slid her shoes back on, gearing for business.

The bell inside the Villa's main office didn't buzz, forcing Lena to knock on the counter. A large woman with a flattop entered from a back room. The sleeves on her shirt had eroded to threads.

"Can I do ya?"

"Need a room."

"How many hours? Don't do thirty-minute rates."

"Hours?"

One of the gal's blue eyes was larger than the other; it drank in Lena's appearance and reconsidered. "Sorry, ma'am. How many *nights* you lookin' to stay?"

"Not sure exactly, least a few."

"Lucky for you, we got plenty a vacancy."

The office door chimed, and Perry walked in. The woman paid him no mind. "Two nights for both of ya comes to a hundred ten even."

Lena pulled a credit card from out her jeans and placed it on the counter.

The woman turned to Perry. "Hubby or Daddy?" Before he could answer, she snickered at Lena. "I'm just foolin'. Mind my own business."

Lena said, "We're traveling the state. Meeting up with old friends. Hey, you wouldn't happen to know a Joe Delancey—stays here on occasion?"

"Don't sound familiar. What he look like?"

Perry put a hand out below his chin. "About yay high—looks like he could be Italian or Mex. Big talker—*funny*."

"Sir, you just described eighty percent of my clientele. Now, if you'd said funny-lookin'...that'd describe the whole lot." She gave a smirk. "He comes in here, I'll holler."

Lena: "Thank you…?"

"Barb."

"Thanks, Barb. How late does that bar stay open?"

"Closes for law at two a.m…but," she winked, "I'm also the owner, so…The Dorado Saloon's open whenever you need it to be."

Lena smiled at the woman; Perry took the room key.

As they broached the door, Barb hollered, "Just let me know if you need more nights, now. Checkout's at noon. Mind the hot water!"

The room was stale but not nearly as bad as Lena had anticipated. A/C unit was busted, lights a dim orange. Perry walked in, unsurprised, trampling a cigarette-burned carpet, heading straight for the toilet. Lena grabbed the TV remote, its batteries held in place by a lone strip of duct tape. The ancient Zenith powered on, revealing a spinning globe from *As the World Turns*. Perry's bowels made their first notes of the trip, prompting her to punch up the volume. She pulled a chair from out a small corner desk and sat, its cushion omitting a foul cloud.

Better learn to love it.

This is the easy part.

8.

"So, yeah…she's my bottom bitch, and shit be like that for some time now. You ass me, 'X-man, why dis' ho ya bottom ho?' X-man say, why not? Bitch's barely five foot, *white* as *fuck*, tight cropped blonde hair—her fashion sense may not be on point, but I ain't Hugo Boss neither—and, hell, she's thirty goin' on thirteen, understan'? Fools be payin' 'cause—she petite, right—they payin' 'cause she *playin'*. Playin' the part, get it? Frees up the john's conscience, I guess—more so than non-jailbait marks. But what do I know, other than the girl can put a Sultan's harem to shame, working the lots over a decade?"

A thick waitress lingered at the edge of the round, puffy booth, waiting for a break in the slim black man's rant, eyeing his violet velour track suit and polarized Vuarnet wrap-arounds; the sunglasses shielded his eyes (indoors no less). She couldn't tell if he noticed her standing there.

"*Sheeit.* Few months back, X-man was down to only three gals at the Cali Gold 'cause a this princess. And it was breezy too; a stable be hard to keep in line at my age. But Repo's got my plate stacked, so had to let them other bitches go. Not Rayna. That's my girl. What can X-man, say? He likes the game, brothers. And she the best too. Outside a fat-ass bitches and massage parlor *mamacitas*, Rayna's my cherry on top a the whole damn worl'."

The waitress cleared her throat.

P-Stone and Miggy turned to her; X-man remained busy, stirring ice cubes in his screwdriver. Miggy grabbed the menu, perusing the breakfast items as vehicles zoomed down Highway 99 out the window. Farnesi's Steakhouse, Chowchilla. P-Stone lifted a finger to order; X-man cut him off.

"Gimme the steak an' eggs—bloody—runny…with a biscuit instead a toast."

The waitress paused. "Sir, there are no substitutions on our world-famous steak and egg combo—"

X-man's sunglasses beamed her way.

"I'll see what I can do." She panned to the others. "And for you two?"

P-Stone: "Steak an' eggs sounds nice."

"How you like it?"

"Medium. Scrambled. Rye is fine."

"You?"

Miggy: "What you got in the line of a veggie sausage?"

X-man nearly spit vodka. "The fuck?" His hand shot out to the waitress. "Hold on now, girl. You fuckin' with us, right?" His eyebrows bounced out his glasses at P-Stone.

Miggy smirked. "Steak and eggs—same as the last order."

The waitress contained herself, blank-eyed back toward the register.

X-man: "Repo said you was a jokester. I like that too—sense a humor. Carries you a long way in this worl'. Amazin' how many fools lack the trait. But not you, Mig. That was good. That was good."

Miggy took a pull off his Bloody Mary, enough veggies floating in it to forgo vitamins for a week. Reminded him of a comedian he once heard say, "I'm a drunk, honey. Get my calories from the mix." P-Stone sat in silence, not one for bantering with X-man; there was probably some history between the two that Miggy wasn't aware and didn't care to ask. "Where's Repo? Thought he'd be here."

X-man reclined in the booth, expelling a sigh. "Don't ass me, man. Just called, said he got tied up, and told me to head on—so here I am. Still got his car too." He pointed to the parking lot at a two-tone Cadillac Seville (burgundy and silver). "She's a '94, I think. Good shape too. I'm fixin' to swoop Rayna tomorrow, take her for lunch over at that Red Top Café—let her dig on that wall of aquatic oddities they got and whatnot. Girl loves that freaky shit. A wall of weird fish—in the butthole of the state? Come on, man." He chuckled.

P-Stone said, "It's actually a museum."

X-man countered, "Bitch, please."

The men sat frozen, faces locked on each other.

Miggy said, "X—said you *had* two other girls, besides Rayna?"

"Matty an' Tenicia. They green as fuck, but sweet as Cool Whip. Shame to let 'em go."

"I met a girl out here once—beautiful—went by the name of Ro. Know her by any chance? I'd love to get a date with—"

P-Stone read from his iPhone: "An institution devoted to the procurement, care, study and display of objects with lasting interest or value. It's a fucking museum."

X-man exhaled, as if he were about to howl. "Nah, I dunno no Ro."

P-Stone: "Roe? Like fish eggs?"

Miggy: "No, this lizard—"

P-Stone: "I thought we were talking about fish?"

X: "We was, bitch. *He* talkin' about some lot ho."

Miggy: "Well, I'm not positive she worked the lots—kinda assumed."

X: "Museum, my ass. *Sheeit!*"

P-Stone: "Better watch that tone."

X: "Is that right?"

Miggy: "Gentlemen, please."

P-Stone deflated.

X-man reclined into his seat. "Now, I lost my train a thought. Oh, the Caddy! Yeah, Repo takes good care a his baby. You treat him good, he returns the favor. Check me out, working for Helm since day one, baby." He took a long slurp off the cocktail, licking dregs from his upper lip. "Tell me somethin' now, Mig. When's that next shipment coming up—I mean, X-man ain't pryin', just askin' for a friend."

"Repo?"

X-man grinned, cocktail straw in his Tic-Tac teeth.

Miggy lied. "I'm hearing good things from my guys down there—a week. I dunno. Maybe faster."

"Faster's always better, but you know that."

P-Stone: "He's good for it. Sampled the last batch. It's worth the wait."

"Oh, I'm sure Repo knows. Just told me to ask is all. Break bread, shoot the shit, see where we at."

A busboy delivered their toast and X-man's biscuit.

X-man hollered, "Bring some jelly, bruh. Grape or somethin'."

The waitress returned with their meals, balancing heavy plates in both arms, a consummate professional. X-man and P-Stone attacked, snouts down, cutting and shoveling. Miggy hadn't noticed till now, but X-man was missing a middle finger; he imagined the story behind it, wondering if the guy was naturally left-handed or trained himself after the incident. He looked down at his breakfast, blood glistening about scrambled eggs. The scent of gristle should've crazed him the same as these two knuckleheads, but he hesitated, thinking of those boars back at Trench's ranch, wishing he was truly vegan.

"Everything fine here?"

Miggy gazed up at the waitress, noticing she'd drawn that mole on her cheek. "Perfect, darlin'. Everything's just perfect."

They leaned against the bustleback tail of Repo's Seville, bellies full, hearts pounding: a trio of successful men. X-man sparked a joint with a torch lighter, siphoning hearty puffs before offering them the roach. P-Stone smoked a Backwoods and strolled the parking lot. Miggy buttoned his denim, bracing oncoming gusts of wind, eyeing X's missing digit. Alone with X-man, he saw a window to bleed some info, knowing the guy loved nothing more than talking about himself; he belched and broke the silence.

"I'd eat here again."

"Yeah, well, it ain't Lucca's, but whatchoo gonna do, right? Place closed down. Same as Mammoth Orange."

"Mammoth what?"

"Orange. Burger joint. Sold 'Alaskan-sized' patties from out a large wooden orange."

"Strange idea for a business."

"Not really. They had orange shakes an' shit like that." He pointed. "See, someone dug up woolly mammoth bones across the way—and a smart sombitch took note, set out to capitalize. Knew folks would be out to see the site. Figured all these travelers would get hungry. *Boom*. Mammoth Orange."

"No shit?"

"True. But everything changes, my man. One day you're eating choice burgers beside an orange monster—now you're paying triple for the same damn beef 'cause you indoors at a white clothed table."

They brooded for a beat.

"What happen to that foot, Mig?"

"Got careless on an overnight drunk." He wanted to ask about X's finger but thought it could be too much, having just met the guy. "P-Stone's been filling me in on Gallows Dome—"

"Right on. What you think?"

"I like it so far. I mean, from the tapes I've heard. Repo's got a way with words."

"Gotta hand it to the dude. Knows his shit. Sharp as nails too. Then again, after a certain age...suppose anyone can stop what they're doing in life an' become an expert of *anything*—so long as they say so. Who's gonna call an old man a liar, right? You know Mook Gipson?"

P-Stone returned to the party. "He don't know Mook."

"Well, me an' Mook been having this conversation—usually

over a beer or two. You know what's wrong with spirituality in this fucked up worl'?"

Miggy shrugged.

"Everyone out hawking their goods has an outdated business plan. They out hustlin' faith based on '*known*' doctrines. Known as in *fact*, son. 'This was written in *this* book, way back muhfuckin' when, so it *must* be true'—proof our doctrine's the shit, right? Well, The Dome do just the opposite. Repo ain't claiming proof in a damn thing. Trench ain't a god, and Gallows Dome ain't even a religion. It offers up the *unknown*, see? Only truth that *is* a fact—human race don't have a clue how they got here. Mook comes at me sayin', 'X, what about them archeologists? They say we been 'round since—' Boy, shut the fuck up, I say. Every ten years, they be digging up something new that prove we been 'round for another ten thousand years, then another ten thousand, then another. *Sheeit.* Who's to say we ain't been around for infinity? Birth. Rise. Decimation. Rebirth. That's The Dome in a nutshell. Scientists can only see back as far as a last catastrophic event. Who's to say that ain't been happening, over and over and over, again?" He paused to regroup. "Now, say that's the case. Humankind rises to great prominence, only to be destroyed by some comet or whatnot—then repeat—a never-ending coil of beasts. Now, look at the state of the worl'—look at it for what it is. We've made technical advancements unseen by our kind, son—we at the pinnacle of *our* being. If history can tell us anything...pretty soon," he chuckled, "we're all gotta be dust."

Miggy: "That's a pretty harsh outlook, don't you think?"

P-Stone: "You gonna sit around and wait to die, Miggy? Or plan to take a stand, embrace the end of days—go out guns blazing? Those of us that pursue The Dome—we're extreme outliers, man. Never mind thinking we're all headed into some future dystopia—look around—peep *this*-topia. Should be focused on anything you ever wanted to do in life—any pleasure—any 'sin'—*that* is what Gallows Dome has to offer. Buncha folks tired a being bent over...now they wanna fuck the world. Freedom comes to the few willing to do *whatever* they *will*—"

X: "While they can." He tossed the roach into his mouth and chewed. "Funny shit is, Mook Gipson don't even believe in science, right? Always going around, hollerin', 'God is good—God is great.' When I see his twisted ass face, an' he blasts me with that tired-ass shit—I tellim, Back up, *boy*. Save your salvation for the suckers."

P-Stone smirked.

"Feel me, Miggy. It's a new worl'—one that braves a fresh way a thinkin'." He opened the car door and slid in, rolling down the window, his Vuarnets lasering Miggy. "If Gallows Dome be wrong, brother—I don't wanna be right."

The Seville launched out the lot.

Miggy turned to P-Stone, already walking to his truck.

"Hey, you got something to tell me about you and this guy?"

"Like what?"

"Come on, man. It's obvious."

"He's talkin' shit on me to Repo—least that's what I heard. He'll never admit it though. Dumb, motherfucker."

Miggy sensed jealousy, P-Stone wanting to take X-man's place beside Repo in an instant. "What's with his nickname?"

"X-man? Repo asks him to do *X*, as in anything he says, and the guy gets it done. Started calling himself that years ago. I think it's lame, but whatever."

Miggy made a gun with his hand and placed it to his temple. "*Anything* Repo says?"

P-Stone didn't acknowledge the act. He didn't have to—his eyes gave Miggy the answer.

The auditorium roared. Worshippers clawed at the heavens, howling in praise, tears boiling out their faces. A portly woman fainted atop two shaky teens, overcome by seizure, lost in trance. Grown men collapsed, one after the other in rapid succession, as if a choreographed dance routine. Hundreds of similar traumas transpired while music blared out the sound system—biblical allegories reminding those in delirium just how special they were to witness these healing miracles, live, on stage, beneath an impressive light show.

Repo adjusted in his seat, notepad on a knee, jotting down the ticks of this traveling road show. Hell, the price of admission alone would've been a fine score for the preacher and his posse. But that was only a ticket for the ride. If Broadway plays guaranteed such physical transformations through spiritual salvation, maybe they could tap into this crowd—the slick money—the dirt. After all, art was in the eye of the beholder, right?

The song ended. Exhausted parishioners returned to their seats, sweaty and winded. The organist struck calming chords while the preacher swiped his brow with a silk handkerchief—same one used to heal those flocking his podium, face after face slapped, their bodies dashed into a vegetable state. Repo's phone buzzed. A text. X-man needed to talk. He pulled a prepaid out his duck vest, dialing.

The preacher jumped in place, harvesting new powers. A second voice out the speakers barked, "There is a lost soul with us today. Rise up and be counted! Whom amongst us must bear witness to His glory—saved from the wrath of Perdition! Stand! Repent! Accept His glory into your heart!"

Repo closed the notebook and rose from his seat.

The crowd went wild—organist kicking back into gear.

Everyone watched as he squeezed down the aisle, stuck the phone to his ear and walked out a side exit.

X-man answered.

"What's up?"

"Just had lunch with your boy."

"And?"

"He sayin' a week at the latest."

"Alright. Have Stone keep with him, stay on top of things. We need his shipment, but if it means dealing with promises in bad faith, then fuck him. We'll cut him loose."

"So far, he been on the level. But you right."

The auditorium roared in the distance as Repo walked through the parking lot.

"Say, where the hell you at right now?"

"In the field. Doing research."

"How'd that transport go? Goods was *intact*, right?"

"Yeah. Trench was happy. You did good."

"Dat's all X-man wanted to hear."

"Keep me posted on our Miggy situation."

"Okeydoke, boss. Talk soon."

9.

Three days had passed since Lena and Perry pulled into the Villa Motor Lodge with no lead on Joe Delancey's whereabouts or a single direction they were headed in. Lena spent her days at the Cali Gold, loitering in the game room or pretending to wash laundry. Place was a festering compound, reeking restrooms, moldy laundromat—every square inch in steep decline after forty-plus years of use. The movie room consisted of Rubbermaid chairs before a Panasonic big box—arcade junked with broken '90s gems. But Lena wouldn't let defeat rear its head, her proactive choice of being out here, trying to make something happen, was enough to get her through another day.

Most folks she came across were just passing through, their faces like petrified wood. With all the talk about lot lizards, she had yet to see anyone half-naked, strutting their wares. Maybe Perry was having better luck today. The sun would be down soon. She decided to head back to the room for a power nap, wanting to hit the Dorado Saloon and mingle till closing.

At a far wing of the Cali Gold sat its general store. Perry was busy digging through clearance bins of cassette tapes and damaged Louis L'Amour paperbacks. Years ago, this place had a decent music selection; nowadays, the entirety of their CD aisle barely filled an end-cap. So far, he'd lucked out, finding a copy of G'n'R's *Lies*, now busy looking for something Lena would like. He palmed a Lou Reed tape with a blue cover, flipped it and began to read the song list.

"That's *really* good."

The girl's voice struck him dumb, his eyes panning from her tiny bare feet—toes with chipped pink polish—upwards to wide green cat-eyes. Hadn't seen anyone with makeup like that since his mother in the '60s.

Perry said, "What's so good about it?"

"The title for starters. *Rock and Roll Heart*. Not every day the name of a record turns out to be that of its best song."

"Wouldn't you think that'd be the case?"

"Oh, many have tried and failed."

Perry tested her youngblood wisdom. "Like who?"

"Oh, I don't know. Let me think for a sec." She fiddled with the strings of her zip-up hoodie. "Look at The Ramones?"

"Their debut was self-titled."

"Of course. But take *Rocket to Russia*. Great album. Should've been called *Cretin Hop*."

"Says you. All the cool kids would've called it *Teenage Lobotomy*."

"I'm definitely *not* cool."

He disagreed, eying her tattered bell-bottoms—the chrome tops off cheap lighters clamped to pockets. "You're definitely a Janis in a world of Kardashians."

She smiled.

Perry shook the tape's contents. "Thanks for the suggestion." He returned to digging; her hand shot out before the bin. He returned to face her—tight cropped blonde locks styled by bedhead and a lemon-yellow clip.

"I'm Rayna. Nice to meetcha."

"Perry. Pleasure."

"You in the mood for some *commercial company* this evening?"

The term eluded him, the girl so petite and wrinkle-free, didn't take her for a prostie at first. He surveyed the general store, searching for accomplices of hers; if this was some kind of roll, he'd like to know what was coming.

She put two fingers into his pant pocket. "Heard in prison, they make bitches walk around the yard, linked to their man like this."

"I wouldn't know. Never been."

"Me neither. Just saying. How about you take *me* for a stroll?"

Perry tried not to let the girl know she'd thrown him for a loop. "How 'bout this? We go and grab us some drinks—get to know each other?"

A pouty face beamed back at him. She said, "Time's money—ain't that how it goes?"

"'Nother day, 'nother dollar, is how I remember it. But I'll pay for your time."

"Alright, mister. You're on."

They approached the counter. Perry paid for the cassettes, avoiding eye contact with the cashier, knowing what the kid was thinking. But that wasn't important. If this girl worked the lot—maybe she'd have some information that could be useful? Maybe she'd seen Delancey? Maybe she knew him? It was more to go on than he or Lena had discovered since they'd arrived.

What did he have to lose?

This cashier's respect?

Fuck him.

Perry discovered two things on their walk back to the Dorado: 1.) The girl was barefoot because she'd left her rollerblades at the store's entrance, having been reprimanded on several occasions for riding them inside; 2.) With her sweatshirt hood on, Rayna turned into a panda bear, all black and white, tiny ears atop her skull, playful eyes at her temples. With her arm in the crook of his elbow, he towed her down gravely streets, zooming headlamps off the highway lighting their path. She was twenty-nine—at least that's what she'd been telling folks for the past couple years. Perry would've guessed nineteen or twenty, but by the way the girl spoke, he knew she'd been around the block. She asked him why he found himself in such a spot, and he lied, saying that he was newly retired and trying to enjoy the time he had left. She took that as a flirtatious gesture, asking if he could spare a cigarette. They smoked in silence as the wheels of her skates grumbled a tune. The Villa's neon was crackling—the saloon's door slightly ajar with music seeping out. He checked the parking lot for Lena, noticing the light flicker off in their room before entering the bar.

Gentle yelps: An animal trapped. She searches through her house, looking to save the thing distressed. The tips of canyons peek through every window. Tess' bedroom. In the hamper, wails resonate. She opens the lid, revealing a whimpering puppy—a Yorkie, no less. She hugs and kisses it—its fur soft and comforting; the puppy slobbers her with licks. Sweet puppy breath. She calls for Tess, wanting to show her this new surprise—an addition to their family...But her calls go unanswered. The puppy begins to grow, rapidly, its body expanding, the weight becoming unbearable. She lets go, only to find the dog standing on two legs before her, eye to eye—something out of a horror flick. Before she can scream, the house disappears from around her, blipping into a black void. Now, she's in the Cali Gold parking lot, trapped among a sea of Freightliners and Kenworths, their horns blaring, exhaust pipes coughing. The mutant puppy is no longer there—now human. Scanning up from its hairy legs, she recognizes it as her daughter, aged far beyond her years—features hardened, legs like her mother's (part-spider). Tess is walking the lot of some future wasteland, sashaying her scantily covered goods through howling truckers. She follows Tess through a maze of eighteen-wheelers—a coiled labyrinth of steel. After several turns, an image conjures through a fog of headlights. Tess, on her knees, servicing a customer, her tongue slurping ecstasy. As she runs closer, the man's features became clear.

Perry.

She tries to cry out to her baby girl, but her vocal cords are severed. Her collapse gets Tess' attention, turning from her john, blood seeping out her lips, staining sharp teeth. "Tastes yummy, mommy! Hahahahaha—"

Lena jolted awake, clawing bedsheets until realizing where she was; as her adrenaline dumped, it brought a surge of tears that seemed endless, yet still not enough to wash the horror from her brain.

Lena climbed into the RV, hunting through cabinets for anything that could pose as dinner. She peeled back the top of a shrimp flavored Cup O'Noodles, filled it to the line with bottled water and slid it into the microwave. Catching a glimpse of her face in the door's glass, she forced herself to sit down, life's mileage packing a punch. Gone were the days of youthful stamina to charge her through stressful situations. She could still feel the electricity behind some of the worst moments in her life, but they all felt different than today's hell. The first episode happened at an early age and had nothing to do with her parents' divorce. *It was a boy.* Thinking back on it now, it wasn't *just* a boy—his actions forced upon her beneath those bleachers had their seeds somewhere else. Regardless, she was victimized, too embarrassed to come forward. And to whom? Mother was working double shifts with no vacation to spare; Daddy was out doing God knows what with bigger boys—probably same as the one who choked her unconscious in order to have his way...

The stress charging her core those following years became a lifeforce, pushing her to exercise at an unreasonable clip. Plyometrics. Jazzercise. Long distance jogs. Anything to fill the brain and make her feel better...human...again. By the time she dropped out of college, she'd become a specimen of flesh. The fond looks and kind words from others came day after day, but to her, she was nothing more than an empty vessel of hate and loathing. Exercise couldn't save her...

Then Daddy died; later that year, Mother moved to Las Vegas for work and had a stroke. Caring for Mom, she switched her hunger for exercise routines to nightlife activities, experiencing the other side of living for the first time.

Alcohol.

Drugs.

Detachment.

She had it all. The perfect combination to not care enough about anything. When Mother passed, and left her with nothing but an old couch and some baby pictures, she shirked a normal job, allowing life to drag her into the gutter...

Fremont Street.

1999.

Weeknight shifts at the Glitter Gulch were strictly to open doors to real monetary gain. She could dance, her tiny body still fit and nimble. She stood apart from the other girls too. At first, they were just propositions. Gifts of the trade—ones that ultimately begged favors. Selling herself was never in the books, but the constant nags made things worse. Anger began to boil. Rage-filled outbursts in public became common over minor discrepancies: the wrong McDonald's order; a soft pour of vodka. But she learned to channel the rage, siphoning its electrodes into more successful avenues.

All his life, Daddy was on the grift.

It was in her blood.

Her father's words: "Mark is a mark, honey. Any sucker's gonna get played sometime in their wretched life—the only question is by who?"

At first, she'd stake out billiard halls, shoot around with locals for hours, adopting fake personas, waiting for action. And that action never involved her making a single break either. She'd blend in with other railbirds, watching sharks play for hours—days if the take was high enough. With so many master stickmen coming through town, the games became less about skill and more about endurance. Who could dish it or take it the longest? Last one with their wits about went the spoils. And they needed something pretty around to look at while they played, right? She'd be there with a big hug or smooch on the cheek, right at their moment of triumph. Some solid drinks, a few laughs, then back to a cheap hotel. She'd munch Adderall while freshening up in the bathroom, waiting for her stud's body to crash. No sex. Just light touching and innuendo. Soon as the men began to snore, she'd have the whole pot of cash to herself. She was always amazed at how many of them put trust in her over simple acts of flirtation.

Suckers.

Daddy's little girl.

But pool savants were only good for a few turns, there being less than a dozen halls throughout Vegas. She adapted, embracing the city for what it was: a mecca for marks. She'd hit The Strip most nights, Fremont on Mondays (called it Loser's Lunch). Pick a casino, any casino. She'd get cozy playing video poker or penny slots, somewhere with a view of the high-end tables. Winners. Losers. Didn't matter. These fools had the bankroll to sit down and play. She'd place herself perfectly, barging into their lives through a spilled drink or pretending she was lost. From there on out, it was easier than outlasting the best of sharks. She *became* the shark, taking foreign businessmen or Texas oil jerks into deep waters before drawing blood. Cash. Credit cards. Jewelry. She was a ghost, in and out of their lives without a trace. What were they going to do? Call their wives? That haul went on for years.

Until one sloppy weekend, capped by a one-night stand, reversed her role.

Then Tess.

The microwave dinged. She opened her eyes, waiting for that electricity to come back and take her into the night. She'd embed herself further into this sad world, a thirsty tick on a healthy deer.

***

The music inside the Dorado turned out to be "karaoke." From their barstools, Perry and Rayna watched a flood of deluded patrons squeal into the mic as they sipped Mexican lager, tossing back an occasional tequila shot. The joint was murky, a positive for a bar in this corner of the world. A large Statue of Liberty loomed near the entrance—its presence an overlord to all that frolicked inside. After having been here for the past few nights, Perry had gotten a creepy vibe off the French lady, similar to those of Jesus pictures with jaundiced eyes that followed you around a room. Rest of the place was your basic juke joint—pool table and ruddy booths to fill its guts. Rayna cheered at a rotund patron, clad in an Indiana Jones hat and flip-flops, as he howled:

If I can just get off of this L.A. freeway—without getting killed or caught...

She hooted and whistled.

Perry panned for the barkeep who'd disappeared on a smoke break. The song came to an end. Rayna raised her hands in applause as Indy gave his bow. She turned her attention back to Perry.

"Forget how much I love this place."

Perry smirked. "*This* place?"

"Same as every other bar I've ever been to. So, yeah...guess I love *all* bars, really."

"I work in one, back home."

"Seriously? Thought you were retired?"

"I am. Helps pass the time."

"Wish I had a job like that."

"A wish isn't necessary. You can. Believe me."

"Easy for you to say. I know the limits of my skills. Believe *me*. This' the best life my tiny ass can buy."

The barkeep returned with dilated pupils; Perry nodded for him to prep another round.

"Been working this beat a long time, huh?"

"Yessiree, Bob. See, you stop in an area too long, a girl like me can draw the wrong kinda attention. That's exactly what panned out...by design."

"There's always more options out there than you think—if you ever wanted to switch occupations."

"Sure, but Del Taco don't pay as much."

"Hey, I'm just sayin'..."

The barkeep slid their hooch. They toasted, tapped the counter and swilled.

She fidgeted with a napkin. "I hear you, Perry. Truth is, I been thinkin' along them same lines lately. There's a shelf life when it comes to working these lots—any lizard will cop to it. Pretty soon my juice ain't gonna be worth the squeeze."

"Shit, look who you're talking to. I've already sang *that* tune."

"Ain't dead yet."

"True...on the outside."

"Ready to give me a squeeze?"

"Honey, I could be your grandpa."

"I've fucked older."

"I bet you have."

"Ouch."

"Now, hang on. That came out wrong. I'm enjoying myself— really. Let's take it slow."

"Don't fuck on first date, I suppose. A *true* gentleman." She scoffed, "What a tease," grabbing her cell beside the beer, quickly realizing it was dead. "Man."

"Your boyfriend lookin' for ya?"

"Hell no!"

"Ah. Plan to tweet something about me then."

"I don't do that shit either."

"Why not? Everyone your age does."

"Well, I ain't *everyone*. Don't get me wrong, I tried it for a minute. But social media just let me see how sad and lonely my heroes truly are. Total downer—and I got enough of those in my life as it is."

The girl beats her own drum, alright.

"Can I borrow your phone?"

As he slid it from his pants to raise it toward her, a juggling act ensued, hand slippery from the frosty bottle. Before he could catch it, the phone bounced off the bartop, splashing into a sink for dunking pints.

"Holy shit." Rayna lunged over the bar to retrieve it. Dripping between her fingers, the screen was completely black. "Oh, man."

Perry palmed the broken device, livid with himself.

"They say to put it in a cup and fill it with rice. Should dry it out."

"Who's *they*?"

"Folks smarter than us."

A new patron approached the mic; Fleetwood Mac bled out the speakers.

Perry slid the phone back into his jeans. "I need a fuckin' smoke."

"Perfect timing."

They rose and hit the front door.

"Just look around you. Everything decays," Rayna said, chomping a piece of peppermint gum to "mentholize" her Marlboro.

Perry took a final drag off his cig, ears filled with whatever popped into the poor girl's head. She had a decent heart, he was certain—but her talking and talking...Reminded him of his ex-wife. When she paused for a breath, he interjected.

"You being an expert on these parts—ever come by a fella named Joe Delancey? 'Bout yay high—big talker, like yourself."

"What he look like?"

"Hard to finger his nationality—your generation would say he's got a pretty almond hue."

"What he drive? Freightliner? What color? I remember my dudes' trucks more than their faces."

"I really dunno—used to ride a Harley."

"I know a Captain Joe Ubik. But he's as tall as he is round with a pecker resembling a cashew. Pretty sure he's from Livingston, Montana too."

"Nah."

"Let me think. There's J.R.—but he's white as a snowy owl. Joe Kemp ate it on the road near Frisco last year—damn near decapitated when they found him—ejected into oncoming—now, why the hell am I telling you all this? Um-um-um-um..."

Perry spun to open the door, nearly knocking into Lena approaching the entrance. He barely recognized her—makeup a bit seductive, clothes a tad skimpy for this night's chill. "Howdy."

She looked over his shoulder at the girl. "How's your night going?"

"It's going, all right. Rayna, this' Lena."

Lena put her hand out.

Rayna barely squeezed it. "This your man? I'll have you know he's been a perfect gentleman this evening—although he did accidently break his cell phone, Lena. Hey—Le-*na*...Ray-*na*...That's funny. Not every day I run into someone with a name so similar. You wanna know something else funny? Rayna means *pure*, clean. Ain't that the nut? What does Lena mean?"

"No clue."

"Huh...should look into it."

Lena smiled at Perry and walked inside, jarring eyes from about the room. Perry and Rayna went back to their stools to finish their drinks. Rayna hung out for another round then split; they agreed to do it again sometime, enjoying each other's company. Rest of the evening, Perry nursed suds, watching Lena pound beers and run the pool table, hamming it up with every person that came inside. Could sense she'd done this sort of routine before—he'd seen several ropers in his time at the 36 36, working the short con, scratching for dollars. Not to mention all the railbirds at every pool tournament in Yankee Doodles. He watched her demeanor, flinty and shameless as she fished for info among the sea of drunks: *an actress in the role of a lifetime.*

And she was good too. He remembered the way she shot into character back at that office supply place, pretending to be a *Times* reporter…

A grifter.

That's what Lena's past life entailed.

10.

"That ain't no shark!"

X-man slid down his sunglasses a touch, leaning over to read the stuffed animal's inscription. "Says so, right here, Rayna. *Goblin* shark. Check out the beak on this fella. Freaky deaky."

"It's skin's all pink and gross."

"Yeah, well…I'm bettin' the taxidermist went a bit heavy with the paintbrush." He licked beads off his vanilla soft serve, about to drip down the knuckles.

They took in the treasure trove of fish (many of which Rayna found suspect: an eerie cyclops, a starfish with feathers), then headed for a bench in the adjacent field to enjoy their midday dessert. Rayna looked nice, sporting the sundress he'd bought her on his last trip to Los Angeles; she tamed down the makeup on her creamy features, blood-red Ray Bans over her eyes. They sat on the tabletop, boots resting on the bench seat, watching trucks refuel at the café's gas pumps. She imagined that some girls did fun stuff like this with their fathers, but she wouldn't know.

"So, what's good?"

"Same old Gold, X. 'Nother day, 'nother dollar."

"You cool on money?"

"Yeah, I'm makin' ends. Met a new dude yesterday. Old guy, heading through."

"Did you have to—"

"No, no. We just talked. Bought me some drinks."

"He pay you?"

"Mm-hmm. What can I say? Mr. Lonelyhearts. Reminds me of my Uncle Stanley."

"The *cool* one?"

"Introduced me to *everything*. The Stooges. John Waters. You name it."

"*Every*thang, huh?"

"Don't be an ass. I'm telling you this old man's harmless. You'd like him the most."

"Dude got a name?"

"Said it was Perry, but I'm not so sure I believe him yet."

"Yet?"

"He's staying at the Villa. I'll see him again."

"Huh."

"What?"

"Nothin'."

She slid her sunglasses down her nose. "Aw, you're jealous."

X-man leapt from the table, tossing his cone in a trash bin, stretching his legs. "Ain't jealous. Just wanna know who's hangin' with my baby is all. You know me, I get protective."

"Don't worry, dear. Know I'm your girl."

X pulled two smokes from his pocket, handing one to Rayna.

She tossed her cone, exhaling after he torched her cig. "They got those in the Bahamas when you were growing up?"

"What? Freaky fish? Come on, girl."

"Soft serve ice cream."

"You're talkin' a lifetime ago. Left the island when I's eight years old."

"So?"

He contemplated childhood treats. "Can't remember ever havin' one."

"Me neither."

They puffed.

"You're a good one, X—too bad no one gets to know that."

"Well, honey, X-man's got a reputation to uphold in these parts. *Sheeit*. Gotta walk wit' a limp, talk like a pimp…"

She chuckled as he strutted around the table, doing his famous George Jefferson. This was the friend that she'd loved—the pal that had helped her get through so many lean years on the lot. Protecting her from predators. Lending an ear. They were birds of the same nest, wings clipped, thumping every branch on their way down.

And she knew what he was capable of.

She'd seen it firsthand, heard stories. But they didn't talk about violent things. They rarely spoke about their past too, her bringing up her uncle just now even threw her for a loop. Once, on a drunken spring day, X had accidently mentioned a wife and daughter that had left him when he was a "young buck," back in Burbank…or he left them…or someone died—either way, the court forced him to a stint in the army soon after. But that mess happened a good thirty years before Rayna was even born, so she didn't count it toward his character. Being judged purely on the decisions she was forced to make in her lifetime defined a different person than who she'd become. And this version was better than the alternative. She took his hand and stepped down from the picnic table, walking toward Repo's Seville; its paint reminded her of a cinnamon Jolly Rancher. X told her how he might be leaving again, if Repo said. She just nodded, rubbing his nubby middle digit, letting him know he'd be missed—afraid for him and whatever he was about to do. Repo was capable of tremendous things. He opened the car door for her. She gave him a hug before climbing inside, whispering, "Thanks for everything, Big Dog."

A cloud of sage hit Repo's nostrils the moment he walked through a beaded curtain into the Psychic Eye Bookstore. With the walls painted black over dense crimson carpets, the shop took on a cavernous tone, filled with amulets, statues, manuscripts and oddities—all tied to ritualistic endeavors of the ages. Repo perused the merchandise, not hunting for anything specific. A jangling came from the back room; he turned from admiring an Egyptian tomb replica to find an older woman behind the cash register, tarot deck in hand. She spoke in a thick foreign accent.

"Need any help, kind sir? Just call out to Madam Sophia."

He nodded, moving on to the vast array of black candles.

"Could I interest you in a reading?"

Repo approached the register, his gaze locked with the psychic. "How much?"

"Twenty for a fifteen-minute read."

"With these cards? No crystal ball or nothin'?"

"Crystal ball is sixty."

He nodded, unconvinced.

"Sir, tarot is the storybook of your life—a mirror to the soul— the key to inner wisdom."

"You put it like that, twenty bucks seems like a steal. Alright. Shoot."

The woman gave a wan smile, cutting the deck like a Vegas pro, spreading them before him, fanning each, evenly spaced. She ran her hands over the cards, eyes closed, lids twitching.

"Sir, please do as I am now. Move your palm above the cards and, with deep focus, pick one that compels you. Lay it down, face-up, before me."

Repo slapped his palms together, harnessing sweet juju. He did as the woman instructed. Soon as his card hit the counter, Madam Sophia's face went flush, mouth agape. She hesitantly leered back at him, hands beginning to tremble. Repo smiled, knowing exactly the horrors conjured behind her eyes. Before she could utter a word, he tossed the twenty atop the cards and walked out.

The raven black Cadillac was fresh off the lot, merely eight hours old—the first large purchase he'd made since being able to wash dope money via The Dome. Felt good, living like a king— flaunting. He'd envisioned this lifestyle several times over, and now it was here. *Success*. In the car, he dialed X-man with a fresh burner. The moment X answered, Repo said, "Been thinking about our friend, Miggy Rojas. I want you to press him—not on the dope, but on his stomach. Want you to show him what we do to folks who fuck with our money. Once he gets the big picture, should deliver the dope pronto." X-man agreed. Repo ended the call, catching Madam Sophia staring at him through the shop window. He blew her a kiss and drove off.

The Speckled Hen Inn, Los Banos.

Joe Delancey, crammed into a busted phone booth, dropped change into its slot as a gaggle of children chucked rocks at a dead crow in the inn's parking lot. Every day for the past few months he'd chastised himself for not checking in with Becca, but some things were just best to keep her in the dark about. One: to manage her stress level. Two: to ensure her safety. The phone began to ring; he plugged his naked ear with a finger.

Four rings.

"Come on, Becca."

She answered, out of breath, the shouts of a drill sergeant blasting behind her. "Hello?"

"Becca, lower the television!"

The exercise commands got softer. "Dad?"

"Hey, sweetheart."

"Don't *sweetheart* me. Where the hell are you?"

"Still up north, tracking a lead."

"Jesus, you take off and don't even—"

"I know. I know. I'm sorry. How's everything down there?"

"Okay, considering. Few customers per week. No more vice raids on the block. Things are cleaning up around here, sort of."

"How you doing?"

"Great. Down to one twenty-six."

"Shit, that's flyweight. Bet I wouldn't even recognize you."

She didn't respond.

He knew he'd touched a nerve but had to ask a favor—the real reason he called. "Listen, I need you to do something—"

"Here we go."

"Relax. It's nothing big. I've been checking the papers for raids done by a Sergeant Mel Brown of the LAPD. Haven't come across anything in the past month. If you could, call your *friend*, the cop, ask him if he's heard anything. He'll know what you're talking about."

"Cop friend? He *was* my fiancé, Dad. But, yeah. I'll call. What's this for? Another job?"

He lied. "Kinda."

"Did you find that Boyd girl?"

"I did."

"Funny, we didn't get a check for it."

"That one was on the arm."

"Great, more freebies. Hey, Perry Quell stopped by looking for you."

His heart sunk an inch. "How's he doing these days?"

"Looked like shit, but not any worse than last we saw him."

"What he want?"

"Had some lady with him that would actually *pay* for your services. Has a daughter went missing."

"That so?"

"You're up there still trying to find Rochelle, huh?"

"Thought I had a lead on something, but—"

"But it's been far too long, am I right? Nothing linking together anymore?"

"That's a fair assessment. But I'm still optimistic."

"A wise man once told me, 'Time's the enemy when it comes to these kinds of cases.'" She listened to him breathing. "Well, Perry left his phone number. Said to give him a call. Knows you're up there."

"How?"

"I let him into your office. Saw papers on your desk."

"Oh."

"You want his number?"

Joe didn't feel like rehashing the disappointment he'd had with himself for letting the man down, but knew he had to call. "Sure."

Becca rifled digits.

"The woman he was with—did you get the daughter's name?"

"He wrote it down here. *Tess.* Tess Madadhi."

"How you spell that?"

She slowly relayed the letters. "You gonna start in on her case then—seeing as it's cash money?"

"Soon as I finish up here. Kinda swamped."

"—"

"Alright, sweet—"

"When you coming home?"

"I'm not sure."

Becca expelled a sigh, swallowing a lump in her throat. "Be careful, 'kay?"

"I love you, Becca."

"Love you too, Pop."

He hung up the phone, composed himself and dropped more change. The number Perry had left went straight to voicemail. "Hey, Perr'. It's Joe. Becca told me you came by the motel. I'm out on the road, undercover—so no phone. But if you call The Speckled Hen Inn in Los Banos, they could patch you into room ten. Late nights and early mornings are best. You know how it goes. Hope all is well, my friend." His fingers ended the call on the receiver. He exited the booth, watching the kids heave stones at the bird's carcass, all the way back to his room. The thought of another missing girl's case was the last thing on his mind. The environment out here had him on overload. Nothing but barren fields and sorrow. Once he figured out how to get more pills, things would ease up. Had to find out about this "Ro"—after all this time, the what if was far too great to head home now...

And he owed it to Perry.

He owed it to himself.

11.

Perry climbed down from Dreamboat's innards, holding his toiletries and a towel, careful as he walked in leather sandals atop the Villa's torn gravel lot. The RV was cozy, and though they'd agreed to swap sleeping arrangements every day, he'd come to enjoy life in the moving vehicle. Reminded him of the *Bessie Mae*; never thought he'd feel uncomfortable in conventional housing, but after decades spent in a hull the size of a large dumpster, there you have it. He yawned, checking his watch; it was approaching three p.m. He knocked on the door to Lena's room. After what seemed like an eternity, she opened it, makeup smeared, hair disheveled, wearing the same outfit as the night previous.

"Salutations!" Perry grinned. "Hungover, are we?"

She didn't address him, lumbering back to bed, slamming down on it—face first.

Perry was finishing up in the bathroom, combing his wet hair, administering beard oil, when he heard Lena return to life. He figured in her weakened state, now would be a good time to ask her a few questions—ones that had arisen last night, watching her play the saloon like a pro. He hung his towel and got dressed.

Lena was hovering over the trash bin, eyes glazed, willing

herself not to throw up. Hadn't drank that much in years, and even though it was mostly beer, the clip lasted until far past closing, making the number of pints she'd consumed one of the world's newest mysteries. She didn't have to look, feeling Perry's presence lurking over her shoulder.

"You were in rare form last night."

"How so?"

"Oh, I think you know. I've been working bars since before you were born, kid. Seen a few grifters in my time."

She went to argue, but pain jolted the back of her skull.

"Can't lie—you were damn good. Could've robbed the place blind, if that were your intention."

"Was trying to find Delancey."

"I'm sure you were. But watching you run the room that way got me to thinking...What say you weren't tryin' to play *me* the same way?"

"Fuck off."

"Not saying you are. Tess is missing, and I believe that. Guess what I'm getting at is...can I see your driver's license?"

She nodded to her purse on the floor. "Knock yourself out."

"Don't think shitty of me, Lena. We just have to be on the level, kid."

"Quit calling me *kid.*" She retched into the bin.

Perry shuffled through her bag, careful not to touch any feminine products, finding her wallet. It was all there: *Madadhi, Lena Rose, F, 5'-1", 106 lbs., Eyes BRN, Hair BRN*...He read her date of birth and dropped it back into her purse. "You're right. You're not a kid. Rochelle would've been the same age."

"Maybe she still is?"

He spun, eye to eye, mouth quivering.

"Hope is all we have, Perr'."

He stormed out to the RV.

Lena rose to shut the door, but saw Perry, frozen, gazing at Dreamboat. Then she saw it too. "What the—"

Someone had tagged the entire side of the beast with thick

black spray paint.

Perry: "Fuckin' Christ."

The cherry on Barb's Winston might as well have been a clown nose by the way she reacted to the defilement of Dreamboat.

Lena: "I don't see what's so damn funny."

"That's a shame."

"Does the motel have surveillance?"

Phlegm crackled in Barb's laugh-cough-wheeze.

Perry: "Not like it'd do us any good, Lena. Back in the city— some tweaker breaks into your car, steals the radio—a call to police would be ridiculous."

"I get it, Perr'. Just don't think it's funny—us being victimized."

Barb contained herself. "Relax, lady. I got a buncha paint in the saloon's upstairs storage." She toggled through a large key chain, the look on her face boasting that she knew every door each opened. She cracked a gold one off. "Here. 'Round back, there's a red door at the top of the stairwell. Know we got white and a shit ton of others from over the years. Brushes, rollers. Help yourself."

Perry: "Thanks, Barb."

Lena: "Sure you don't know anyone that could've done this?"

"I look like troubled youth?" She popped another Winston and commenced slouching through the day.

Lena couldn't tell if the temperature had shot up or she had the sweats, but the Dorado's storage room was fouler than Barb's office. As she waded through mops and buckets, the scurrying of vermin could be heard. She shrugged the chill up her spine, eyeing a metal shelving unit on a far wall that held nearly a dozen gallons of paint. With the light on her cell, she viewed cap labels, brushing off dust or rat pellets, finding just about every color but powder blue. An idea struck. It was her RV after all. She began lugging gallons outside, along with a bucket filled with brushes.

Didn't take Lena long to remove the words with white paint, coating the entire side, creating a blank canvas. She hadn't done a mural in at least ten years. Would take on work to pay the bills, back when she and Tess were struggling in Downtown. Taking a step back to drink in the whole sidewall of the RV, she contemplated what to paint and how to incorporate the side door into it. Most of her pieces were surreal, evocations of the subconscious during meditations or dreams. She closed her eyes, conjuring happy images of when she and Tess were together. Soon as inspiration hit, she began opening cans and stirring paint.

Perry was swiping mustard from his beard outside the Cali Gold, a bit careless with his ninety-nine-cent "Patriot Dawg," when he noticed an older Cadillac with one of those weird behinds pull into a parking slot. Thing was hard to ignore since every other vehicle around was moving freight. He watched as Rayna, seated shotgun, leaned over and gave a slim black man a peck on the lips. She didn't see him standing there; he lit a smoke to justify his leering. The car's door opened. The driver eyed him intensely as Rayna got out.

"Hey there, stranger."

Perry greeted her with bouncing eyebrows. "Hard at work?"

"Hardly working, these days. How's the phone?"

He reached into his back pocket and pulled out a box of Rice-A-Roni. "Just bought this. See if it works." He tossed his smoke to the ground. "You keep some interesting company."

"You an' me both, buddy. That was just my pal, X."

"X as in Xavier?"

"X as in X-man."

Perry spouted smoke through his nostrils, containing a laugh. "You give him all your money—or he let you keep a few bucks?"

"He ain't my pimp, Perry. Just a good friend."

Perry nodded in disbelief.

"Serious. He knows everyone in these parts too. I bet he might know that fella you were askin' me about..."

"Joe Delancey."

"I'll ask him next time I see him."

Perry softened. "Buy you a patriot dawg?"

"Just ate—an' I don't care for lips and assholes. But thanks for the offer." She burped. "Take a grit though."

"A what?"

"A grit...a smoke...a cancer stick."

"That's what you kids call 'em these days?"

"That's what *I* call 'em, but I'm hardly a *kid*."

Perry told himself to stop using the term, not knowing why he'd started. Out here, everything made him feel old. He handed her his soft pack.

"What's the retirement life got in store for you today?"

"They're playing a couple monster movies in there. Prolly stick around for one."

"Which ones?"

"*Predator* and *The Thing*."

"Oh, snap! You kidding? We gotta stay for both."

Her enthusiasm brought a smile.

"Perry, you don't understand. It's usually superhero crap or John Wayne flicks all the time. This' something special. Let's grab us some booze an' candy—get us a primo seat."

"There's no one in there yet. I just checked."

She cashed her grit on the concrete, smoke seeping out her wet, red lips. "Even better."

She held onto his arm for most of the first movie, occasionally slipping her hand to his thigh, then back. She shouted at the TV, hollering when that dude from *Rocky* got his arm blown off. They passed a pint of Evan Williams between them, chasing the burn of bourbon with Milk Duds and black licorice. She looked nice today, her dress and cowboy boots—but he didn't mention it. He just sat still, catching peeks of her during fight scenes, willing away an erection. The girl was something alright and having physical contact with another human felt nice. Her fingers slid down to his thigh, this time lingering for a bit. He could feel her stare but didn't turn to meet her. Her fingernails began to crawl toward his zipper. He stopped her, moving her paw back to his arm.

The sun began its descent as Lena put the finishing touches on her mural. Due to the tools she was working with, the linework of the images was crude yet beautiful, similar to that of an ancient Chinese scroll, only using the colors black and red. She tossed the brush into its bin, wiping sweat from her brow with a shirt sleeve, paint smudges up her arms to the elbows. At its center, the painting featured the giant head of a Yorkie, its red tongue part of the RV's side door. The pooch was in full sprint, trailed and flanked by a pack of wild dogs, their expressions nearly cheerful. The whole piece looked like a minimalist comic book panel, the words DREAMING OF YOU plastered at the lowest portion of the side wall. After resealing the paint cans, she turned to walk back into her room for a shower and was startled by Barb's presence, smoke dangling from her bottom lip, studying Lena's creation.

"That's incredible. I mean—I watched you the whole dang time, honey. Never seen anything like that."

Lena kept walking toward the room. "Thanks."

"No. I'm serious. It's beautiful. I've been meaning to redo the interior of the Dorado—would you be interested in doing some artwork on the walls?"

"Depends. How much you paying?"

"I'm sure we can reach a deal—free nights, a booze tab."

"I'll do it if you let me pick up some late-night shifts, bartending. Just want to have something else to do around here. I'll paint in the daytime, drop in after eight at night?"

"Guess we could use a little more help behind the bar."

"I'll start tonight. Let me write you a list of supplies I'll need to begin on the interior tomorrow. Think of what you want the place to look like too—a theme. Then I'll start sketching."

"Sounds good."

Lena shook Barb's hand and went inside the room, happy with her decision. A lot more was heard from behind a bar than she could drag out of strangers from a stool. One thing she knew firsthand, barkeeps were like priests in confessional booths—some stranger bending their ear, easily dishing absolution since they never had a pony in the race. She'd get a lot closer to finding Delancey this way.

"Best ending *ever*."

"Ever?" Perry buttoned up his windbreaker as they walked through the truck stop's parking lot.

Rayna mimed the infamous final scene. "*'Why don't we just…wait here for a little while…see what happens?'*"

Perry passed her the last of the bourbon, the same gesture between the film's surviving characters, MacReady and Childs.

They walked along the interstate's shoulder, same as the night previous, reliving the double feature, questioning what other flicks they loved in common. The girl was well versed, a self-dubbed cinefile, spitting out names like Joe Spinell and Umberto Lenzi. Perry, although having once thought he'd seen all the great movies Hollywood had to offer, was given a lesson in obscure cinema.

"And how'd you learn about all these kinds of exploitation films?"

"My uncle. Stanley. You remind me of him."

"Good guy, I hope?"

"The best. He lived in my grandma's trailer, and every day after school I'd head over, rummage through his record collection or watch some bizarre VHS. He didn't filter anything for me either. If I wanted to watch *The Exorcist* or *Pink Flamingos*, he'd just throw it on. Learned a ton about this kinda stuff from him. Taught me how to escape."

"From what?"

She shook her head, eyes letting him know she wasn't about to get into it.

He thought about her idea of cinema and art, not as entertainment (like he'd always looked at it), but as a kind of medicine—to help escape the trappings of one's predicaments. He wanted to reach over and hug her but knew she wanted nothing of the sort at this moment. The way she brooded reminded him of Rochelle. But his daughter always had aspirations to do big things; the way Rayna gleefully perked back from the dark place in her head made him think she never had a chance at a single dream to lose.

"Whoa. What'ya do to your motor home?"

Perry saw the mural and was staggered for a moment at the grandeur of the piece. The fact Lena completed this in a single afternoon was insane. *Every bit the artist.*

They paused on the RV for another instant, then continued toward the saloon.

The sight floored Perry: Lena, dunking pints, jawing with customers. They approached the bar, Rayna taking the same stool as yesterday, Perry waiting for Lena to acknowledge his twisted face.

"What you two drinkin'?"

Rayna turned to Perry, not sure what to order.

Perry: "Hold up. What's the deal, Lena?"

"No deal. Barb said I could take on a few shifts per week. See the RV?"

Rayna: "It's gorgeous. How'd you learn to do that?"

"Through decades of failure."

Perry: "Sure this' a good idea? If we gotta up and leave, you won't be putting Barb out, right?"

"Nah. She's comping the room on nights I work though—

gonna have me paint some artwork inside here too."

Rayna: "More dogs?"

"Barb wants stuff about America."

Perry: "How 'bout a nuclear winter behind Lady Liberty over there—maybe a few Russian flags by the juke?"

Rayna slapped his arm.

Lena slid drinks before them as a break crashed at the pool table.

"When you gonna see your pal again? This X-man."

"Dunno. He's hitting the road for a bit, so it might be a minute. What you looking for this guy for anyway?"

"He's an old pal. A private investigator."

"Holy shit—like Kojak?"

"A bona fide dick."

"Cool."

"It's a shit job, if you ask me. Lousy hours. Tugs at the heartstrings. A good PI is worth more than an honest mechanic though."

"I can believe it. He expensive?"

"Why? Got someone who needs finding?"

"My son."

"How old?"

"Be ten by now. State took him."

They both swilled awkwardly.

"I have a daughter."

Rayna pointed her bottle at Lena.

"Not her. My daughter disappeared in 2009."

"Like, ran away?"

"No."

"Jesus. What happened?" She saw a shift wash over his face. "Strike that. Don't have to tell me. It's too painful."

"Should talk about it more, it being so damn long ago…"

She turned her body on the stool, giving undivided attention.

***

The juke switched from Buck to Dwight as tears bombed down Rayna's cheeks, her winged eyeshadow now a bleeding mess. Perry exhaled a sigh of relief, him being able to regurgitate the whole incident without letting his emotions take the reins. He was sure Lena heard him and wondered what she thought, him letting some lot lizard into the darkest nook of his heart. He respected Lena's situation too, not divulging anything about Tess. That, and there was no code of conduct when it came to such familial calamities; Perry just assumed. Reliving the event didn't revive his hope of finding Rochelle either; however, it did bring his mind back into focus. What they were searching for—fighting for—was *family*. The strength in numbers when it came to bloodline that Lena and he (even Rayna) had been stripped. Watching Rayna's tears flow, he knew that only one in ten were for him, the rest were personal.

Everyone takes family for granted until members get erased.

Rayna blew her nose into a cocktail napkin. "I'm not sure when I'll see X, but I can text him, if you'd like?"

"If you don't mind."

She pulled out her cell and smiled. "It's dead. I'll do it later, okay? Hey, there's someone else that might know your pal. Meet me out front of the Gold, tomorrow at noon. I'll let you know what X says, then take you to go see Mook."

"Mook?"

"Mm-hm." She touched his shoulder and slogged toward the exit.

12.

One thing X-man loved most about the outskirts of Los Banos was its cloak of darkness at night—the ability to lurk and prey within a dense fog of shadows. The Seville was parked behind a team of sycamore trees, directly across the highway from The Speckled Hen Inn. Soul jams seeped out the speakers. When Rayna was in the car earlier, she'd commandeered the stereo, messing up Repo's dials, stinking up the cut with hippie bullshit. Staking out Miggy Rojas' motel room, X-man found time to fix them all. Rayna was a trip. He recalled a time when he felt such love for another human being—a long, long time ago. Back when he was young and dumb, throwing away the love a wife had tried to give him, forfeiting the responsibility of fatherhood. *Everyone has their devils.* But with Rayna, he saw a second wave. First time they met, at least eight years ago, they'd hit it off, goofing on each other about this or that. She was a baby. They became schoolyard buddies with a lifetime age gap between them. Threw him off his game, for sure. Last thing he ever thought would happen: him feeling paternal for some poor white trash. But he went with it, enjoying the window into an alternate universe he'd always dreamed of. The duality of life: friendship by day, bloodshed by night. When Repo orphaned his stable, moving onto the advance-ment of Gallows Dome, X-man saw an opportunity. He'd never pimped a day in his life but had been around plenty of lizards—

knew their plight. With Repo's blessing, he took on some girls, letting them all go after a few months in order to hang with Rayna full time. He never demanded a thing from her but expected truth between them. The girl made him feel like someone he never was.

Someone good.

Rayna was an escape from his gruesome reality—one that currently had him slumped in a car, in the dark, waiting for a *pendejo* to give him some clues, proving his gut instinct was right.

Miggy Rojas was too good to be true.

X couldn't put a finger on it but knew when he was right. A person his age couldn't be alive in this racket for so long without a whispering angel. And Repo had a hunch too, asking him to press the dude's stomach, see how much game Miggy could take—show the fool what befell poor fucks who messed with Repo's money. He held up binoculars to room ten, watching Miggy glide behind ratty curtains, a free-floating specter. He'd had Miggy's license plate run with the help of a cop on Repo's payroll by the name of Elkins. Miggy's El Camino came back being owned by some dude down in Los Angeles. Hopefully, the car was stolen, clearing a little more air, exposing Miggy as being of their kind. Song out the speakers switched: *And do I love you, my oh my?* The door to the room cracked open, Miggy stepping out with an empty ice bucket. At first, the act seemed insignificant, but on second glance, X-man's gut did the twist.

Miggy was barefoot (sans walking cast, zero limp) as he strolled across the second-story balcony.

Bitch ass—

X-man lit the engine and began to creep toward the motel's entrance.

With both hands, Joe splashed through file documents across his room's bed, trying to locate a sheet of paper that had his login scribbled to access the L.A. Public Library's database. He was hours deep into researching the history of Sergeant Brown and two other cohorts via newspaper clippings, trying to connect dots on information Becca had left (via a message at the front desk) from her ex-fiancé, What's-his-face. Turns out Brown wasn't the only worm in the apple, two more names of cops were supplied, both supposedly having dipped their claws into the honey jar during the last biker bust. Word on the street was that these two, officers Davis and Little, shared a storage unit near LAX and were sitting on whatever was inside. A PI buddy supplied him the address. Odds were, Joe could finagle his way inside and pilfer whatever stash they had—hopefully more of the same, but at this point, any type of narcotic would do. The moment he found the sheet, a vehicle's high beams torched the curtains. Could hear a car door open, footsteps, then what sounded like the car's hood unlatching. Before he could reach the window, a car horn blared. Behind the curtain, down below, stood X-man, waving up at him, hollering something inaudible. Joe put up a finger, letting X know he'd be right down. He scrambled to wrangle the documents back into their file, sliding them back into the vent alongside that Saturday night special. He hurried to dress, then slipped into character.

"Stone told you I'd be here?"

X-man grinned, lowering his shades for a better view. "He mentioned it. Repo's Caddy took a shit. Just so happens, X-man was nearby. Thought this would be a good place to pull over—there being a friend here and all."

Miggy strolled over gingerly, his walking boot thudding asphalt. "What's wrong with her?"

"Was making some sputtering noises—thought I saw smoke. Man, I dunno shit about cars. You?"

"A little."

"Take a gander." X lit up a joint.

Miggy peered into the engine, not recognizing anything suspicious. "Start her back up."

X-man sat inside and cranked the ignition. He watched as Miggy's eyes darted around the engine, wondering if the dude was bullshitting about his mechanic's skills too. Didn't matter, he was lying about the car being busted.

Miggy gave a thumbs up, closed the hood and leaned into the driver's side window. "Looks ship-shape to me."

"Can never be too sure, am I right? If it were my Caddy, would've just parked the bitch and walked home. Was on my way to grab a drink though. Should hop in and join me."

Miggy peered back at his room, the lights still on, door unlocked.

"What, you busy or somethin'? Got a bitch up there, don'tcha?"

"Nah, I just...Gimme a sec to grab my wallet."

"Sure thing, jelly bean. But hurry. X-man be thirsty as hell."

Miggy ran back upstairs. X-man pulled two weapons from the center console, a Glock 9 and a .45, inspecting each. Two minutes later, Miggy was back in the Caddy, listening to X-man sing Marvin Gaye as they hauled up the highway.

A pillbox structure sat ahead on the right as the Caddy approached the Golden State Highway; Miggy squinted to read the sign over its door, pickup trucks catawampus in its dirt lot. The Mint Tavern. He assumed X would pull in and park, this being the first bar they'd come across since leaving the motel, but he didn't.

"Got a better spot, Miggy. Hold tight." A grin split X's face as he punched the gas, merging onto Highway 99.

They pulled off at the outskirts of Chowchilla, making their way down rural roads, entering a track of manufactured homes called Juniper Grove. This late an hour, nearly every home sat darkened. Miggy remained silent as X tore up the driveway of a lavender multi-sectional with a Ford Bronco parked out front. As the engine cooled, a deep quiet enveloped the cab. X-man removed a pair of taut leather gloves from under his seat and proceeded to stretch them on.

"Don't touch anything when we go inside."

"What?"

"Here." X-man opened the console and handed Miggy the loaded .45. "I'm sure you ain't a stranger to one a these..."

Miggy tried to remain calm. "Thought we were grabbin' a drink?"

X-man scratched his temple with the Glock. "We are. *Damn.*"

They gazed out at the home, its porch light now ablaze. X-man racked the slide, adjusted his shades and opened the car door. Miggy followed suit.

The owner of the residence was a big man, least six-three, two-seventy. From the porch, the inner home décor appeared to be purely Native American. The man rubbed sleep from his eyes, unfazed by X-man's smooth greeting. They knew each other—least, Miggy hoped they did. Soon as X introduced the fellow to Miggy as Bear, tensions eased. They entered the residence.

The living room bled southwestern prints with Kachina dolls frozen in dance about every shelf. Bear sat on a La-Z-Boy, petting an unkempt Pomeranian. Miggy stood by the front door, per X's request, the gun concealed in the back of his waistband. X-man rifled through a kitchen cabinet filled with liquor, the bulge of his Glock noticeable inside its holster, beneath his track pants. He removed a bottle of J&B, showed it to Miggy, eyebrows bouncing, making sure he'd made a fine selection. Miggy nodded, palms getting sweaty.

Bear asked, "What happened to your leg?"

X: "Tellim, man."

"Got drunk. Fell down a flight of stairs."

X: "Fell or you was thrown?"

Bear laughed.

"Way you can walk on it like that, bet it's close to being healed, right? Won't be needing that boot no mo'."

"Hope so. Stopped wearing the boot when I'm lounging at home."

Bear squirmed in his chair; the lap dog scrambled not to get pitched. "Listen, X, I told Repo everything I know. And I'm sorry about this whole mix-up, but shit happens—"

"Oh, we're starting in on this now?" X-man tossed the bottle to Miggy and stood over the big man, the gun bulge nearly brushing Bear's left ear.

Bear said, "That's why you're here, ain't you?"

"I brought my friend over for a drink, say hello, enjoy some Native hospitality…but since you done brought up this mess, best we hash it out." X clapped his gloves together in a way that made Bear (and Miggy) jump. "Lemme fill in my associate here on what the fuck it is we be talkin' 'bout."

Bear slunk further into the recliner.

"See, Mig. Bear here was in a similar spot as you is now. What you supply Repo, Bear?"

"Crystal. Sometimes Molly."

"How long this been going on, Bear?"

"Year or two."

"And what happened with that?"

"My nephew—the chemist—got pinched. Doing ten years, and I dunno how to make the shit. Supply's all dried up. I'm out the biz completely. Ain't got a line on nothing else."

X-man turned to Miggy. "Can you believe that?"

Bear: "It's the fucking truth, dog!"

"*Dog*? You tryin' to win my heart with cultural 'propriation?"

"No. I just—"

"Just what? Heard other Chumash toss around that slang out on the streets? *Sheeit,* I ain't never heard no Red use it."

"I'm sorry—I…"

"Where's the money, mothafuckah?"

"I don't have it. Swear on my dead son. Told Repo—cops took

everything when they nabbed him."

Miggy watched as X bent over and pulled a makeshift garrote from out the lining of his athletic sock. Appeared to be some kind of electrical wire fixed with plastic handles—looked like a kid's jump rope, only miniature.

"Bear and his dipshit nephew were paid up front for a shipment they only delivered half of, Miggy. Without the full supply, Repo wants his investment back. It's a reasonable request." He splayed the wire between his fists, concealing it behind the La-Z-Boy. "You get one more shot, Bear. No dough, then I'ma have Miggy here put the squeeze on ya. Show him, Miggy."

Miggy pulled the .45 from out his pants, pointing it at the floor.

"See, Mig's the new kid on the block. And you know about them new kids...always gotta be showing off to earn respect." He smirked at Miggy.

"Told you I ain't lyin'—"

The garrote wrapped around Bear's trunk of a neck—X pulling both sides, hovering behind the big man, maximizing his leverage. The dog yelped and ran into a bedroom. Bear's eyes bulged as he clawed at X's shoulders, unable to fully grasp him, blood spewing out his nostrils. As X-man squeezed, his shades slid off, eyes lasering Miggy, veins bulging his neck, spit dribbling off his chin. As Bear went under, a scream erupted from the bedroom. Miggy raised the gun, aiming beyond X, at the hallway. X-man didn't panic, staring into the barrel of the .45, holding the garrote till Bear stopped convulsing, went limp, then lifeless— soul sent back to his spirit world. A tiny Hispanic woman rushed in with a leveled rifle, nearly the length of her body. Miggy froze. She'd run past X-man, blinded by the stranger at the door holding a pistol.

She cried, "Get out!" The rifle trembled.

Before Miggy could make a move, X had his Glock to the back of the woman's skull. Miggy began to shake his head no, turning back into Joe, images of Becca flooding the brain. He closed his eyes, heard a blast, then felt the woman's warm fluids pepper his mouth and cheekbones.

At the car, X-man immediately took the .45 back from Miggy, thinking he should've just given the fucker a banana, would've gotten the same protection back there. Miggy wiped his face with a hand towel, one X-man had ganked from out Bear's kitchen; its scent of the home lingered about Miggy's nostrils. They were driving back toward Los Banos, X-man taking slugs of scotch and passing the bottle. At first, X-man tried to address the issue in the car but held back once seeing Miggy's demeanor. He was in shock, or something damn close to it. As for Miggy, weird thing was, he didn't feel a thing for Bear or that woman, only the urge to vomit being that close to death himself. This was a test, and Miggy/Joe wasn't sure if he'd passed or failed. Didn't matter. Miggy was in too deep now. That meant there was only one direction Joe was headed.

"Wasn't supposed to go down like that."

Miggy swigged the liquor.

"But now you know the business you keep."

Miggy took another pull.

"When's that shipment coming, Mig? Don't bullshit me now. Repo's counting on it." He turned his gaze from the road. "Missed a spot." He grabbed the towel and swiped flesh from the side of Miggy's head.

Miggy switched to Joe then back to Miggy. He bluffed. "I'm heading down, first thing in the morning."

"This morning?"

"Nah, tomorrow."

"Tijuana?"

He stammered. "No, San Diego—a meet-up."

X-man nodded. "When can we expect you?"

"A day—maybe two."

X-man gave a long, silent stare. "Bring back that shipment,

Miggy. No muss. No fuss. Make Repo a happy customer. I don't enjoy doing shit like that to guys like Bear—but whatever Repo wants, Repo gets."

Miggy didn't believe X disliked his job, the euphoric look on his face once Bear's body caved to death, tongue out, eyes bulging. A denser fog had set in. They tranced on a frenzy of white lines in the road, trapped beside each other, unable to focus on any periphery. Reminded Miggy of an endless hamster's wheel—one that Joe Delancey regretted ever jumping onto. A ghost truck screamed past, eastbound. Miggy immediately recognized the hauler: P-Stone. The rig held two familiar canisters in its bed.

X-man didn't even look at him when he said, "Well, ya already know where the hell he's goin'."

By the time the Caddy pulled back into The Speckled Hen's lot, it was well after last call, making their bottle of scotch the only drink of the night. Miggy lumbered out from the vehicle, heavily buzzed, climbing his way upstairs. X-man watched, making sure Miggy got into his room alright; he knew for sure what the guy had just experienced was foreign to his being. The way he tensed up when that bitch ran in with the shotgun. *Can't all be cold blooded. Maybe he only slang dope after all?* His cell lit up on the dash. A text from Rayna.

U know a dude named Joe Delancey
Private investigative, hangs at the Villa
Askin for Perry he tryin ta find him

Investigator

The name struck like a brick. He rifled through his track suit, retrieving the piece of paper he'd scribbled specifics on Miggy's false license plate. *Joe Delancey, 1533 Pacific Coast Highway, Harbor City...*He looked up at the room, its windows now dark.

Private investigator? He exited and opened the trunk, grabbing a small GPS tracking device from out a pleather satchel. Strange days were upon him. If Miggy Rojas or Joe Delancey or whoever the fuck this dude was had plans on picking up their supply soon, then X-man would track him for peace of mind. Right now, the most important thing was that Repo got his stash. All this other bullshit could be dealt with afterwards, if necessary. He approached the opal El Camino and secured the device deep into the car's undercarriage. Back in the car, he returned Rayna's text, contemplated calling Repo but thought better at this hour before lighting a final joint and heading home.

13.

Dunno no Joe

Rayna squinted at the cell's screen, eyes heavy, having fallen asleep before X-man responded to her late-night text. She checked the time on her phone: 11:18 a.m. *Damn!* She jumped from her cot, rummaging through a cheetah print suitcase for fresh clothes. The room she rented was shared by two other girls, one a lizard like herself, the other a runaway still trying to find her place. Neither roommate was on their respective cots, allowing Rayna to be as loud as she wanted. There'd be enough hot water to shower with too. She grabbed her toothbrush, towel and soap, ready to start the day and help her new pal, Perry.

Perry pulled his cell phone from out a fountain cup filled with dry Rice-A-Roni. He punched buttons to spark it to life but was met by a cracked black screen. *Fuckin' hell.* Still time before meeting Rayna at the Cali Gold at noon; they had a payphone in the laundry room. Could get there early, grab a decent coffee, some Ding Dongs, try to call into his voicemail—see if anyone phoned in the past day. He flung a Marlboro into the air, caught it with his lips and climbed out Dreamboat.

***

Lena had slept in longer than she'd liked, her first night tending bar extending deep into daybreak. She didn't mind, taking the chance to meet locals and pick their brains about all sorts of topics; however, when prying about Joe Delancey, all she received were drunken blank stares.

A quick ramen breakfast and back out to the Dorado.

She opened the door, omitting a smell of stale plumbing. It was after one o'clock, a good three hours after she'd planned on getting started on the first mural. Folks would be thirsty soon; doors opened at four. She grabbed a folded tri-cornered Old Glory from off the bar counter and walked out to the flagpole. Dreamboat was parked in the distance; she admired her dog pack while raising the flag, halting at half-mast. Wasn't sure if the country still recognized that last mass shooting…

Perry slammed the payphone onto its receiver, nearly repeating the act again and again. Mounting frustration had hit a crescendo. After several tries, he couldn't get into his voicemail; pass code after pass code came up short. Was it Rochelle's birthday, or the date he got divorced? He exhaled, trying to focus before calling again. Before he could pick up the phone, he noticed Rayna's tapping toes on the linoleum before him.

"Ah, shit. It's noon, isn't it?"

"Twelve ten."

"Sorry."

"No worries. Who you callin'?"

"Voicemail—can't remember the code to get in though. Do me a favor, Rayna?"

"Shoot."

"Never get old."

She winked. "Hey, X don't know your guy."

"Great."

"Well, he ain't the end all be all. We'll find Joe." She unzipped her fanny pack, removing a cassette tape and handing it over.

"What's this?"

"Copy of a tape my uncle made for me back in high school. Got a buncha great stuff on it—The Flesh Eaters, The Saints, Roky Erickson."

"Love his song about a cold night for alligators. Got it on the juke back home at my bar."

"This has 'Don't Shake Me Lucifer.'"

"Thanks."

"Thought it might perk you up. Shall we roll?"

He sighed once more at the payphone. "Kinda name is Mook anyway?"

"Dunno. What kind of name is Perry?"

The sun felt good on Perry's face. Wasn't exactly sure where they were headed, ambling roadside. Only thing in the sprawling landscape was a pop-up fruit stand. "Sure we don't need to drive? I can haul out the RV, save us some sweat."

"It's right ahead, lazy bones."

"That fruit stand?"

"A fruit *and* nut stand. Gipson Farms. Mook runs the joint for his grandparents."

"A grown man with both grandparents alive. That's a first for me."

"Not exactly." She smiled, speeding up her wheels, launching ahead.

At the stand's entrance a young boy—couldn't have been more than sixteen—approached, holding a carrot and a black bunny; boy's fireball hair bled out the corners of a beanie cap.

Rayna said, "Hey, Mookie."

Mook handed her the bunny.

Perry perused the merchandise as Rayna and Mook caught up; they hadn't seen each other in a hot minute. She asked him how he was doing; kid replied, "God is good. God is great." The stand held nectarines, plums, walnuts and pistachios. Perry gobbled free samples, amazed by the freshness—the power of vegetation at its source. He panned the orchard: migrant workers, nearly a dozen, picked walnuts at a feverish pace.

"Nice farm you got here, Mook."

"Been in the family three generations. Who knows how many more, with all the water rights garbage these days?"

Perry pulled a cigarette, gave one to Rayna and offered another to the boy, who declined. They lit up. Perry turned to Rayna. "You ask him?"

"Ask me what?"

Rayna exhaled a plume. "You know a fella by the name of Joe Delancey? He's a private investigator that's roamed these parts, out on a case. Ain't that tall, got dark features…"

Mook racked his brain. "He got a moustache?"

Rayna looked at Perry.

Perry said, "Not the last I saw him."

Mook shook his head. "There's a guy with a 'stache I've seen, drives an old El Camino. Been catching him through here—past few months. Never stops for produce, but definitely ain't from these parts. That's the only guy I can think of."

Perry nodded, huffing nicotine, wishing the butt were big as an exhaust pipe; he was sick of dead ends.

Rayna: "Mookie, your grandad still making that bathtub hooch?"

"It ain't bathtub, alright?"

"I didn't mean it that way. Come on. Go an' grab some. I'd love you forever and ever."

Mook removed his cap, scratching what looked like a legion of fire ants. He walked into a back room of the shack.

"What's he gettin'?"

"Best damn gin you'll ever taste."

***

Lena worked on the first wall of her Dorado interior design for hours, but so far, she'd only been able to coat it with white paint. She opened the front and back doors to air out the joint from the stench, then poured herself a Cape Cod, marinating in thought.

America?

She sat at a table near the karaoke stage, trancing on the blank wall, conjuring cliché images of a nation punch-drunk on greatness. Barb had given her free rein of the images, yet Lena still felt nervous about what she *really* wanted to paint.

'Merica?

She sat up straight, closed her eyes, slowed her breathing and slid into a meditative state. After thirty seconds, her eyes opened in defeat, the only image she could conjure was of Tess' smile—from newborn to teenager, that glint of innocence in her eyes—then footage of her abduction.

The walls closed in around her.

Her drink smashed to the floor.

She slammed her face atop the table and wept.

14.

Vic & Anthony's Steakhouse, Las Vegas, Nevada

Repo Helm dipped warm bread into the steaming blood of a bone marrow appetizer. The restaurant was candlelit, formal—lobster tails the size of child brains being whisked to and fro by bow-tied waiters in crisp aprons. A family of five leered from the next table, ogling Repo's companions: two high-end escorts, one redhead, the other a heavyset Brazilian. They smiled at him every few minutes, sipping cosmos. Talking was not in the arrangement, he made certain when ordering them online. A waiter swept crumbs from the table as their entrées were placed accordingly. Repo checked the time on his Rolex, adjusting a gold cufflink. His steady flow of clean income was being utilized. *Top of the world, Ma.*

Research had brought him to Vegas last week. When it came to hedonism, what better place than Sin City? He'd been holed up in his Golden Nugget penthouse suite, recording sermons and reading nonfiction tomes on masterful diviners—twentieth-century soothsayers that had successfully intoxicated the masses: Semple McPherson, Crowley, Jones, L. Ron, Oprah...Their extreme differences in platforms was not of interest; he was searching for a single thread woven throughout each's agenda, a fortitude of clarity, an overlap in extremes. There was one trait the idols shared beyond charisma, deceit and greed; each had the ability to pinpoint a growing *need* within a subculture and meet that *need*—one the public didn't even know they had. In the past few days, his sermons gravitated in this direction, hyper-focused on the fellowship's absolute break from conscience to breed felonious, self-serving lives. Their *need* was pandemonium on Earth; Gallows Dome would serve it on a platter.

The mountain of steak before him sparked salivation, the flesh practically still *moo*ing. He went to cut the beast when a man at the hostess' booth caught his eye.

No fucking way?

Darcy.

His brother followed the hostess' manicured finger. Their eyes locked. Repo waved him over with a smile.

Of all the gin joints...

Darcy appeared disheveled, tie-slackened, sweaty. He sat beside Repo, breathing heavily, eyeing the escorts, whispering for them to be sent away.

"The hell's wrong with you, Darcy? No hello. Not even surprised to see me?"

"Yeah, like I didn't mean to find you."

"Say what?"

Darcy's eyes bounced to the girls.

Repo said, "Ladies, can you give us a moment—go an' powder them pretty noses."

The women left napkins on their seats.

Darcy waited for them to enter the restroom. "Give me your phone."

"What the fuck is—"

"Just hand it over, and I'll explain."

Repo slid the cell from out his suit pocket.

The moment it hit Darcy's fingers, he dropped it into a carafe of water on the table.

"Hey!"

"It's been tapped."

"By who?"

"Feds."

"How do you know—"

"Thought we agreed not to ask questions about each other's business. I got people that reached out, a client I do work for. Guy has a connect in the DEA, tips him off from time to time. Your name came up somehow—this guy knows you're my client."

"Are you sure—I mean, is this guy's source credible?"

"How you think I found you?"

"Shit."

"Indeed."

"Well, I never use my personal for business. If they wanna hear me discuss grocery lists with the wife, then fuck 'em."

"Still. You need to slow your roll with everything, the distribution," he flicked the Rolex, "heavy spending—at least for a few days, see what comes to light. Now's not the time to sleep on the fundamentals of your dope enterprise. Make sure all is well on that end—no slipups. You have to remain one step ahead of the game."

"What about Gallows Dome?"

"I asked about that. So far, there's been no connection—we did use your middle name for all of the documents. It's bullet-proof on paper. I mean, sure, these feds are probably pretty smart and digging for dirt, but come on...at the end of the day, I wouldn't worry too much."

Repo contemplated telling him about the ceremony's grim details, the sacrifice, then refrained. The less Darcy knew about The Dome's doctrines and rituals, the better.

Darcy flagged the waiter and ordered a Sazerac. "Here's the bad news."

"There's worse fucking news?"

"Kinda—for me at least. I have to sever ties with you. Can't get tangled in whatever these fucks are trying to pin you with. It would compromise, not only my future business, but also the trust of my long-term clients. I can't afford it. As of right now, me and you are back to being strictly brothers. I'm relieving you as my client."

Repo exhaled, stewing in what he'd just heard.

The cocktail was slid in front of Darcy; he downed half in one pull. "If I were you, I'd ditch everything and head home. Don't call your wife—we don't know if she's been compromised as well. Get there, tell her in person, have your affairs in order and sit tight."

Repo took his prepaid and stared at it before tossing it into the carafe. "Can never be too sure. I'll grab a new one tonight."

The escorts sauntered back to the table, their skirts leaving little to the imagination.

Darcy finished his drink and rose.

"At least stay for supper. This might be the last time we see each other for a spell."

"Can't. Have a flight to catch. Only reason I came out here was to speak with you, face-to-face. Anyway, I hate Vegas. Got no self-control—seduced by the slots, pussy, free booze. You know me. We'll get together soon as possible. Head down, finally see that ranch of yours."

"I'd like that."

They shook hands.

Something told Repo that this would be the last time he ever saw Darcy, in person.

"Get this meal to go and head home, Repo. I'll contact you in a few months, if I think it's safe." He buttoned his suit jacket, turning to the escorts. "Ladies."

They watched as he walked out the restaurant, through the sparkling casino floor.

"Well, fuck me," Repo muttered.

The redhead replied, "Okay."

15.

They sat in the cool shade of the walnut grove, Perry swilling from a mason jar, feeling like a bear with honey. Mook and Rayna were playfully drunk, tickling each other, telling dirty jokes. Not a single car pulled off the highway for produce in the three hours since they'd arrived. Mook jolted up and went sprinting through rows of crops.

"Where's he headed?"

"Forgot he has to help with his grandma."

"Oh. Where's she at?"

"A good mile that way." She squinted, focusing one eye before pointing south.

"You got the stink eye."

"What?"

"You're hammered."

"No way!"

Perry took another long swig, eyeing the strange potion, a magic elixir that had stunted all the stress of searching for a lost cause. And Rayna. He'd forgotten how it was to be in the company of a younger woman, a compassionate silliness that hadn't returned to his life since 2009. *Nearly felt like fatherhood, again.* A bolt struck: *2009—of course!* That was the voicemail code he'd forgotten. *Wasn't a specific date, but the year Rochelle...* The epiphany brought a smile.

"You look happy, old man."

"I am, I guess."

"Not sure, huh?" She crawled over to him, head resting against his ribs. "Pass me that."

He handed the jar slowly. Gin dribbled down her chin. They sat in silence, leaves rustling overhead. Perry felt drowsy, lost in that velvet fog of inebriation.

"Can I tell you something, Perr'?"

"Go for it, girl."

"I only told this to one other person…"

A breeze swept in.

Silence.

"Did they die of suspense?"

"I'm trying to be serious here." She fixated on birds flying overhead, taking another pull of gin. "My son, Gilby. They took him 'cause I was a bad mom."

Perry figured, but didn't harp. "You were a kid yourself. We all are, deep down—no matter how old we get. Take comfort in *that.*"

"Yeah, but what eats me is that I just didn't care enough. Couldn't. Never felt like he was mine. Was like he'd just appeared there, *poof,* before me. A little alien, you know? And I felt *nothing.* Not a single thing. That's crazy, right? First, I thought it was the baby blues, turned out I just never knew what true love was. Still don't, I guess—outside a stranger's touch…I mean, maybe I could've been a good mom if I knew, right? Kills me inside—that I'm nothing but a giant turd in this life. Maybe in the next one, I'll be a hero or somethin'. I dunno. Anything but another sad whore."

"*Stop.* Can't all be saints, honey. There's a place for everyone. Good or bad." He yawned, not wanting to address where exactly he fell.

"Perry." Rayna turned to face him.

He was passed out.

She smooshed back into his gut, the chirps of birds serenading serenity.

***

A fond memory returns...

He's back in his teens, that beach bonfire in '76. Some of the fellas took dried Christmas trees from out neighborhood trash bins and hauled them to the inferno. Everywhere along the coast, kids drink, smoke and mingle. He feels sauced to the gills, leering at a thick girl in a striped bikini—one he's seen in algebra. Dottie something. She's too cute, well-built, skin prickly by ocean air. He looks down at his own body, hairless, rippled, gaunt. Being too skinny was a curse—chum for bullies. She approaches. He flirts. She guides him toward a lifeguard tower. He barely knows her. Never spoke in class. She rubs the outside of his corduroy shorts, placing a kiss on his chapped lips. He grows in her hand. She loses the top, plump nipples, rosy and hard. She slides to her knees. He grabs the tower, trying not to faceplant. Her tongue crowns his head, then takes it whole. His skull tingles, fighting every urge to erupt...

Perry's eyes cracked open, discombobulated by the lucid dream, not sure if it'd ended. Bouncing on his lap was Rayna's bare ass, grinding, hot, wet. He moved to posture; she sat down harder, taking him deeper, panting as their parts slapped beneath the trees, moonlight casting shadows.

"Stop." He whispered, still lost in the gin drunk.

She ignored him, fingers caressing her clit as she rode.

"Stop it!"

She grunted, dimpled cheeks shuddering as she strummed herself to finish.

As she went lax, he pushed her off, flailing to slide up his pants, jumping to his feet.

She spun, winded—confused at the rage in his face. "What's the matter?"

He was tongue-tied, brain swimming. "Why?"

"What'ya mean? We were laying there, I started to rub your cock and you moaned."

He leaned against the tree, eyeing the girl, upset at their now tainted friendship.

"What's your fucking problem, Perr'? I thought you wanted to…"

He scoffed. "How much do I owe you?"

"Never charge my lovers."

"Said I reminded you of your uncle?"

"You do. I love you."

Drunk tears came, but he swallowed them back.

"I love you, Perry."

One fell.

She got up off her knees, still bare from the waist and grabbed his shirt. "Say it back to me."

He sucked snot.

"Say it, Perry!"

He pushed past her. "You ruined it."

Staggering out the grove, Perry's ears filtered her every shout. When he got back to the Villa, he'd tell Lena that he was done and heading back to Long Beach first thing tomorrow. If Lena wanted to stay, good on her. He was done with caring for others.

What a fucking waste of time.

Perry splashed water on his face in the Cali Gold men's room, hating the person glaring back at him in the mirror. A rusty dispenser peddled French ticklers and cartoon smut pics above a damp cotton towel roll. He dried off, stomach growling.

In the general store, he wolfed a roast beef sandwich and potato chips, washing it down with a Mountain Dew. A hangover was in the works, but food and caffeine held it at bay. He strolled to the stop's laundromat, finding the payphone empty and dropped change. When prompted, he punched *2009*.

You have three new messages.

Perry! It's Dottie. Where the fuck are you and when are you coming back to work—

He deleted it.

Perry—Dot again—

Delete.

Hey, Perr'. It's Joe...

He nearly puked.

...if you call The Speckled Hen Inn in Los Banos, they could patch you into room ten. Late nights and early mornings are best...

He replayed the message two more times before jogging back to the Villa. Late night hours were closing in.

He had to find Lena.

16.

Lena carefully hauled Dreamboat west, down Route 152; dense fog and a scarcity of lighting made the road even more treacherous, not to mention the occasional roadside memorial every few miles. Perry sat with his fingers coiled on his gut, eyes closed, trying to pull it together. Lena didn't give him any grief for his stupor, after the way he came at her the other day for being haggard. How could she? He stormed into the motel room with music to her ears. Her body buzzed with anticipation. Should she introduce herself and make pleasantries with Joe, or just fire right into the situation—see if he'll get started immediately? The RV's high beams flashed a tractor crossing sign. Music out the tape deck screeched.

She turned to a snoring Perry. "Perry, wake up."

He opened one eye. "What?"

"What band is this?"

"That's why you woke me?"

"Well, we're almost there."

He held the cassette case, reading Rayna's scribbled words. "The Germs."

"I like it."

"Good for you." He slapped his cheeks and lit a smoke, hoping to quash brain cobwebs.

***

X-man hummed along to The Temptations, scoping Miggy's room through binoculars, the Seville parked beneath sycamores again. Through the fog, he couldn't see a damn thing. Since leaving Miggy (or should he say Joe) back here last night, he'd done some online homework. There was little to go by, only a few mentions in news outlets and some crime TV show. Turns out Joe Delancey was a private investigator based in L.A.'s South Bay, specialized in missing persons, cheating spouses—that type of mess. Wasn't an ex-cop, like most dicks. Per an obituary, he had a daughter named Rebecca and a dead wife. A picture of Delancey sealed the deal. Why the man was out here posing as Miggy Rojas was beyond X.

"Jus' my 'magination..."

His gut said the dude was out here working a case.

"Runnin' away with me..."

But maybe not.

"Jus' my 'magination..."

Maybe he had a side gig slanging pills—the false persona used to keep both lives separate. *And why not?* Being a PI didn't pay shit.

He texted Repo's new number this morning; when he called back, X relayed the odd news. The tracking device he'd put on the El Camino hadn't moved a blip all day. X suggested to Repo that he trace the fucker and make sure he was picking up the haul he'd promised; pill connects were drying up faster than the Central Valley soil these days. They agreed not to make a fuss out of him being a PI, unless it was necessary. Who cared what his true identity was? If Miggy could deliver, he was their rainbow to a pot of gold. If he didn't make good, or say, if this Joe Delancey was on a case involving Repo somehow...X-man would just take the bastard out. Repo would be bummed on the lack of goods, but there were a few others out there. He'd just have to work a little harder to find another dealer, preferably one with rocks for brains and a healthy supply. Time was the variable, with Gallows Dome nearing.

Headlights flashed along the highway; a large RV lumbered

past, its side painted with toy dogs.

"Da fuck?"

Immediately, he recognized the passenger in shotgun—Rayna's dude—one from the Cali Gold. *Perry*. Some woman was at the wheel. *Not Rayna*. He watched the motor home glug into The Speckled Hen's lot, smoke spitting from its tailpipe.

Looks like Perry found his damn man.

He fumbled with the binoculars before tossing them to the back seat, firing up the Caddy for a better view. The Seville slipped into fog like a snake to water.

"Get in, get in." Joe closed the door behind Perry and Lena.

As Perry embraced his pal, Lena stood at the foot of the bed, gazing at Joe as if he were some A-list celebrity—a character who'd come off the screen and into the theater. Perry introduced her. Joe shook her hand and looked her in the eye.

Perry said, "The hell you doing out here, Joe?"

"Funny you should ask." He grabbed the case folder from out the air vent and began shelling documents to Perry, describing the context of this investigation: his informant Devon and her learning of a lizard named "Ro"; the serendipitous link he'd made between Trench and Somerset Boyd.

Perry: "You think this *Ro* could be—"

"So far, I can't confirm and it's not looking good. Too much time has passed, Perry. But I don't have to tell you that. It's the best lead we've ever had though. Had to follow up on it."

"Why the fuck didn't you tell me? You know I would've dropped everything."

"It's more complicated this time."

"How so?"

"I managed to embed myself—undercover as a pill pusher—a middle man named Miggy Rojas."

"You're *Rojas*?" Perry scoped Joe's attire, not having thought much about it yet, figuring the guy just might be into rodeos these days. "That explains the moustache. The hell happened to your foot?"

"It's part of the disguise."

"Subtle." He pulled out a cigarette. "We actually went looking for him."

"Who?"

Lena said, "Miggy," taking Joe's desktop note from out her purse.

Perry: "If you're Miggy Rojas, then what the hell does that scribbled address and STAMPS have to figure in all this?"

Joe grabbed the note, having forgotten what he'd written. "This store? Think it's called 9 Muses."

Perry: "Yeah. What about it?"

"Just the place I had stamps made for my business documents."

Perry shook his head at the joint's insignificance, their wasted time. "So, that's it? You're out here shaking trees, trying to find someone called *Ro*?"

"Initially. I mean, that was the first domino to fall."

"And now…"

"Got caught up in something else."

Lena: "Another case?"

"I wish."

Perry's eyes pierced Joe's.

Joe struggled to articulate his current predicament, stuck in the gears of Repo Helm's dope machine. After some stammering, Joe finally spilled his guts.

Perry fumed. "Why'd you go an' do somethin' stupid like that, man? Could've gotten yourself killed!"

Joe smirked, knowing that death at the hands of Repo wasn't behind him.

Perry berated him about not thinking of Becca before taking such a risk—regardless of the cause. Between the two of them, there was already one family member missing. Joe relayed remorse, not divulging any more info, switching topics.

"Speaking of Becca—she said you had another case?" He

turned to Lena.

Lena outstretched a red plastic folder with the documents she'd brought for him.

"You mind if I go over these when I get back?"

Lena tried not to deflate.

Perry said, "From where?"

"L.A. There's something I gotta do tomorrow. Be back soon though."

"A job for this Repo fella?"

Joe shrugged. "Wouldn't happen to know any drug dealers, would you?"

"Jesus fucking Christ. You're in *that* deep?"

Lena: "Do what you have to, Joe—but *please* hurry. Sooner you start on Tess' case the better—I'll pay whatever."

Perry: "Pigs got no leads. *Shocker.* Time's a wastin', Joe. Poor girl's out there somewhere...cold...scared..."

Joe nodded, tossing the documents onto the bed. "Yeah, I'm on it—soon as I get back. Promise. Anyone like coffee?"

Lena and Perry passed. As Joe loaded the complimentary coffee maker, Lena tried not to let Perry see her despair, tinkering through Joe's paperwork on Rochelle's case, trying to stay positive.

"Well, then introduce *me*—say I'm you're connect down in Mexico! It'll buy you some more time. Let me deal with these clowns. It's my daughter you're looking for! Let me in on this, Joe."

Delancey sipped coffee, legs crossed at the room's lone table chair.

Perry paced, chain smoking.

"It's too dangerous, Perr'. Don't let me drag you into this."

"Think about Becca, dammit. I have nothing left to lose. I'll finagle my way into this picture somehow—so help me."

Lena studied Joe's intricate notebook on his new findings

since being out here. The depths of crime were on a level she'd only read about in headlines. Every page was hard to take in. The names of people: P-Stone, X-man…If she was reading the notes correctly, Joe had definitely put himself in a tight spot.

Joe: "When I get back, I'll see what I can do, okay? Maybe introduce you as a partner or something—that is *only* if I can deliver the goods they're expecting."

"What if you can't?"

"Then you both stay as far away from here, and from me, as possible."

Lena rose off the bed, notebook in hand. "What's this here?" She pointed to a page. "Gallows Dome?"

Joe refilled his mug. "Some scam Repo's running. The details are spotty, but from what I know so far, it's some kind of gathering for troglodytes."

Perry: "Speak English."

"A simple-minded crowd, convinced the end of the world is near—plan to spawn a new Babylon. Probably involves sun worship or a flat earth. If you ask me, Repo and that woman, Trench/Somerset Boyd, are somehow using this group to establish a religion to avoid taxes and launder dope money. The event, Gallows Dome, is to proclaim a Savior of sorts." He rifled through his briefcase, removing the cassettes P-Stone had supplied. "Here. Listen to these—Repo spewing mumbo-jumbo, fishing for select converts to attend The Dome and drown in debauchery."

Perry pocketed the tapes. "This event might be a good time to bring me into the fold."

Lena: "When is it?"

"Few days." He began stacking the documents on the bed. "The event is invite only, supposedly. I have yet to get the nod, but plan on being there. Chances of you getting in might be slim to none."

"See what you can do."

"Listen, I gotta get at least an hour of sleep before the sun comes up. I'm driving to Los Angeles, remember?"

Perry said, "What you driving these days? We can take you."

"El Camino down there. And thanks, but I gotta do this on my own."

Perry smirked at Mook's dead-on description, pegging Joe without him realizing.

Lena made her way toward the door.

Perry followed, shaking Joe's hand, pulling him close. "You got my number. Call me. And be careful."

"I will." He smiled at Lena, her gaze to the floor. "Was nice to meet you, Lena. I'll try my best for Tess when I get back."

They shook hands.

Lena and Perry left the room.

Perry shouted, "Call your daughter more!"

Joe slammed the door and set his alarm. He sat back in the chair and closed his eyes. No sleep would come and he knew it, no matter how hard he tried.

Oh, what he'd give for a beautiful dream.

X-man crouched in the car's suede seat, watching as the motor home slugged through fog out the lot, back onto the highway. He was curious how the woman driver factored into all this. Didn't even know why Perry was looking for his private eye buddy either. The Caddy fired up and headed back toward the sycamores. Dash beamed 4:18 a.m. Rayna was sure to be asleep, but he called anyway. She answered on the second ring, beyond perky. He could hear her teeth gnashing. This wasn't good. She only freebased when something was wrong. After minutes of her relaying what she'd seen on an infomercial regarding the "Power of Positive Thought," X managed to get a word in. She motor-mouthed how Perry was a "fucking asshole" who'd lost a "shitty" daughter and that Joe was "the prick" on her case. As for the woman—some "uppity bitch" named Le-na ("like Ray-na, right?")—she "didn't know nothing" about her, other than being a travel companion of "that cocksucker," Perry. Rayna's molars began to squeak, forcing X to pull the phone off his ear. He promised, at least five times, that he'd call her later. She was blathering about "her blood being itchy" when he hung up. He rolled down the window and lit a cigarette, worried about what Perry had done to his baby. *The girl set herself up for heartbreak in order to feel alive.* He'd deal with it when he got back from wherever Miggy/Joe was taking him. Hopefully, San Diego—like he'd said. *Maybe get to take a breather down there—grab cocktails at the Hotel del Coronado— catch one of those killer whale shows about to be banned.* Yeah...San Diego. He eyed the GPS monitor, willing it to blip and get this show on the road.

INTERLUDE
POWERS THAT BE

Outside, the cabin's firewood pile was getting low. Trench bent over to gather an armful, a chill in the air biting her earlobes. Night was coming to a close. Birds weren't singing yet, the woodland confines surrounding the home a vast emerald curtain. The girl would be awake soon. Trench had little time to get things in order for another day. Regardless of all the cases she'd read and studied the months leading up to receiving their Savior, nothing could prepare her for the workload of captivity. There was an art to transforming another's will to seek comfort in the care of their abductor. Medical studies helped supply a timeframe, six days being extreme but accomplished in Sweden by armed robbers and their hostages during a 1973 bank heist. The girl had been in the cabin for well over a week, the results so far being satisfactory. Back inside, Trench loaded the fireplace, torching an inferno to life, filling the home with a hint of sweet smoke. From that first day Trench "found her in the barn," she never presented herself as any sort of abductor—just the opposite, a heavenly caregiver. A divine intervention to a horrendous happening.

A savior to their Savior.

The girl couldn't recollect how or why she had gotten there; she was clay in Trench's fists. Repo made sure his guards didn't disturb them during this crucial time, having each monitor the ranch at its perimeters. A calm setting, downright heavenly, was necessary for Trench to accomplish the act.

Coffee percolated. Trench diced cantaloupe into a mixing bowl to accompany their Fruit Loops breakfast. The girl would barely eat, but that was understandable. The amount of heroin that had coursed her veins by the time she was delivered couldn't be confirmed, although Trench knew firsthand of X-man and his lack of human regard. Repo sending him on this mission wasn't her idea, but she tolerated it since there was no better man for the job. There was one stipulation though: X couldn't rape the girl. And regardless of his reputation, he was a man of his word.

Today, the heroin didn't matter anymore. Trench was helping restore the girl's health, taking a motherly approach, supplementing Oxys and Percocet to keep the girl comfortable. Trench opened the door to the girl's bedroom. She was angelic in slumber, petite features like a porcelain doll's. Trench sat quietly at the edge of the bed, gazing at her creation in progress, thinking in a perverse way that this is what motherhood must entail: complete dedication and unwavering care. But she wouldn't know, never having had a *true* mother or a child. For a few more days, this girl was her life's purpose. She brushed wisps of hair from the girl's sweaty brow, startling her awake.

"It's okay, kiddo. Your angel's here."

The girl's eyes darted in frenzy until remembering her surroundings. She began to cough uncontrollably, her body spasming into contortion.

Trench held out two pills in her palm, along with a small glass of fresh-squeezed orange juice. The girl allowed for Trench to place the painkillers in her mouth and slowly pour fluid down her throat. Trench stroked the girl's hair, holding her close, waiting for the medicine to make her well. The girl wept in her arms. Trench smiled, thinking of the impending grandeur of Gallows Dome, shooshing her doll into silence.

Trench truly had dreamt of the girl. Her features, her beauty, her innocence. Maybe not *this* girl exactly, but damn near close. Once Repo solidified the plan of action for Gallows Dome, it was apparent that the movement would need a face—a foreign being to rally around, someone supernatural—out of this world.

The Dome's crucified Christ.

Repo's plan was simple: start a movement, offer salvation through sin and excess, reap tithings from the devout, launder dope money and ride the wave; however, once this Savior was sacrificed, Trench's plan was quite the opposite, retreating deep into Mexico with enough cash to set her up for a decent life filled with sunshine and mezcal.

No more truck stops.

No more dead soil California.

This was her motivation: a new beginning, far from the curse of this life. And she knew it would happen. She could visualize it. All her life, she'd always felt the outer realm, seen things—strange invocations that always came to fruition.

Her powers.

The night she fled that final foster home of her youth, a guardian angel had appeared before her, commanding her to take charge of her life. *Freedom willed*. Weeks later, the same golden spirit prophesized her meeting a strong, brilliant man that would protect her from despair; that night, Repo approached her at the Cali Gold and whisked her on an adventure through Los Angeles, sweeping her off her feet. *Protection conjured*. Her dream of this girl, the Savior, was another omen, a foreshadowing of Gallows Dome's impending success. The repercussions of the poor girl's death at the gathering weren't of her concern; this would be the exact moment she would abscond. She could see Repo up there, preaching to his devout—the guards busy patrolling the grounds. It was perfect. She'd be gone before the gathering's conclusion. All that mattered was for her to serve as The Dome's beacon toward Babylon, like Repo had intended. Soon as he got up on that stage, she'd bolt, taking whatever money she'd skimmed ($110,000 so far) and catch that plane to Cuernavaca...

When it came to this girl she'd dreamt of, Trench used social media to find someone like her, the teen's image seared into her brain. She knew the right one would have to live a good distance away (Los Angeles or San Francisco), so there would be no local trail once she vanished. Trench perused Facebook profiles for teen girls that met the dream girl's description. After days of searching, she came across a doppelganger: Tess Madadhi. All of the girl's info was there: what school she attended, her favorite movies, books, food—photographs of everyday life that provided a loose timetable to her weekly schedule. Her mother was a little-known artist with no distant relatives. Everything fell into place thanks to modern technology. Tess was perfect; she'd glow on the pedestal that they would place her on before The Dome's fellowship. All that was left to do was snatch her up, break her down and mold her back together. Trench's new lovely life depended on it.

The dining room table was set for breakfast; Trench put on a DVD of *The Goonies* in the living room, one of Tess' top three favorite films. With the girl's current state, Trench tried her best at creating an atmosphere that would be soothing and comfortable. A safe zone to work on her. Again, social media supplied every detail, from the boxes of Fruit Loops to the CDs for the boom box to the types of art supplies in her bedroom—the cabin was custom equipped for the girl's impressionable teenage mind. Trench heard the shower turn off and sped to supply a warm towel.

They ate in silence, Trench reading the newspaper and sipping her coffee while the girl chewed cereal one piece at a time. So far, this morning was like the others. Any minute now, the girl would inquire about what had happened to her, again—a broken record that was becoming quieter by the day. Reprogramming the girl would take time and patience, but Gallows Dome was approaching.

The girl set down her juice.

Trench paused from finishing an article, prompting the girl to speak. "Something on your mind, dear?"

The girl fidgeted.

Trench projected a soft disposition.

"Am I dead?"

Trench smiled, warmly as she could. "Not anymore."

"But I was?"

"Yes."

The girl fished a green loop with her spoon. "And then what?"

"I took human form and appeared before you."

"To save my soul?"

"Yes, dear."

"A guardian angel."

Trench touched the girl's hand. "Call me Mother."

Tess looked out the cabin window at the dense foliage across the land, sunrays creating an aura about. "Am I in...Heaven?"

"Not quite."

"Then I'm in—"

"No, no, no. Somewhere in between. Your work on Earth is not done yet."

"Work?"

"Do you remember who you once were—your past life?"

"I was a student. I lived in Los Angeles."

"That's correct. And now, you are beyond. In order to achieve an afterlife, you must first help others—living humans, to see the light that is within you."

Tess chewed, stupefied.

"Only then will your soul be free."

The girl marinated in thought, mind cloudy from weeks of mind-altering substances.

Trench got up and gave her a hug. "Don't worry, dear. I've been put here to guide you." They met eye to eye. "Soon it will be time, and I will make sure you are ready."

The girl rested her head on Trench's bosom.

"Do you believe?"

"Yes, Mother. I do."

***

The girl had been sketching in a notebook most of the day, listening to The Stones, sipping cola. Her attempts at drawing the outside landscape had failed miserably, forcing her back into a comfort zone of Yorkies and poodles. She thought of her mother, the one who taught her how to draw in her past life—of what she must be going through without her only child. Pain swelled within her core. She struggled to recall what the woman looked like. A tear bombed the paper. She reminded herself that she would be in a better place soon, one where they could be reunited someday. She flipped the page to begin another sketch when the grating sound of an engine came out front. She got up from her bed and walked through the cabin, a gentle breeze fluttering the curtains. Her new mother was out front, speaking with a man in a large ominous truck. She pulled up a chair and watched as the visitor pulled over to the barn and removed two steel canisters with a dolly from the truck's bed. Mother entered the house.

"Who is that?"

Trench cursed P-Stone under her breath, the fool too stupid to know he couldn't make drops at the ranch in the daytime with the girl here. She composed herself. "Just another lost soul. Not like us though. A fallen angel."

The girl's eyes popped.

"We must pity them, the ultimate price they pay."

"What's he doing?"

"Disposing of the wretched—those destined for an eternity down below."

They watched as P-Stone poured a canister's contents into the pigs' trough. The girl gasped at the contents, holding her mouth, trying not to retch; Trench patted the girl's head, reminding her that all was normal in this realm. There was a sordid beauty to the horror.

"Mother, those are—"

"Hell is all too real, dear. But if you follow my every word—every single thing I ask of you, then—and only then—"

P-Stone carelessly crashed the canister into the bed of the truck.

Trench lost her train of thought, fuming. She'd get in touch with Repo about Stone's bullshit.

"Then what, Mother?"

"Then this will be the closest you ever come to its fire."

The girl turned away, sickened by the sight. "Guide me, Mother. *Please.* Lead me to the light."

"Your light is within."

PART THREE
CREEPING RITUAL

17.

P-Stone was in a pissed-off mood, hauling his truck from Greenfield back to his home in Fresno. The entire ride he fumed, disgruntled with the way his services were being treated by Repo, X-man and, now, Trench. The other night, he was in his goddamn PJs, half asleep, when, guess who calls saying he needs two bodies picked up and a home burnt to embers up in that new community, Juniper Falls? If it were just an X-man request, he would've hung up and turned off the light. But with it being an order from Repo Helm...there were no other options; he leapt into the truck and screamed the engine toward the problem.

Was hardly a problem either, the large Chumash and his tiny girl—although he did have a time stuffing the bastard into that steel canister. The manufactured home went up faster than a haystack, so fast he barely got that yapping dog outside to safety. He wasn't a monster after all—just the help, slaving away to clean up the mess of monsters. And Trench. The woman didn't even offer him a soda or to use the head when he pulled up at the ranch today. No one gave a shit about him, and he knew it. Just look at the way Repo treated X-man—like some spoiled brat. But what could he do? Cry his jealousy to Repo? Find some chump job hauling copper or aluminum? *Please*. There were medical bills to pay, his ailing mother to think about. A familiar tune bled out the speakers. He inhaled a deep breath and cranked the stereo, trying to calm himself. When the chorus hit, he rolled down the window and belted the lyrics from deep in his gut.

"Life is a highway. I wanna ride it. All. Night. LONG!"

The Ford glugged through the Tower District, Fresno's historic retail and restaurant core. He lived with his mother in a quaint two-bedroom craftsman—its view out every window of sprawling asphalt parking lots. The Tower Theatre's starburst neon ball cast their front lawn in spectral hues. Pulling up the driveway, he didn't notice the unmarked sedan in the adjacent lot. Didn't think twice of the police cruisers at Sequoia Brew Co. either, figuring boys in blue needed to eat dinner sometime too. As his key slid in the front deadbolt, he could hear mumbling inside. He turned to the truck, his pistol and knife snug in the glove box. He went to sprint for them when the door swung open. Two detectives were inside—his mother and her oxygen tank on the sofa. Looked as if she were having another episode. Stone rushed past the officers, tending to Momma.

"What happened? You okay, Ma?" He spun to the strangers. "Did she fall again—a neighbor call you guys?"

The slender man in a flat charcoal suit closed the door; he had Irish features, but who the hell knows? The other was Asian, wearing a navy sportscoat and auburn slacks. Stone looked out a window and saw cruisers mobilizing toward the house.

"Fuck is all this?"

The Asian flashed his badge.

Feds?

"Need to have a word with you, Preston. Mind coming with us?"

"I have a choice?"

Irish: "No. But I'm sure you'd rather not involve your mother in any of this."

"Can I make sure she's taken all her medication first?"

"Sure thing. We'll wait right here for you."

P-Stone swiped a tear from Momma's cheek, adjusting her oxygen tube back into place and grabbing a tub of prescriptions on the kitchen counter.

"Listen, I told you guys already. I'm kept in the dark, man."

"Jesus fucking Christ. Okay, let's run it back. This time, open your goddamn ears, Preston."

The interrogation room's bright bulb blasted his eyes soon as the Asian pulled back from shouting in his face. The officers were Powell and Watanabe. DEA dicks. They had a case compiled against Repo, dangling a carrot before P-Stone, trying to make him slip his neck into their guillotine.

Powell slid a chair uncomfortably close to P-Stone and leaned in. "Our investigation has been ongoing for the better part of a year. This isn't some long shot here. Repo Helm will soon be arrested and charged with drug trafficking—enough to put him away for a long time. Not to mention the remarkable coincidence that several of his associates have suddenly gone missing. Here's where you come in, Preston. You have the fortunate opportunity to decide your own fate...ask yourself, do I take the life preserver these guys are trying to toss me, or am I going down with the ship?"

Stone rolled his eyes. "Fuck outta here."

Watanabe cursed.

"Before you decide," Powell said, "there's something we'd like you to listen to—so you know that we're on the level."

Watanabe pushed a digital recorder into the center of the table and pressed play. Two voices resonated, distinct, familiar: Repo and Trench.

Repo: "I'm hearing that he's getting sloppy with some of the details."

Trench: "I've warned him once already about being careful with the disposals. Fucker showed up today and was spotted by our guest. Sloppy is right."

"This could be a liability. We have to treat him as such. Nothing can get in the way of the gathering."

"Have X keep an eye on him. If he slips again, then he needs to be snuffed."

Crackling silence.

Repo: "I had hoped that P-Stone could be a good boy, but you're one hundred percent right. I'll send word to X—"

Lee pressed the recorder to stop. "We've had their cell phones tapped for some time now. This' what your loyalty has bought you so far, Preston. The recording is from Trench's cell. We know your role in all this too. An errand boy. Your testimony could put Repo away forever—that is, if you live to see the trial."

Powell: "Think of your mother. Where will she end up if you don't take our rope and pull yourself out this ditch? What's more, how will she cope with burying her only son? It'll fucking kill her, and you know it."

Stone shook his head in disbelief. All these years at Repo's beck and call. Viewed the man as the father he'd always wanted. It was clear who the favorite son was. If X-man was ordered to off him sometime soon, then he'd be ready. "I might be able to help you."

Watanabe perked up, eyebrows bouncing at Powell. "Good. For starters, give us the name of this X and we'll put someone on him—to protect you."

"Don't need protection, but I'll gladly fill you in on everything I know about X-man."

Powell said, "X-man? Good Lord. And what about this 'gathering' that was mentioned?"

"Gallows Dome, a ritual to evoke the end of days."

"Here, I thought *we* were doing just that for Mr. Helm. You're serious?"

P-Stone's eyes answered the question.

Watanabe smirked. "You sad fucks are a silly bunch, know that?"

Powell: "Let's start from the beginning and work our way

back. How'd you link up with Repo Helm and, better yet, where the hell is he?"

"You're telling me you smart guys don't know?" P-Stone huffed. "I ain't seen him in well over a month. Could be any-where."

"He doesn't give you orders face-to-face?"

"You tell me. Thought his phone was tapped."

Watanabe: "Yeah, well, his personal cell recently went quiet."

P-Stone: "Grab me a coffee and one of those cheese Danishes I saw out there. Cigar would be nice to."

"Then you talk?"

He nodded, fixated on his fists, recalling all of Repo's dirty work that they'd helped destroy. "And I'll be free to go after, right?"

"You'll be on our leash, but yeah." Watanabe turned to Powell.

Powell said, "Free enough to get yourself killed. We'll look out for you though. After we have Repo in custody, we'll talk about a reduced sentence—but that'll depend on how much you contrib-ute."

P-Stone shut his eyes, wishing this were all a bad dream. Watanabe bounced for coffee. Powell took out a fresh legal pad and three black pens.

A tight spot indeed.

18.

X-man cruised the Caddy through a Flyin' P parking lot near Gorman, a stone's throw from the Chevron where Joe Delancey had settled for gas. X's tail began at an early hour, Delancey being straight about leaving first thing in the morning. He wished he would've gotten a little more shut-eye but figured so did Delancey. This truck stop was by far his favorite in California, its bombardier pig logo always bringing a grin. He stopped in whenever sent on missions to what idiots refer to as The City of Angels. Closest thing L.A. had to a blessed angel was its snaking fault line, promising a glorious death of biblical destruction. He loaded up on snacks, filling a tall tumbler with French roast. Nearing the counter, he saw an enticing image: a cartoon boy with doe eyes hoisting a chocolate-dipped soft serve. He thought of Rayna and felt bad for not spending more time with her the other day, not sure how long he would be gone this time. He'd check in after giving her a few days to mellow out; whenever she was on a bender, it never lasted long. He dropped cash on the counter and signaled the clerk to start dipping that cone.

It was a juggling act to the car, treats stuffed under both arms, balancing hot coffee in one hand, ice cream in the other. Could feel the phone in his back pocket begin to vibrate. He dropped the food on the car's hood, set the coffee on the roof (a splash of which burned his missing digit) and checked the cell to see where

Delancey was driving. Still south. Maybe he was going to San Diego after all? He tossed everything into the ride, hopped in and gunned for the highway.

Joe Delancey was tired, running on fumes as smog cloaked the San Fernando Valley. His El Camino sped down the 405, approaching America's worst interchange (the 101). He was nearing his destination; soon as the El Co charged over the Sepulveda Pass, a legion of sparkling planes would pepper the air, gearing for touchdowns at LAX. But charging over any freeway was a pipe dream these days. Even at midday with some traffic relief, it could still take a good hour to go the eighteen miles necessary. He slowed to a stop past Sherman Oaks. Driving was more comfortable now that he'd ditched the walking cast for the trip, his left foot free, able to be scratched at will. Radio spouted a Dodgers' doubleheader; a smoldering vehicle died on the shoulder, up ahead. He needed to piss but there wasn't time. He'd relax and eat soon as his objective was in hand. Nerves wormed his intestines. He emptied water bottle dregs out the window and unzipped. Relief washed over the moment he released, admiring a row of undead palm trees (a rarity); juxtaposed by the red sea of brake lights, he saw beauty.

Trapped in paradise.

GPS had Delancey carving a snail trail through the Sepulveda Pass; X-man was hungry, craving a burger and beer. Traffic wouldn't let up for a while. If Delancey was set on petrifying in gridlock, that was on him. There were plenty of ways to head south to San Diego from the Valley, X-man's old stomping grounds from when he was a young buck. He exited at Burbank Boulevard, cruised south at Lankershim, then east down Magnolia. The old neighborhood still held its awkward charm, even with hip shops and high-end eateries that had destroyed an era of mom-and-pops. He knew of one place that still had a pulse. At the corner of Naomi and Magnolia sat Tinhorn Flats. At first glance, the saloon appeared to be a generic cowboy bar, equipped with swinging doors and a wild west motif—but that wasn't the case. Place had been in business since '39, its wooden interior home to damn fine burgers and cheap pints. X-man took in the structure, recalling the many nights lost inside during his early twenties. The saloon doors thwacked as he strolled in, greeted by cow skulls and wagon wheels; a lone bartender cut lemons beneath a mirrored wall of hooch as a fry cook prepped beef in the rear kitchen. X-man sidled the bar, checking his phone for Delancey's whereabouts before grabbing a menu.

Place still smelled the same from the last time he was in here, thirty-plus years ago. The barmaid was a local, he could tell. He'd bet she never wanted to be a movie starlet or musician, like barkeeps on the other side of the hill. Her face wore the legacy of several sweltering summers. He ordered a jalapeño cheddar burger, fried pickles and Miller Lite on draft. As the barkeep placed his order and returned to chopping citrus, X sat in deep thought, recalling that last day he spent on this very stool. The afternoon he made a conscious decision to walk out on his family and risk it all for a life on the hustle. No more bosses to take shit from. No more wife to answer to. Zero responsibility—a split from society into a nomadic sea of chance. *And how did that pan out?* He thought of what his twentysomething self would think now, seeing himself as an old man, the casualty of a crime-filled life. Was curious if his daughter still lived in town, knowing her mother had passed from an aneurysm years ago. What would it be like if he looked her up, rang her doorbell, unannounced? Would she even know who he was? Should she? But he never would, steadily haunted by the possibility of what he had ruined. Better yet, what would his parents think of him these days, if their hearts were still beating—their courageous voyage out the Bahamas when he was a child, only to be trapped by the cold western cage of the Pacific. Had their boy done good—a self-made man? Was he living the American dream? He pretended they'd be proud. A bell dinged from the kitchen. The food was placed before him. He ordered a shot of bourbon and took in the smells. Sunlight broke through saloon doors. The cell began to blip; Delancey had pulled off near Marina del Rey. His brow scrunched. *A slight detour?* He tore into the burger and watched the phone intently, trying to determine what the hell Delancey was up to.

The storage facility sat just off Century Boulevard, the back lot of what used to be a magnificent strip joint—its massive sign boasting Nude Nude Nudes. Joe remembered autumn nights in the place, swilling rotgut whiskey, peeping young co-eds—even the cockroaches danced on stage. He parked the El Co in a neighborhood, one block west. Under the car's tonneau cover, he removed brown slacks, a brown button-up and a mesh UPS cap. After sliding the clothes on, he fished the truck bed for a flattened brown box, restored it to form and searched for a roll of tape. Once secured, he placed his leather gloves and lock pick case into the parcel. He briskly walked east—the faster the strut, the more unnoticed he became; no one on the street blinked twice at a busy delivery man.

The facility was on the cheap side, open air, only the units' sliding doors securing valuables from the outside world. Joe removed a scribbled note from his shirt pocket with the info Becca had given him. The unit was on the third tier. He lowered the brim of his cap and used the box to obscure his face, cautious of security cameras, if there were any. He'd noticed a small guard shack at the north entrance of the facility; not sure if it was for this place or a neighboring hotel, he went out of the way to avoid it. His boots prowled catlike up the metal staircase. About halfway down the third floor's unlit corridor, he found unit 314.

With an eggshell touch, he slid a tension wrench into the

unit's deadbolt, massaging the steel before advancing the pick. It had been a while since dealing with this type of lock, but after five minutes, he managed to unlatch it. The door rolled up, quieter than he'd expected; however, the sight inside was anything but exhilarating. Five Rubbermaid totes sat at the rear corner of the deep unit. Joe rushed inside, sliding the door halfway closed behind him. The first four totes were empty, rat fecal matter atop their lids. His stomach sank. Upon kicking the fifth, a heft perked his interest. The lid cracked gently; items that he was looking for (any kind of dope) weren't inside. *But there was something better.* He pulled out a dense brick of cash, easily fifty g's. At a glance, there had to be a quarter million. He quickly transferred the green into his parcel and jetted out, securing everything inside the unit, as it was.

Felt like he was sprinting on air as he charged toward Century. He was nearly there when a shout came his way, followed by a strange wheezing noise. He turned to see a security golf cart pull up, its driver the size of a baby walrus. Joe tried concealing his face, but it was no use.

The guard removed a phone from his ear. "That a delivery for 5701? I can sign for it."

"Nah, Spectrum Storage."

"Oh, well I can take it if you like? We're neighbors."

He thought fast. "It's a COD."

"Whoa, they still have those?"

"Apparently."

"Shit, that's how I outta send my Christmas presents next year!"

Joe forced a smile.

The guard beeped his horn twice, put the cell back to his ear and zipped in reverse.

After ten steps, Joe craned to make sure the guy was gone. The cart had stopped; the cold gaze of the security guard, speaking into the phone, was unsettling. Joe walked at a faster clip.

***

The Palm Motel, Harbor City.

"Jesus, Pops! Where the hell did you come from?"

Joe marched inside the manager's suite, placing the box of cash on the coffee table before giving his daughter a squeeze. He ignored her inquiries about the parcel, holding her tight, taking in her scent, similar to when she was a baby. She pulled away.

"Seriously, Dad. What the hell's going on?"

"Nothing, really. Was in the neighborhood—"

"*Stop*. Tell me the truth."

He eyed the box. "Let me put this in my office and we'll go for a bite—catch up."

She eyed her sweaty workout gear. "Lemme change first."

He nodded, bolting out the door, upstairs.

Turned out, he was off by fifty grand: There was a cool three hundo in rubber bands after all. Street value on the pills he'd supplied Repo last time approached a hundred K. He took half the money, transferred it into a backpack, then stashed the extra in a wall safe behind a Dodgers' pennant. As he descended the stairs, he could see Becca speaking with customers—two gentlemen at the night window. He tossed the bag into the El Co and walked over. By the posture of the men, along with their German convertible parked in the lot, Joe assumed they were a couple, maybe a jock and his power bottom, hoping to score an hourly rate. As he got closer, the look on Becca's face said otherwise. It was all too familiar—same as when he taught her to ride a bicycle: absolute fear.

The jock spun.

Joe recoiled at the pistol in his fist.

The Seville glided in front of Bill's Liquors, directly across from The Palm Motel. Delancey's El Camino was in the parking lot, but X-man was more transfixed on the two men rough-housing Joe and a girl into the manager's suite. Curtains to the unit were wide open; cars zoomed down PCH, oblivious. X fished for binoculars on the passenger floorboard and lurked.

It didn't take long to know the score. He exited the Caddy and opened the trunk, taking inventory on what supplies he had for chaos. He removed a gas can and baseball bat, tucking his Glock into its waistband holster. He casually walked to the corner, hit the pedestrian button to cross the street and waited.

"If this is a hold-up, take what's in the register and get the fuck out."

The power bottom secured Joe's wrists behind his back with a leather shoelace and tossed him onto the couch beside Becca, already bound and gagged. The jock began rifling through the home, emptying drawers and cabinets. The bottom now had the pistol; he kicked the exercise ball before them and sat down, bouncing.

"Don't be stupid, Joe. You know why we're here. Just tell us where it's at and all will be forgiven."

Joe's brain did the Watusi, uncertain of which crime he was being accused.

The bottom scoffed. "You think Brown didn't have cameras hidden all through his pad? *Please.* We saw everything, Joe. There are no hows and whys—just a where. We've had this motel staked for some time now, Joe. I'm tired of watching your daughter lose her baby fat. And we don't care where you went, just that your back, understand? Now, where are the fuckin' pills?"

At first, relief washed regarding the storage unit cash, then panic returned, watching Becca's face glistening with tears. "I...ugh..."

The bottom lunged and pistol-whipped Joe, splitting flesh at his ear, trickling blood onto the couch.

The jock came in from the bedroom. "There's nothing here."

Before the bottom could reply, a large *whoosh* came from outside. Lips of fire danced out the window.

The jock sped over, immediately seeing the guts of his Beamer up in flames. He rushed to the door.

The bottom asked, "What the hell is it?"

No answer came. Soon as the jock launched out the door, his septum met flush with the meat of a Louisville Slugger.

X-man watched the dude timber, like a sack of dirt tossed to asphalt. He retook a batter's stance, awaiting the little dude, knowing curiosity would draw him out. After a few more questions shouted to his partner, the barrel of a pistol slowly broke the door's plane. X-man brought the bat down on it, knocking the steel to concrete. Before the guy could retreat inside, X charged in with a massive blow, its connection with the back of the dude's dome so effective, the Vuarnets nearly slid off his nose. He tossed the bat and untied the girl. Before Joe could say anything, X asked, "Who's she?"

Joe, in shock at the sight, thought fast (as Miggy). "Just the manager."

He pulled the Glock out his waistband. "Ain't lyin' to me now, Joe?"

Joe! His bowels sank. "Don't...X...please."

Becca's eyes gave her dad a *you-know-this-psycho* stare.

X didn't level the gun her way and spoke calmly. "Call the police, honey. Tellim you was bein' robbed—but leave us out the equation, awright? Say some vigilante stumbled upon the scene, saved your pretty ass and took off—didn't leave a name, not wanting to be a hero." He turned to Joe. "I love those type a stories. Don't you?" Joe went to nod, but X already had his bound hands cranked up his back, going out the door.

Outside, Joe flailed to be released, ear still bleeding. "What the fuck? Untie me, man."

"Later. I like you better this way, Joe."

Joe! "Wait, wait—wait!"

"Don't you see that burnin' hooptie? Them two dudes out cold, half dead? No time, Delancey."

"Listen. Let me explain."

"Can talk all you want on the car ride back north."

"The goods are in my car. Backpack on the seat."

X-man stopped marching him, turned to the El Co and doubled back for the take.

Joe pleaded again for X to untie him as the Seville tore up the 110 North onramp, hugging the shoulder past a galaxy of brake lights.

"Jus' try an' relax, feel me? Let's get to talkin', first. Why's there cash in that bag instead a the dope you promised?"

"Shit went south. I didn't want to worry Repo until there was *something* to worry about. Thought I could pull it off. Turns out, I couldn't—but my penny landed heads up. That's all for him too—fifty k more than the street value of the dope I brought him before—I want him to have it since I fucked up, no heavy lifting, worry free—"

"How so?"

"Let's just say, the dickheads who stole it won't be reporting it to police. It's off the cuff. Free money."

"No such thing, Joe. Belonged to those dudes back there?"

"I dunno who the hell that was."

"I bet." X chuckled.

"How'd you find me?"

"Oh, *Joe.* I'm a resourceful fella." His fists wrung the wheel. "*Crazy* Joe...Crazy Joe Delancey, *PI!* Never thought I'd ever come face-to-face with a real-life gumshoe, but here you go. *Sheeit*, if I had a helicopter, we'd be made for Hollywood." He smirked. "Miggy Rojas musta thought he was dealin' with some dumb muhfuckas, am I right?"

Joe sighed, squirming in the seat.

"Miggy, Miggy, Miggy...Personally, I didn't trust the bitch—but

Repo felt some kinda way about him. Don't wanna think what he's gonna say about all this—but I'll let Crazy Joe do the talkin'."

"Can you *please* untie me. Hands are numb. Can't feel my fingers."

X pulled the Caddy off near Downtown, his shades never once panning in Joe's direction. After a few blocks, he swung into an empty parking lot of the once legendary Grand Olympic Auditorium. Boxing every Thursday; wrestling matches Wednesday and Friday. These days it was converted into some mega church. They sat in silence at first, staring at the monstrous structure as if it were still in its prime—a house of war—not stained with a huge mural of the King of Kings.

X-man lit a joint and muttered, "Jesus Christ."

"That's him alright." Joe turned to give X his tied hands.

X-man used a torch lighter to scorch the ligature.

Joe yelped as the lace snapped, rubbing his wrists back to life.

"X-man ain't been down here since the doors closed in '87. Don't even drive by when I come to L.A. no more. Still hurts. Some of the best days a my life, watching men pour their blood in there."

"Caught a bout between longshoremen here once. Two Mexicans. Called a draw. Second tier crowd tossed beers into the ring. Riot nearly broke out."

X blew a plume. "Who were you bettin' on?"

"Shit, I can't remember their names."

"I mean in all this...Miggy or Joe? Whose agenda were you pushin'? To me, I had a hunch you was in this for the money, but that don't seem to be the case with that bag right there. Anyone money grubbin' would've fled with the loot—and something tells me you hadn't even considered it. Naturally, now I gotta hear it from the horse's mouth. What's your angle, Joe?"

He contemplated an answer, settling on the truth since there was nothing left to hide. "I was out on a case, looking for a missing girl..."

X-man's sunglasses darted in alarm.

"...taken off the street a decade ago."

X's shoulders relaxed at the timeframe. He recalled Rayna blathering about this incident, last time they chatted. "So, what happened?"

"Girl vanishes up near North Hollywood, truck driver is my only lead—me and her father head up through truck stops and nothing comes of it. Few years later, get another lead and it brought me back out to the Cali Gold. Figured she might've worked the lots—maybe someone knew her. Repo ran the lots back then. Had to get in close to find out."

"A lizard, huh? What's her name?"

"Rochelle."

X-man confirmed Rayna's coked-out rant as truth, then racked his brain, remembering that lunch at Farnesi's Steakhouse. "That's why you was askin' me about some 'Ro' chick?"

"Yeah."

X-man chuckled. "Ain't that a bitch? An' here, I thought you might be up to something nefarious. You a knight in shinin' armor, Crazy Joe. *Sheeit.*"

"Not exactly."

"Bet your parents are proud of you doh?"

"They wanted me to be a postal worker."

X-man choked on the doob. "Then your daughter be happy, right? Rebecca. That was her back there, the manager?"

Joe didn't respond, his ear throbbing. "Let me get a hit off that."

X passed it over, eyeing the bag of money again. "I'm guessing you stole that first batch of pills you brought Repo too, huh?"

"I do what I have to do to get inside on a job. Sometimes it can get a little out of hand."

"You think?" X peered at Joe, a bloody mess, his good intentions on solving his case now beaten into dust. "It's a long drive back to Los Banos. Hopefully be there by midnight."

"What the hell you waitin' for? Let's get this over with."

"Man, you ain't even thanked me for savin' your ass yet."

"Thanks, pal. I owe you one."

"More than one, but I'll take it. So, this is what helpin' somebody feels like nowadays? You can keep it." X took one more look at Christ's weepy eyes on the defunct gladiator dome.

Joe killed the J.

The Caddy hit the road back to Hades.

19.

...Through Gallows Dome, we are immortal. Now's our time to assault a new era—one dictated by a chosen few, bound by blood—in honor of our forefathers—

Perry killed Dreamboat's tape deck once he'd heard enough; Lena sat beside him, mouth ajar. Perry exited into the Villa's parking lot to light a smoke. Could feel Lena's eyes, burning him from behind. "It's a buncha baloney, Lena. Zealot hoo-ha. Don't look too hard into it."

"It's just, I don't know—that whole spiel creeped me out. What year is this, and where the hell are we?"

"Shitsville, baby. And it don't matter the year when cash is king. It's a damn hustle—any fool can see. And if they don't...fuck 'em."

Lena pondered if this was the initial response given to the religion she'd been baptized—all those doctrines (till recently) that she'd given her whole heart in search of redemption. What difference did it make, preaching love, hate, when it was all in the name of infinite wealth? She felt like one of the fools Perry was talking about as she strolled back toward the motel room.

"Back to bed already? It's not even supper time."

"Have to get to painting. Might as well get this mural done while Delancey's gone, keep my mind off things."

"He'll be back soon. Don't you worry."

***

Lena took her paintbrush to the far wall, dancing it about: her magician's wand. The image had struck her on the way back from meeting Joe Delancey. An expansive landscape, either Yosemite or Yellowstone. From that base, she would carve out something topical about the US of A.

For the next three hours, she painted feverishly, as if in a dream state, her arm flowing with ease, heart pounding. Once she stood back to admire her work, she realized the piece could be finished by morning. Two monolithic rock formations loomed at its parameters; dense ponderosa pines, incense-cedars and white firs jutted along the bank of a rippling creek, its rocks afire by the sun. She smiled at a thought.

Yeah, that will finalize the piece...

The saloon was bustling for the first time Lena had been on shift. At least thirty revelers took to the well, slurping shots, smashing billiards—scratching their heads at odd blues arrangements out the juke. Lena hustled to clear tables of soiled pints and tumblers. Among the laughter and riffs, her mind was refreshingly blank.

A big man with a shiny head pummeled into the joint. She'd never seen him before. He sat at the elbow of the bar, eyes on his hands, troubled with thought. Lena took a towel to the wood before him.

"Can I get ya?"

"Tequila. Well." His eyes never left his knuckles.

"How you want it—on the rocks, neat...in a bowl?" She giggled, trying to alleviate the mood.

"Neat. Bud back."

Fetching the man's juice, she eyed him intently, introducing herself upon delivery. He thanked her and apologized for his demeanor. They shook hands. When he told her his name, she was immediately struck; P-Stone was scribbled throughout

Delancey's notebook. *An eerie surprise.* She left him to his thoughts, deciding that she had no choice but to befriend him. After all, he was a player in an evil game that could answer questions about Rochelle. It was the least she could do for Perry, letting her drag him all this way just for a chance to speak with Joe. She poured him another shot for lubrication, on the house.

Perry hadn't seen Rayna around the Cali Gold since their drunken incident and began to worry that he'd done something damning to her psyche, a rejection of the only thing she'd wanted in life: *love.* As he sat in Dreamboat's captain's chair, scanning channels on the CB, he tried to believe this mishandling of Rayna's feelings was what prompted him to start inquiring about her over the airwaves. After all, he knew she would often score johns this way; maybe she was listening, or another driver had seen her around town. But that wasn't his primary motivation: He had to ask her about this "Ro" girl that had worked the same lots as her, a few years back.

For most of the evening, he pestered haulers suffering from "Beaver Fever" or searching for "High Speed Chicken Feed" and "Pickle Parks." There was a smorgasbord of terms he couldn't understand, but just as he was about to give up, a female voice came through the receiver. The girl claimed to be a roommate of Rayna's. Perry had never considered Rayna's living conditions and grew curious. It soon became apparent that this roomy did in fact know Rayna and was trying to poach whatever proposition Perry had in mind. He asked if Rayna was with her, and the girl balked. She haphazardly gave him her address and told him, "Come see fuh ya'self, cowboy."

He hauled Dreamboat down the interstate, relying on a foldout map for guidance. He pulled up before midnight, an older residence located a stone's throw from a Walmart. Its flat roof was in disrepair, along with a rusted Plymouth on blocks in the driveway. There was no porch light—or any lights on inside for that matter. Girl had mentioned a back house. He grabbed his revolver, tucking it into his jacket. As he approached with caution, the sight of rollerblades strewn on the rear lawn brought a wave of relief. A lamp glowed through the rear unit's front window. He took a breath and knocked on a decrepit screen door.

The rowdy bunch at the Dorado began to disperse after midnight. P-Stone remained slouched at the elbow, eyes glossed, shoulders lax. Lena slid another beer before him.

"So, what's the P stand for?"

"Huh?"

"P-Stone?"

"Preston."

"Well, Preston. Have the place all to ourselves now. Wanna shoot some pool?"

He eyed the surroundings, not realizing they were alone.

Before he could say no, Lena had already punched two quarters into the bar-sized table, clacking balls out the gate.

He walked over to the stick rack, beer in hand.

"Only ones somewhat straight are the 19 and 21."

"Nineteen?"

"Ounces. What, you never played pool before?"

He shrugged, feeling the weight of the cue in his hand.

"Well, don't worry. I won't embarrass you…much."

He smiled for the first time.

She racked the set and chalked her cue. "Now, watch and learn, mister. After this beating you can tell all your boys that you were humbled by the infamous Machine Gun Lena." She bent over the table, back arched, hips swaying. Could feel his eyes on her. The rack crashed, dancing about dingy blue felt with two small balls about to drop.

***

The CB gal answered the door in a torn negligee ripe for a small-town stripper—ill-fitting, bright enough to cause migraines. She was short and stout with a face reminiscent of a thumb. Perry humored her invite to come inside. She turned down a hallway, leading to her bed, then noticed he wasn't behind her. He began loudly calling out to Rayna. The girl, in desperate need to salvage any potential monetary exchange from Perry, intentionally blocked a door to what appeared to be a bathroom. She attempted to coax him by rubbing his chest. Perry contemplated pulling his weapon, then pushed her aside, wadding up a twenty-dollar bill and tossing it to shag carpet. The girl relented, scooping up the cash. He slowly opened the door, heat lamp flickering inside. Rayna was in an empty bathtub, naked, vomit clogging the drain. Her face was ashen, lips chapped—discolored. There was a glass straw, torch and charred tinfoil atop the toilet. He lunged to check for her pulse. Before fingers could touch her, he noticed the swelling of her abdomen. She was breathing! He propped her upright, trying to shake her awake. As her neck plunged like a wet noodle, he noticed a team of scars across the crests of her breasts—slash marks—superficial yet deep enough to scar. Some were fresh, though the majority were not. He turned on the shower; she awoke in frightened grumbles, cold water glistening. He swiped a towel from its rack and wrapped her up, carrying her to the living room, laying her on the carpet. The roommate watched from the kitchen, heating a Hot Pocket; Perry shot look-daggers.

"Get her fucking clothes, put everything in a garbage bag."

The microwave dinged.

"Now!"

The girl ran to the bedroom.

Perry held Rayna as she wailed, disoriented, a newborn flush out the uterus.

After a few minutes, the girl returned; she helped get Rayna into her pajamas. He slung Rayna over his shoulder and grabbed the bag, charging out the house. After placing her on Dreamboat's rear mattress, he ran back to snatch her rollerblades.

By the time he hit the highway, Rayna was already back asleep. He kept one eye on the road, the other on the rearview, scared that she might burst to life and try to jump out the window. He chastised himself for being so harsh to her in the walnut grove, but he was hurt at the time, drunk. And that's what animals do—lash out under duress. But she was just a kid in his eyes. He should've known better, and what did that say about him? He was a damn kid too, emotionally. The neon swan-diver welcomed Dreamboat back to the Villa.

Rayna nibbled a grilled cheese, not sure if she could hold it down. Her brain felt like a bag of concrete being mixed—her body, a stiff, achy mess. Perry gave her time to process the predicament, then brought her up to speed on their whereabouts; when she woke in the motor home, could've sworn she was in some time machine, barreling backwards through a gauntlet of failures. She wouldn't talk about her troubles though, only stating that sometimes it helped her to shake up this life by walking a ledge. He hypocritically disagreed, asking her if she wanted help, assuring that he was there for her. She knew he'd seen her scars too and felt fortunate by this reaction—a first. But she wouldn't address them either, a lifetime of feels.

"Can't you answer me one thing, missy?"

"Depends."

"You didn't do all this 'cause a the other day did—"

"Anyone ever accuse you of having an inflated sense of self, Perr'?"

"Just the ex-wife."

"Well, her brain prolly cut glass." She fidgeted with the bottlecap. "This isn't about anyone but stupid ole me."

They ate in silence, the occasional burp from Perry melting her heart.

He was her friend.

Not even X-man had ever come to her place and helped her out a jag. He'd wait it out, sure—act surprised that she was still alive the next time they met. Never once did he truly show that he cared for her, outside of the occasional lunch or a new dress. She'd read Perry all wrong and felt ashamed. Then again, how was she supposed to know? Not every day that a man considered her for anything more than her profession. She reached out and touched his hand. "Thanks, Perry. I mean it."

The eight-ball ran from one rail to another, finally banking into a side pocket. After nearly a dozen games, Lena had won all but one. This one.

Without the table beneath him, P-Stone might've plummeted through the floor. "Told ya, honey. Hit better when I see three at a time—smash the ball in the middle."

"I'm truly impressed."

He slouched onto a nearby chair, hand fishing across a table for a bottle that wasn't there.

Lena attempted to keep the conversation going, wanting to pry some kind of info from the dude, but all that tequila became the big winner of the night—P-Stone slurring unintelligibly. She pounded the rest of her drink and hollered for the other barkeep to help pry Preston to his feet.

They walked him to the Villa's office where she asked Barb to let him sleep it off in exchange for some of her pay. As they careened the brute to a room that smelled like a sarcophagus, P-Stone became an annoying parrot, squawking about "bastards that wanted him dead" and "sweet fuckin' revenge" and "damn Gallows Dome"; Lena focused to mine anything of use, determined to confront him again when he emerged, beyond haggard, in the morning.

"Think hard, Rayna. Joe said she worked the same lots as you, maybe five to ten years ago."

"And they called her Ro? And you don't have a description?"

"All I know is that another gal had mentioned her—a Somerset Boyd."

"Now, I'm all messed up. Boyd? My memory sure ain't what it used to be."

"Think some folks 'round the lots called her *Trench*."

Rayna's face went flush. "That's Repo Helm's old lady."

"Yeah—and he used to have a stable at the Cali Gold, right? This Ro was a part of it. Weren't you?"

She slowly nodded yes. "I know him well." She thought of X-man's best friend, his capabilities. Just when she figured the monster could definitely be responsible, a name popped into her head, one that she hadn't thought of in years. Problem was, it wasn't the name Perry wanted to hear. "Pretty sure it's Rosalee Moss—this runaway from Arcata, up north. Teamed with us for a minute, but she was pretty off in the head. Got a bad john, lost her shit. Ran into oncoming traffic out of nowhere one day. I didn't see it, but the other girls said it was like watching a mosquito smack a windshield."

Disappointment washed over Perry's face. "You positive?"

She shrugged. "You asked if I knew anyone…I'm sorry, Perr'."

He boiled, chastising hope, leaving the RV for a smoke. It wasn't Rayna's fault. Just another dead-end street to his dead-end life.

20.

Back in Los Banos, Joe ascended the stairway to his room, followed closely behind by X-man, holding a box of donuts with his four-fingers. They'd gotten in much later than expected thanks to exhaustion forcing them to doze at a rest stop in Gorman; the whole time X had his Glock leveled at Joe, even when snoring. Delancey was afraid X-man would have a nightmare and fire the rod into his abdomen. Yet, every time Joe opened his eyes, he was met by X's listless stare, uncertain if his eyes were open behind those polarized wraparounds. Not liking his chances, Joe decided to pass on pushing his luck by reaching for the weapon. He was worried though; once Repo was in possession of this new money, and the truth came about there being no real Miggy Rojas, there was no guarantee things would be square.

X-man slid their breakfast onto the table. Joe put on coffee and went into the bathroom to clean up his ear and shower. X made him leave the door open, pinky-swearing no funny business. The shower blasted. X-man called Repo on his new cell, but ended up leaving a voice message, trying to set up a time they could meet later. He sat on the bed, gun placed beside. There was a pile of folders and notebooks spread before him. He began to peruse their contents.

"This all your work stuff out here, Delancey?"

Joe stuck his head out from the flamingo shower curtain.

"What?"

X spoke louder. "Your work stuff? On the bed."

"Yeah, mostly notes that amounted to nothing. Move them to the floor, if you want."

"This be some superhero shit right here. Crazy Joe's Bat Cave."

"That's one way to church it up."

X flipped through barely legible script, handwritten—hundreds of pages. Felt like he was gazing through a window into the other side, a good guy and his process to help make the world right. The man's work routine felt oddly similar to X-man's habits. Joe appeared to go the extra mile to make things precise, same as he did. Throughout the years, X would take notes on styles of firearms used effectively in certain situations: drive-bys, long-distance targets, simple hits. Knew the right amount of rope, gasoline, explosives or heroin to handle most of Repo's tasks. It was a good job ethic that today's youth didn't seem to strive for anymore. Here he was rifling through his bizarro brother's things, realizing they weren't that different. One could argue the only hiccup between them was their askew views on death: Joe's with human regard; X-man's without.

Joe rinsed quickly, exiting the shower, leaving it on. He listened as X-man rifled through documents, placed the towel on the toilet seat and gently climbed to the air vent. Quietly, he unscrewed the bolts, reached in and grabbed the Saturday night special. It wasn't like him to be put in such a powerless situation. Now, the playing field would be a little more even from here on out. The showers humidity forced him to wipe dampness from the gun. He placed it inside the front pocket of his hanging pants, killed the water and dried off.

X-man reclined with a cigarette, holding a red folder that was different than all the other documents; its scribbled tab, the work of a female hand, enticed him. He opened it carelessly, puffing away, never considering that the innards would sink his gut.

The girl.

Gallows Dome's Savior.

She smiled back at him from a glossy yearbook photo—same one he'd seen on the news, days after. *Tess Madadhi*. He turned the picture over, revealing the next page, a typed summary of the case thus far. Cops hadn't a clue; Joe must be on the job. Delancey had lied about his intent as Miggy. He was trying find the girl and her abductor: him. But how much more did Joe know than the cops about the kidnapping? The next photo summed up X's every fear. He froze on a black and white image of himself—a frame from a surveillance camera—a red circle over his missing digit. He cursed being so careless; crime over time tended to make a man lazy. The shower died. His heart began to race. Joe knew it was him. Or did he? A quick inhale returned control.

Joe said, "Coffee's ready." He slid on his pants, inspecting the busted ear in the bathroom mirror. "Mind if I take that jelly donut?"

X-man said, "Go for it."

"You sure?" Joe fingered the pistol in his pocket, contemplating scenarios when storming into the next room, weapon leveled. Could he take X's gun, walk out the door and disappear into Los Banos? Maybe Perry could pick him up somewhere—take him home? But X knew about The Palm Motel—about Becca. It would be a life of constantly looking over his shoulder—worrying about Becca every waking moment she was not by his side. Unless X was dead, then Repo wouldn't find out about Miggy Rojas...He finished getting dressed, drew a few deep breaths, palmed the pistol and went for the donut. "If you want the damn jelly, just say so. There's two strawberry crullers and a Boston cream."

The moment Delancey broke the bathroom's doorframe, he juked for the box of donuts, spun and fired—the report omitting a strange *pop*. Peril immediately seized him, seeing X's confused face, knowing damn well he couldn't have missed from this close.

X-man recognized the sound of a squib load, bullet lodged in the barrel. Before Delancey could flinch, X shot him in the face.

Blood spat across tired wallpaper as Joe fell back into the bathroom, crashing to linoleum, body full spasm. X walked and stood over him, thanking every god in existence for the bitch gun's misfire. A damn shame. He liked the dude, a long-lost brother...but survival was king in this jungle.

He took quick glances out the window to make sure no one was stirring from the blast; aside from a pack of kids throwing rocks at a stray cat, all was calm. He'd covered Delancey's body with the bed comforter, not wanting to be judged by the man's marbled eyes. This situation needed to be taken care of pronto. He placed Tess' file onto the bag of cash, grabbed his phone and called P-Stone. There was no answer. He tried and tried. All straight to voicemail. As he was texting a final attempt to get P-Stone to The Speckled Hen, his cell began to ring. He almost answered it blindly, thinking it was Stone, then thought better. Screen beamed *Rayna.* He swiped the jelly donut and killed her call, contemplating his next move. As warm cherry oozed through his teeth, Crazy Joe's blood seeped through the blanket.

A joint flared between X-man's lips. He used a Zippo to light the corner of Tess' file and splashed Delancey's paperwork throughout the room. It had been ten minutes since sending the text to P-Stone, and X was getting antsy. This was the closest thing to a Viking funeral that Joe would get; X felt slightly noble for thinking of it that way. Not only could he bring an end to this situation, at the same time he would honor this fallen bizarro brother. The fire would chirp alarms, even set off the sprinkler system, but by then X-man would be long gone. Would take the cops weeks to identify the man checked into this motel as Miggy Rojas. Lips of flame danced through X's shades. He tossed the folder once it was fully engulfed. Cash bag in hand, he walked from the room as if he were stepping out for supper.

Halfway down the stairwell, he heard gravel crunching in the parking lot. He watched as an unmarked cruiser with two suits inside pulled next to the Seville. The driver used a flood lamp to illuminate the Caddy's interior.

"Sheeit."

He turned and briskly walked to the back side of the motel, out of view. He glanced up at the structure and saw smoke beginning to billow. As he darted across the street and up the block, fire engine sirens could be heard in the distance. He sat at a bus bench and watched as the trucks raced by, boarding the first bus that stopped, having no clue where it was headed.

Didn't make no sense.

X-man huddled over a screwdriver and T-bone steak. There was an all-night diner at the fringe of town; he got off once the bus doubled back on its route. *Why the hell would an unmarked be all over Repo's Caddy?* Of course, there were plenty of reasons for him to think of, but none that the police should know. After all, Repo had most of them, in these parts at least, snug in his pocket. He took out his phone and searched for a contact, their favorite cop on the take. Ran license plates for him—tipped Repo off about drug and prostitution raids. *Elkins.* P-Stone, along with every other cohort of Repo's (aside from himself), was kept in the dark about such individuals—and for good reason. Never knew when a situation like this would bubble to surface. A safety net of sorts. He called.

"Hola."

"X-man here."

"Can I do you for?"

"Need some info."

"Shoot."

"Find out if you got an unmarked patrolling Los Banos to-day?"

"Gimme a sec."

The waitress dropped his check, splashed with hard candies.

"Nothing on our end."

"Huh."

"Feds have been around though. Could be one of theirs."

"DEA?"

"Yessir."

"What they be doin'?"

"They don't tell us shit. Get to use our station for whatever they want. Mooch all the coffee."

"Anything else strange I should report to Repo?"

"Nah."

"Alright then. Thanks."

"Wait."

"What?"

"You know Preston was in here yesterday?"

"Booked?"

"Nope."

"Just hanging out at the station?"

"Dunno what the hell he was doing here, but you might wanna ask him."

"Sniff around. See if anyone else there knows what he was up to."

"Sure thing."

X-man hung up and marinated in thought.

Silence from P-Stone today, the first time ever when called for a cleanup...

Was chillin' at cop headquarters yesterday...

He tried Repo again, a second number he was given recently. And why the fuck was boss man constantly switching out phones? Again, no answer. He left another message: "We might have ourselves a problem..."

X-man pushed the steak aside, appetite lost. There was only one thing that he was hungry for: answers.

21.

Sunlight burst into the saloon, startling Lena awake; she'd fallen asleep at one of the tables, exhausted after finishing the mural. She held a hand over her eyes, trying to focus on who was standing before her. *Barb.* She rose from the chair and stood behind the woman, now ogling the wall, slack-jawed, fresh cigarette dangling from her bottom lip.

"Well...what you think, Barb?"

Barb's head toggled, taking in the immensity of the piece. The Yosemite landscape was pristine and glossy, gorgeous pines, rippling water—a dime store postcard. It was an image at the creek's bed that had Barb perplexed: a toothless vagrant, disheveled and smiling—his busted shopping cart trapped on a glistening stone and filled with rainbow trout. She tilted her melon, as if a jolt to her brain juices would help. She inhaled to speak but then thought better, figuring Lena for one of those extreme artsy types—someone on another planet—not wanting to let on that she didn't understand the piece. Instead, she took the cigarette from her lips and gave Lena a lukewarm smile.

Lena hugged her. "I'm so pleased you like it."

Barb took in the mural's juxtaposition once more as Lena cracked her rib cage.

The door swung again. Perry ambled inside. Lena greeted him, wondering what time it was. By the look on Perry, something had happened last night. He stood before the mural in awe, his stunned silence taken by Lena as a compliment. She left Perry to chat with Barb and walked outside. A large truck was parked in the same spot as last night, meaning P-Stone was still in his room.

"What the fuck happened?" P-Stone surveyed the suite, still clad in his clothes and boots, mouth a cauldron of muck.

"Well, you weren't in any shape to leave," Lena said. "Don't worry about it. Motel's manager owed me a favor. Saloon's about to open soon. Interest you in some hair of the dog?"

The nodding of his skull brought down a hammer. "Hair of the *god*, maybe. Can't remember the last time I felt this terrible. Never drink tequila—not sure why I decided to start last night." He knew.

"Hey, you tied one on and now you got your bill. Big deal. I'll let you wash up, meet you down there." She exited, ready to introduce Perry to her new chum.

P-Stone noticed a gang of missed calls on his cell and grumbled, "Fuck."

Rayna had her bare feet on the motor home's plastic dash, wiggling toes to the beat of a Blasters tune on the tape she'd recorded for Perry. The hours upon hours of sleep, along with her mind's constant self-flagellation, had helped break through the ceiling of her latest funk. Now, the escapades of days previous were merely a footnote in her forgettable biography. She watched shadows eclipse every blemish upon the motor lodge, contemplating *the sun* in her life. Nearly down a rabbit hole of thought, a large man exiting one of the motels rooms broke her concentration: P-Stone. X-man always bitched about how the guy was a pain in his rear. She'd never formally met the man but heard enough gossip to never want to. He was walking toward the Dorado, looking rough. But who was she to judge? Before the saloon doors could swing, he was greeted by Perry's pal, Lena. Rayna perked upon the captain's chair, peeping the pair's discourse, wondering what in the hell a person like Lena could want with a fuck up like Stone.

Inside the Dorado, Perry sat at the bar, nursing a vodka tonic that he'd made himself. The balance was off, hooch prevailing. He took in the mural again, recognizing the vast differences between his brain function and Lena's. Eventually, his introspection wandered elsewhere. He felt depleted.

Physically.

Mentally.

As his thoughts took the darkest of turns, in walked Lena with some hulking menace. He shielded his eyes to catch a better look.

"Perr', there's someone I'd like you to meet."

Lena introduced the lug. He recognized the name from out Joe Delancey; Lena's bouncing eyebrows signified that she was all too privy. They shook hands, Perry pondering the dastardly feats P-Stone's fists had partaken. P-Stone sat on a stool beside him as Lena ran to serve drinks. Perry fought the notion to say, Fuck it, and leave his daughter's soul to rest in oblivion. But now there was another who might have a different take on this "Ro" mystery, if there still was one. *Rayna wasn't positive of her ID after all.* Lena poured heavy and the trio got to gabbing. The world was madness; madness was their world.

Perry watched as P-Stone rose from his stool, thanked Lena and left the saloon for good. The moment the wood doors swung at his back, Perry turned to Lena and said, "Not much of a chatterbox."

"Hell, I don't really know him at all, but can tell something's got him troubled. Was in the back when I heard you two start yapping. Say anything about Ro?"

"Not a damn thing. Shrugged it off like a sneeze. Said a Miggy Rojas had asked him the same question not too long ago."

"You don't say?"

"He mentioned Gallows Dome—said if there was a Ro that was still in Repo's good graces, she'd be at the event. Soon as I started asking about Repo, he clammed up. What is it with all these fools and this Gallows Dome?"

A voice came from behind.

"You got me."

Perry and Lena craned to see Rayna approaching.

Lena couldn't help but notice that the girl looked like she'd been chewed up and spat out—reminded her of a wet cat. "Watcha drinking, hun?"

"Just a Roy Rogers. Thanks."

Perry asked, "You know of this Gallows Dome then?"

"Got an invite to it."

"How'd you manage to pull that off. I hear they're hard to come by."

"I wouldn't know. Not into any of that mumbo-jumbo. X-man got it for me."

"Any way he can finagle another?"

"I make one phone call and you're in. No questions asked. X is good to me like that."

Lena: "How about two?"

"Don't see why not? Hey, how you know that dude just walked outta here?"

"We don't. Came in last night on a tear. Had to spot him a room 'cause we could barely get him out the bar."

Rayna nodded. "And what, he come in here spouting about Gallows Dome?"

Perry: "I asked him about you-know-who. Said she'd be there if she was still around."

Lena delivered her syrup and cola. "Say you make that call?"

"Now?"

"Better time than any."

"Perhaps." She pulled out her cell from a rear pocket. Her tongue slithered to the tiny red straw as the dial began to ring.

22.

"Yeah, I couldn't talk then, girl. Wassup?"

"Don't call me girl, X. You know how I hate that."

"Listen, Rayna—ain't got no time for confrontation."

"I just called to say, hey. That's all. Aren't you interested in what I've been up to since you left?"

He placed his palm over the cell to address his Uber driver. "Man, bust a left up here." He placed the phone back to his ear. "A course I do—"

"Where in the hell are ya?"

"Just got back into town. Merced. Why?"

"Saw your buddy today?"

"Who?"

"Stone."

X grew in the seat. "Where?"

"Dorado."

"When?"

"Earlier."

"Like fifteen minutes ago, or what?"

"Thirty, but you know I ain't never been good about time..."

"Say where he was headed?"

"Don't talk to that loser. Why? You looking for him?"

"Nah. Just...he was supposed to do somethin' for me and X-man couldn't get a hold a him."

"Heard he was pretty sauced last night."

"He was drankin'?"

"Pickled to the gills on tequila, I'm told."

Never once seen P-Stone bite the worm...

"Hey, that Gallows Dome thing is coming up, ain't it?"

He almost forgot. "Tomorrow."

"Think you could add me for a plus two?"

"For who?"

"My roomies." She lied, not wanting to increase X's jealousy of Perry.

"Cool."

"Thanks, Big Dog."

The Japanese sedan braked before newly built condominiums. X-man exited, promising Rayna they'd hang soon—at The Dome. He entered the complex and rode the elevator to the top floor.

The unit was modest, barely furnished, a lone painting of a nude lounging Latina the only décor. He kicked off his loafers and slid atop the covers of a king-sized waterbed. Thought of turning on the television to hear about that fire, then zeroed in on some birds chirping outside. His body went limp, every knot, all that tension, washed away by the cool pool beneath him. The moment he fell asleep, his phone rang. He answered with his eyes closed.

"Yeah?"

"Elkins here. Word on the street is your boy got pinched by the feds."

"Why you say that?"

"Officer down here, Tarkington, overheard the interrogation. Sounds like your boy is about to flip."

"Bullshit." X sat up, making waves. "About to flip on who?"

"Mr. Helm."

"I don't believe it. You *positive* it was Stone?"

"Feds had Tarkington run out for Backwoods cigars."

"Shit!" X wiped his brow. "You said, 'About to flip'—but he hasn't *yet*?"

"I'm not sure."

"Fuck."

The call ended. He went into the closet and pulled down a large suitcase. With the cards on the table, there was only one hand left to play. He'd head out of town after Gallows Dome; there he could find Repo, give him the money—tell him the shit news (if he didn't already know). He'd see if Rayna wanted to join him, a long overdue vacation. Barcelona. Venice. New York City. Somewhere to get lost, pretend he was someone else. *Someone good.* He bled back to reality. Before that could happen, there was one final mission to accomplish: find P-Stone, brace him—then shut him up...forever.

INTERLUDE
THE BABYLON BIBLE

"Bestow thy blessings…"

"Bestow thy blessings."

"Of your infinite sins…"

"Of your infinite sins."

"Unto me."

"Onto me."

Trench withheld a sigh, masking it with a smile. "Almost."

Tess drooped her head as they walked a dirt trail through Monterey pines at the ranch's northern flank. It was as far as she'd been out of the cabin since finding herself placed in this otherworldly realm. She was trying to sponge everything Mother was telling her, yet the immensity of the forest—the animals, the smells—had her brain scrambled. Similarities between this realm and the other she'd known before death was uncanny. But this one was more welcoming, warmer—as if she were ensconced in cotton balls, sheltered from dark outside forces. If this was indeed limbo, as Mother insisted, then she could hardly contain the joy in envisioning a heaven that she now knew to exist. She returned to focus, knowing that acquiring that bliss would require more work. She closed her eyes.

Trench: "Bestow thy blessings…"

"Bestow thy blessings."

"Of your infinite sins…"

"Of your infinite sins—"

With the exception of a lighter's spark, Repo Helm found himself trapped in complete darkness. Could barely make out the wafting smoke as he exhaled clouds, burdened by thought—the same ones he'd been pondering the past few days. He'd gone off the grid completely, focusing solely on Gallows Dome, its execution. Couldn't help but reflect on all the bloodshed, the loss and pain—created by him, over decades in this spiteful world...That wasn't entirely true. Pa had seasoned him and Darcy to lawlessness, same way Grampy had taught Pa and so on. He sat and waited, puffing away. Tried not to think about the feds either, closing his eyes for a solitary moment, trying to blank his brain but failing. The Dome would be his greatest feat, the dawn of a new era—a legitimate enterprise. If they pulled it off...

And they would. Had to.

For survival.

For prosperity.

To fulfill the dream.

The wood led into a large field, its grass golden, enveloped by an undulating forest periphery. At its eastern edge sat four flat-bed eighteen-wheelers, their trailers parked side by side, conjoined into a giant square. A fifth trailer equipped with a shipping container T-boned the square on the north. Large generators beside towering flood lamps surrounded the jumble of steel. The girl stood curious of its existence. Reminded her of some modernist sculptures she'd once seen at an art show, back then. Mother walked through trampled brush toward them, motioning for her to follow. A pair of hawks glided in circles overhead. She tranced on their grace, walking in Mother's footsteps, leaning to touch prickly blades of bottlebrush. At the field's center, she noticed another odd sight: a team of porta-potties huddled at the western fringe. She glanced back to see Mother atop the flatbeds, arms raised to the sun.

The girl ran toward her.

***

"A stage for the ceremony, silly."

"When?"

"Tonight—right here. Look around you. Imagine lost souls everywhere—here to see you—hear you. You are the embodiment of their salvation—the answer to their desperate prayers."

The girl panned the empty field, nerves tingling with uncertainty. From atop the trailers, it felt like she was floating on air. "But why me, Mother?"

"Because you have been chosen. The meaning of your being here is to enlighten these poor wretches—show them a guiding path to either *the light* or *the darkness*."

She pointed an index. "Up or...down?"

"Beyond."

"And how am I supposed to—"

Mother shushed, putting a finger to the girl's lips. "That's why we've been sent here to help you. To ensure your place as Savior."

"We?"

"Father and I."

"Father?"

The door to the cargo container began to rise, mechanically. Sunlight refracted off something shiny in its innards. The girl squinted, holding her hand as a visor to cut through brightness. At first, she noticed feet—a pair of moss green boots. Then wiry, black denim legs. Mother held a frozen grin as the door climbed, revealing a grizzled man with pebbly eyes seated on a gilded throne.

"It's all for you, my dear," Repo said. "A fluid transition from this place to the next. A door, to be opened by you. Only then can you cross over to infinity."

They were seated at the edge of a flatbed trailer, Tess' legs swinging as father spoke truth to her about their festivities. Mother was inside the cargo trailer, tailoring their attire to be worn—long robes as glistening as the throne to which she would sit. Father's look to her was one of great happiness. Surely, he sensed her discomfort.

"You are having trouble, I hear."

"I assured Mother not to worry. I will be present, rising to the occasion."

"You still don't believe. Do you?"

"I..."

He stood on the platform, raising his arms to the sun. "Watch." He placed a palm in the direction of a tall and wispy Douglas fir, not far behind them. Closing his eyes, he began to speak in broken tongues—dead language.

Trench watched from the container, awaiting Repo's command. The moment he stopped mumbling, she was to detonate an explosive he'd placed earlier at the rear midpoint of the tree; she held a plunging device in her fist.

The girl recoiled at the tremendous blast, splintering the wood into two weeping pieces.

Repo nodded at Trench, who nodded back. He embraced the girl, shaking in his arms. "We are not here to destroy, but we can, you see? Mother and I want nothing but for you to part this veil with ease. Now, what must you do to make that happen?"

"Recite the homily Mother has taught me."

"When?"

"At the conclusion of the ceremony."

"Why?"

"To open a portal for the wretched."

"How?"

"I'm not sure..."

"As their spiritual Hand of Glory—only *you* have the power to open *any* door."

"Okay."

"There's still time. You'll do fine." He patted her head, looking around the field at what was to come. Drugs and drink. Pyrotechnics, music, fire. Hopefully (if he'd done his job), all bodies would be exalted in narcotic transcendence, either writhing in fornication or clashing in violence.

Hedonism at its best.

The girl was fast asleep in his arms. It would work, he thought.

Trench sat beside him, caressing his shoulder.

He met her gaze. "Our time is now, High Priestess."

She ran her fingers through his thinning hair.

Their tongues gnashed inside a sloppy wet kiss.

The moment Repo went to further prepare in the barn, Trench drew a bath for the girl and brushed her own teeth, getting his taste off her lips. As their Savior soaked in bubbles, Trench retrieved a suitcase from out the coat closet, careful none of the guards were peeking inside. She'd already packed it with clothes, snacks and $280,000—a fraction of Repo's freshly washed cash. Couldn't help but wonder which he would miss more: her or the green. Carefully, she rushed the case into the field, stashing it beneath the stage. Soon as The Dome was swinging—sex, violence and gore full-bore—she'd seize her chance, escape through the forest, never to return again. A vision came to her now, that place beyond, a familiar dream—one she'd lived thousands of lives over ten thousand years. She made it back to the cabin in peace, just in time to serve the girl her towel.

PART FOUR
TO THE DOME

23.

With just over two and a half hours remaining to Greenfield, Dreamboat was making excellent time, chugging through Salinas, gearing toward Highway 101. With Gallows Dome set to begin at midnight, Perry's logic was to get there early, eat a solid meal somewhere and regroup before diving head-first into the unknown. A tiny pink sedan cut them off; Lena honked, grasping the wheel as Rayna searched through tapes in the glove box, looking for something good to pass the time.

Rayna said, "Hey, Perr'. Never even opened this, huh?" She held up the copy of *Rock and Roll Heart* he'd purchased at the Gold, first time they met. When no response came, she turned to see him snoozing in one of the recliners. She showed Lena instead. "You mind?"

"Go for it."

"Know he bought this for you?"

"He mentioned something about it."

"I told him to. I mean, didn't know it was for you at the time, but still, a great record. Listen."

The cassette began to churn inside the stereo, a smooth saxophone seeping out the speakers.

Lena held the RV at a steady clip as it shot down the interstate, surrounded by a massive wind turbine farm. "I like it."

"Who couldn't, am I right? Say, this is the first time us gals have had a second to ourselves."

Lena shot a smile, trapped in thought, trying to avoid conversation. The girl looked much better today; she'd showered and changed into a nice floral dress with cowboy boots. Makeup hid blemishes about her face, albeit several layers. "Thanks again."

"For what?"

"You know...getting us invites to this."

"No sweat. I think it's a buncha phooey, but, hey—if I can help Perry in any way, I will."

"He's one of the good guys."

"You don't even know. I was in such a bad spot before I met him. He's really opened my eyes to a lot of things."

"I can second that."

"Any word on your daughter's case."

"—"

"Overheard you and Perry talking earlier. I shouldn't pry. Sorry."

"No. It's fine. Nothing on the police end, but I've got a good feeling about Joe Delancey. Said he'd be back by the event tonight, but I'm not so sure. Fingers crossed..."

"Hope to die. What a wicked, wicked world..."

They gazed at a herd of cattle, free range, munching grass as the sun dipped behind green hills; they stopped talking, entranced by song. Lou crooned, saving them from ugly thoughts: *Ah, I believe in LOVE...*

When they sped past the next rest stop, Lena couldn't help but notice a large truck pulling out, just like P-Stone's...

24.

P-Stone held his arms out like the crucified Christ, seated on a bucket at the rear of a surveillance van. Watanabe taped a wire to his chest and down his torso.

"I don't know why this is all necessary."

Powell said, "That's the beauty of what we do, champ. You don't have to know a damn thing. We're in control. Do as we say and you might just make it out of this bind you've made for yourself."

"Said you had his phone tapped. Told me you had enough to take him down. What the fuck is going on here?"

Watanabe: "When going to trial, you can never have too much evidence. Anyway, I told you, he starched his phone—his wife's cell went cold over the weekend too."

P-Stone swatted Watanabe's hand and buttoned his own shirt. "How come you guys couldn't grab X-man already? Fuckin' ridiculous."

"We found that Seville he was driving, but he wasn't in it, dipshit."

Powell: "Found it in time to stop a fire in progress at a roach motel though. No thanks to you."

"Fire?"

"Looks like some wacko set their room ablaze, then tried to bite a barrel."

"What room?"

"I dunno, top floor."

"What was the name of that motel again?"

"The Speckled Hen Inn."

"I'll bet hard money that that was Miggy Rojas back there. X-man killed him and tried to cover it up with arson since I never answered his call. Don't you see? He *was* there. You blew it."

Watanabe: "Well, he wasn't when our boys stormed through."

Powell: "Or the fire department. And he didn't *kill* anyone. Like I said, they think this fella tried to kill himself. Last I heard, he was listed critical in ICU."

P-Stone chewed through his cigar, bad thoughts pinballing the brain. "If Repo's been tipped off about me talking to you knuckleheads, I might as well bite a barrel myself. He's got a few local cops on the take."

Powell: "Who?"

"Well, he never told *me*, man. But I heard things."

Watanabe shrugged off Powell's curious stare. "Small town cops are the least of our worries. Buncha jocks, been hit in the head too many times. You need to focus on finding Repo at the gathering and trying to squeeze him about these bodies you last dumped. If we can get him on tape with that angle, along with the distribution charge, it's lights out for sure."

P-Stone began to fidget with a cigar.

Powell took it from his fingers, lit it and passed it back. "You got nothing to worry about, Preston. We'll be with you every step of the way. There's surveillance vans like this one all over Greenfield. Soon as the festivities kick off, and we have a solid visual on Repo, then the boys will ride in blazing."

"Why wait? Why not just nab the bastard before the event goes on?"

Watanabe: "Maybe we aren't here to just grab him."

"How so?"

Powell: "Ton of folks expected today. Bunch of other criminals, I bet. When the cavalry charges, we'll have buses waiting to take every participant down to headquarters. Part of that field they got set up for the ceremony just happens to have a creek nearby, owned by the state. We checked, and they never filed for any permit to use government land. Makes the attendees illegal trespassers. That's a shame, isn't it?"

P-Stone rolled his eyes. "Let me the fuck outta here."

Watanabe opened the rear doors of the van, its outside panel proclaiming a laundry delivery service. P-Stone took a step toward his truck. Powell shouted that they'd be in touch and good luck. He flipped them the bird and climbed into the Ford. Driving out the rest stop, he pulled onto the highway—soon as a motor home adorned with puppies glugged past.

25.

X-man was less than thrilled at the choices of rental cars presented to him by a doughy teen that was surely having a laugh at his expense. He gunned the tiny sedan, a sorbet Chevy Spark—some pink fucking clown car—down the interstate, outside Greenfield. Its engine wheezed. His luggage didn't even fit in the trunk, forced to ride shotgun. He weaved through traffic sans blinker, eliciting honks, taking an early exit to drive through a McDonald's before continuing to the ranch. Hadn't been in these parts for a minute—way back when he got instructions from Trench on how to kidnap Tess Madadhi. He planned to arrive well before the event, hoping to find them at their log cabin. If the stars were to align, P-Stone's bitch ass would arrive the moment he spilled the beans.

Trench and the girl were already in place, snug inside the cargo trailer until Gallows Dome was to begin. Naturally, Repo would be the master of ceremonies; their being inside the container was as comfortable as could be, the insides customized for their needs: fully lit, air conditioned with plenty of room to move. After stringing colorful lights throughout, Trench made last-minute adjustments on the sequin robe the girl would be wearing. She'd constructed the robe from scratch over a matter of months, the garment shimmering in emerald green. At its center, a severed right hand covered the torso, each finger a lit candle with flames of blue and orange. *A Hand of Glory.* In between threads, a strange image popped in her brain: a vehicle destined for the cabin. The girl was asleep on her throne thanks to a sedative. The image swelled again: the oddest pink car she'd ever seen. With it came unwanted news—she was certain. But who was the message for? She got back to work, putting the disturbing image to rest; after all, attendees would be arriving shortly.

Repo admired the boars in their pen, snorting through a sloppy dinner he'd provided, covered in their own filth. He took in the treetops, replaying through his mind the tone he'd set this evening to The Dome's fellowship...for the hundredth time. It would be juicy enough to illicit unwavering loyalty, bringing forth the power he'd envisioned all along. Couldn't lie to himself: He was drunk on the prospects, the power, the influence. He understood now. A vision clear as The Dome's High Priestess could see. This was far greater than any feeling a dead president on shit paper could provide. Let the feds scratch together a crummy case. With the wealth he'd amassed...didn't matter. He felt invincible.

A conqueror on home soil.

He checked his watch; it was nearing eleven. He took a step toward the cabin, hoping to get dressed, fall into character. Before he was out the barn, a small car raced into the yard— screeching to a halt, kicking dirt. Two of his guards drew weapons upon it, then noticed the driver and pulled back.

"And you're sure it's Preston?"

"Elkins said so—dug around to be positive. He here yet?"

"No."

The cherries off their cigarettes danced inside the dark barn like fireflies.

Repo turned from X-man and began to pace. "I was told by another informant last week that something was brewing—that I should get rid of my personal cell. Said, in so many words, there was a snake in the grass. Your name was even brought up."

"Me? Come on now."

"I know, but we anticipated the worst. Figured the problem would rear its head eventually, and here you are."

"Yeah, well shit ain't resolved, that's what I'm trying to tell you. I ain't the problem neither. We gotta split for a minute—chill out 'til everything simmers."

"I have a plan in motion."

"Me too."

"What's in the bag?"

X handed over Delancey's loot, explaining the whole debacle.

"But he's dead?"

"Far as I know."

"Is there anything else?"

X-man took a long drag.

"Where's the Seville?"

"I hoped you wouldn't ask..."

"Another casualty?"

"It was at that motel when I hit Delancey."

"Delancey?"

"I mean Miggy Rojas."

"And you think they're going to try and tie this to me?'

"No clue. The Caddy could've just got impounded, not belonging to a guest there. We gotta be careful, is all I'm saying. Get the fuck on, take a year or two. Feel me?"

"After the ceremony."

"A'course. What you need me to do?"

"I already have the crew busy, monitoring the gatherers, torching bonfires...Let's head inside. Have you eaten supper?"

"Quarter Pounder and fries."

"Shit, X. I wouldn't feed that grease to my swine."

"I hear that. Nah, I'm good on food. Gonna head on down, keep an eye out for our Judas. Soon as Stone shows his ugly head...them pigs better be starving, my man."

Repo slung an arm around X as they walked out the barn, the hoots of an owl providing a soundtrack.

26.

The locust descended onto the field.

Steadily, the number of revelers grew, trampling brush toward beckoning flood lamps with large speakers beneath them, droning organ music. Lena, Perry and Rayna watched from inside Dream-boat; parked among freight vehicles, trucks and choppers; the outlying ranch nearly resembled that of the Cali Gold parking lot. Their plan was to split up (Lena/Perry and Rayna) and roam the grounds, canoodle with strangers, ask if anyone knew or had seen this *Ro*. Perry didn't like the odds but had to try just to say they had—that he'd taken this lead on Rochelle as far as possible. Only then could he rest knowing that he'd done everything in his power to find her, before landing in a grave. He retrieved the matte black revolver from out his duffel, placing extra 9mm rounds into his jacket. He told neither Lena nor Rayna of his packing heat, thinking of the piece as a fail-safe if things turned south. They exited and followed the others, old and young, men and women—nomads and squares. A legion of doomsday ushers, clad in denim, leather and flannel. Perry lit a Red, handed it to Rayna, then torched another. To kill the butterflies, Lena asked him to spark one for her too. There was no time like the present, as they were about to find out.

***

The second time P-Stone passed the entrance to Repo's ranch, he'd embraced the fear jolting his entire body. He jerkily poured tequila into his face as the truck bore down the dense, forest-lined road, approaching eighty miles per hour. Large pines zoomed his peripheral into a maddening merry-go-round; he wanted nothing more than to swerve in an instant, careening the truck directly into a thicket to nirvana. But there was Ma to think about. It killed him, the visuals, her tragic end to a meaningless life clouded by the loss of her only child. Why had he begun working for Repo in the first place, if not for her? Liquor burned the esophagus. A tear fell. He slowed the vehicle to an even sixty, circling back toward the ranch. Along with the pistol and knife in his glove box, he added a sawed-off double-barrel beneath the bench seat. Headed into the inferno, he'd be prepared for war. The feds' agenda was the last thing on his mind, survival at the forefront.

He guided the truck through the entrance, driving past a swarm of attendees, their eyes trapped on fireballs igniting in the distance.

As Perry, Lena and Rayna ascended into the basin, the heat off large bonfires brought warmth, five to be exact, positioned in a broad pentagon before what appeared to be a makeshift stage of flatbed haulers. The enormity of the field made the number of attendees seem low. Lena guessed there to be at least a hundred, so far. There were armed men at far points of the field's perimeter, looked to be private security for the event. Soon as they hit the field's center, Perry and Rayna went in one direction while Lena took the opposite. Immediately, a group of men approached her, their eyes frenzied. One offered up a bottle, another a homemade pipe and torch.

She pushed the pipe aside, shouting above the ambient music. "I'm looking for Ro!"

The taller of the four said, "Ro? We only got Tina and Molly. Want some?" He began fishing through pockets.

She veered around them, onward to another group, cautious of the crowd's inebriated state—all the while keeping an eye out for Delancey.

27.

After a half hour of introducing himself and rummaging for Ro, Perry stood at the front of the stage, alone and frustrated at the mind-numbing task. No one knew a goddamn thing. Felt like another dead end that he was trying to delude himself into being something more. He'd lost Rayna to a pack of bikers with several cans of Coors. He watched her frolic in the distance, the open spaces in between attendee clusters not seeming to fill in. The amount of folks walking into the field had dried up too. Not exactly the turnout Perry was expecting. He lit a smoke and was quickly bothered by a kid with one leg asking to bum one. He handed over the cig, asking the kid about Ro, moving along before he got a solid answer, heading to the porta-potties to sit and contemplate his meaningless existence.

Rayna slid the man's paw from her left breast and thanked him for the beer. She watched as Perry lumbered through the crowd toward the shitters; he looked defeated as Charlie Brown. She checked the clock on her cell; the festivities would begin shortly. As she approached the next set of heathens, the glint off a pair of sunglasses caught her eye: X-man. He was at the back end of the stage, actively panning the crowd beside an armed guard, searching for something. She jammed two fingers in her mouth, whistled and ran over.

Repo stood in front of the bathroom mirror inside the cabin, texting via burner with Trench inside the cargo container, gearing up for the ceremony. He was clad in a long forest green robe, a frayed noose as a grim necklace; his face was slathered with mechanic's grease, voiding his weathered features into a sludgy, ominous mask. His crew was to kill the field's flood lights at twelve on the dot, then he'd wait ten minutes to stir the crowd into frenzy—a standard rock band technique—before walking down to the stage at the perimeter of the field, ready to address the devout under a spell of blood red lamps. One of the guards came inside and notified him of the time. Their end of days grew near…

P-Stone placed the pistol in the rear of his pants after wedging the knife sheath into his boot. As he exited the truck, a tearing of tape from the wire on his chest had him yelp. In a fit of rage, he let out a tirade that he knew Watanabe and Powell would hear. The anger gave him an idea. Curious if the feds were bullshitting, he wanted to head into the woods, anxious to see this government-owned creek that played lynchpin to their raid. He plodded down into the basin, veering a hard right before reaching the first bonfire—directly toward the field's fringe of absolute darkness.

"You don't seem too happy to see me?"

X-man stopped surveying the crowd for P-Stone and looked down at Rayna.

"Come on, girl. I'm working right now. I miss you good. Don't be givin' me no shit, 'kay."

She huffed. "Aren't you gonna even ask how I've been?"

He calmed for a second. "You look nice in that dress."

"Thank you."

"Where them roommates?"

She paused. "Around here somewhere…"

"Looks like you came out that bender on top, huh?"

"No thanks to you."

"Why is it my fault every time you go off the deep end?"

"Deep end? Fuck you."

"You know what I mean."

She turned to walk away.

"Hold up. You seen Stone here?"

"Nah."

She tried to bail.

"Wait."

She turned, only her head this time, eyes broadcasting annoyance.

"I gotta leave again—this time for a stretch."

"How long?"

"Dunno. Months. Maybe a year."

"Why?"

"Less you know, the better."

"Then where you headed?"

"Prolly Reno, then keep moving east. Chicago. Pittsburgh."

"So, this' it then?"

"Wish I could say no, but…"

"So much for the warm sendoff." She grabbed his hand, tapping his missing digit, memories of their friendship rocketing through her melon. "What if I came with you?"

"I already thought of that, but it isn't safe, girl. Too many variables in play that could turn things in a bad way. Maybe after a minute, when shit dies down. I'll send for you—let you know where I be—fly you out."

She leaned in to give X a hug, knowing this could be the last time they ever saw each other. Before she could get her arms around him, he started to jump up and down.

She backed off, letting him pogo. "What the hell is it?"

With each jump, he caught P-Stone's large skull bouncing through the parking area. "Wait here. Be back in a few."

Rayna watched as X ran off in a full sprint.

28.

Lena couldn't help but notice the surge of attendees had come to an abrupt halt with only a few more folks romping the grounds than when they'd walked in. *A midnight ramble without many ramblers.* She panned the crowd, looking for something to stand on for a better view, still on the lookout for Delancey. Where was this guy? He planned on being here. She pushed through a huddle chanting *Gal*-lows-*Dome* as they ogled an orgy by a bonfire with more men than women, and bumped into a familiar face.

"Any luck, Perry?"

He shook his head, gazing over her shoulder to scope an eyeful of the unflattering copulation.

As his head shifted, Lena noticed a light within the peripheral darkness behind him—a few football fields up ahead. She squinted, pegging the light to be coming off a structure, its chimney smoke barely visible with the bonfires raging. Maybe that was where this Repo and his crew had their headquarters? Maybe Joe was over there?

"Have you seen Rayna?"

"No. She was by the stage earlier. What about Delancey?"

Before Perry could say no, the large flood lights shut off, leaving the crowd cast in the infernal glow of the fires. Odd music seeped out the speaker system, a chanting of sorts, another language—she couldn't be sure. As the music droned, every reveler began to hoot and howl, dense smoke masking moonlight, erasing every star.

Lena shouted over the raucous, "I'll meet you right over there, by the stage, in a few."

"Where the hell you goin'?"

He couldn't make out what she said, but knew it dealt with Delancey.

She briskly walked past him, parting the horde, onward to that lone radiance in the distance.

Repo moved like a shadow down the forest trail, knowing every safe step, having trampled the path a hundred times exactly for this moment. Under the cloak of darkness, the energy from the gatherers roared, bringing chills to his core. He emerged from the wood to part the crowd without causing a stir. After all, no one besides his Gallows Dome crew of insiders had ever seen his face—and with caked grease about it, not even they would suspect him. He climbed upon the stage's rear, past two guards, rapping twice on the cargo container to let Trench know he'd arrived. The red lamps would blaze shortly for his sermon. He took in the field, lips of flame at pentagram points. The smile fell from his face. Where the fuck was everybody? With all the invites, they'd anticipated three times this amount!

Lena was careful walking through overgrown foliage on her way through trees to *the light*. The closer she got, could see it was a log cabin, a lone bulb afire inside. Through the shouts and roars emanating behind her, she could hear a rustling—twigs snapping, dirt grinding. She ducked behind a large pine, waiting for whatever was coming to pass, hoping it wasn't a feral animal. What she saw could've been mistaken for a specter—a cloaked being with only the whites of its eyes visible. There was a noose, chopped past the knot, around his neck. She held her breath, still as a rock. The thing passed a mere foot before her. By its stature and gate, she knew it to be human. As the rustling got weaker, she came from behind the tree and ran toward the home.

She was careful when peering through a window. The innards were what one would expect from such a place. Cries of animals could be heard nearby. She noticed a barn; parked before it, a Pepto-pink automobile. She crept across the porch, wood creaking with every step. The front door was unlatched. She opened it to see no cohorts—no Joe. Place looked to be empty. Regardless, she moved stealthily, heading first to the fireplace, retrieving a poker as weapon. She held it samurai-style through the home. The kitchen was spotless yet traces of inhabitants were strewn throughout. Behind the first door, a man's dirty laundry lay in a pile, western wear devoid of charm. A second door masked a bathroom; an opened tin of grease sat at the sink. She moved the poker into a spear position, approaching a final door, light glowing around its hinges, bringing heightened caution.

She took a quick breath and swung the door open.

The room was also empty. A child's room.

A girl's.

Her shoulders went lax, poker hitting the floor. She'd accomplished what she came for and hit another roadblock. She was turning to exit the bedroom when she saw it. A drawing. Taped behind the door.

A Yorkie.

She peeled it off, frozen in disbelief. Certainly, it was a coincidence. She tore through the bedroom, searching. Under the bed: more drawings. Inside the drawers: Yorkies galore. But how? She crashed to her knees, afraid she was going mad.

But there was no mistaking the style. The *strokes* of the drawings—ones she'd taught for years to her only child.

Tess was here!

She frantically rushed through the cabin, screaming for her daughter, over and over—tossing furniture, fishing through closets. When nothing was found, she rushed out to the barn, combing every inch, kicking over canisters, then out to the animals—a sty of giant boars snorting at her, gnashing sharp teeth.

What the hell was happening?

Was this for real?

Her heart pounded, tears too scared to flow. She grasped a fence to prop herself, panic attack engaged. Red lights flared above the bonfires.

Was this a hell created specifically for her?

She rushed to find Perry—call the police. With her first movement, she began to pray—a mumbled rosary seeping from her lips with every step. Was the only thing she could think to do for now, a panic mode: Virgin Marys, Our Fathers. She wanted to believe again. Needed to.

Mother of God, pray for us sinners!

She ran like never before—as if every demon she'd amassed throughout life was clawing at her heels.

29.

The field was cast in blood red.

Perry found Rayna at the corner of the stage, smoking a cigarette while spurning the advances of every male within her reach. A fist fight broke out; Perry shoved his way past the row to her.

"There you are." Rayna smiled.

Perry lit himself a smoke. "This shindig's about to begin, or what?"

"Got me, but I'm ready to leave."

"Me too."

"Where's Lena?"

"She'll be here in a few."

"No sign of any Ro?"

"No." He had trouble seeing under the dark spell of crimson.

"Oh, shit."

Perry looked at Rayna, then followed her gaze up to the stage: a cloaked figure, face melting with what looked like tar.

The ambient music died, crowd simmering to a whisper.

P-Stone had his fingers in the cold creek, its flow soothing, calming his nerves. So, the feds weren't putting him on. *Big deal.* Still had a plank to walk to secure his end of the bargain.

A branch rustled behind him. He spun, pistol leveled.

X-man shot his hands to the sky. "Shit, man. It's just me. Whatchoo doin' over here? Looking for snakes?"

"The hell you doing?"

"Lookin' for your sorry ass. Repo asked X-man to find you. Saw you running through them cars. Everythin' okay, dog? Look like shit."

P-Stone returned the gun to his waistband.

X-man approached, uncomfortably close. He hovered over P-Stone's shoulder and took a whiff.

"What you doing?"

"Somethin' smells off, my man." He slid down his sunglasses, meeting Stone eye to eye. "Why ain't you returned any my calls or texts?"

"My ma's been sick. Was at the hospital. Poor reception."

"She okay?"

"Yeah, just getting old."

"A blessed thing—that ability to age. Most folks in our profession don't get the option. Sooner or later, the hammer comes down...You look nervous."

"Fuck outta here."

"There somethin' you ain't tellin' me?"

"Like what?"

X-man shrugged, taking a step back, returning the shades up his nose. "Like...you in bed with the feds." He pulled the Glock.

P-Stone ducked, tossing his boot knife, hitting X directly in the shoulder.

The impact had X-man drop the gun. P-Stone fled back to the truck. X pulled out the blade, grabbed the Glock with his left hand and rushed in pursuit. P-Stone zig-zagged through trees; X fired anyway, bullets ricocheting, striking wood.

P-Stone slid to a stop, opened the truck's door, retrieving the shotgun from under the seat. The second X emerged from the wood, he unloaded. The round missed but sent X to the dirt. P-Stone jumped inside and started the engine. As he took off, a thud came from the bed of the truck. He didn't need to check the rearview to know what it was. He pulled the pistol and fired blindly over his shoulder.

Watanabe and Powell were given the description of the cloaked man on the stage but couldn't be sure if it was their target, Repo Helm. In their earpieces came, "Shots fired! Shots fired!"

They paused, looked at each other.

Watanabe: "Fuuuck."

"You said it." Powell gave the order to move in and break up the party.

Their connection to P-Stone had been lost, but they both would bet either he was the target of those blasts or doing the firing. They exited the van, heading to the field for a better inspection of the melee.

Repo stood before the microphone, all eyes on him. He raised both palms in praise. "Brothers. Sisters. The time has come to unmask the reckoning of days."

The revelers cheered.

He slid the noose from his neck, hoisting it for all to see: the tool he'd wield to sacrifice their Savior...with his bare hands. "Today we take action. Today we chew through the noose of modernity—we hoist our own gallows and watch as the world hangs!"

The crowd went berserk.

"Through the powers of our High Priestess, a Savior has risen..."

Cheers washed in waves.

Repo waxed poetic, surging an urge for blood. The cargo container's door began to rise behind him.

Loud bursts—projectiles—fired into the field. Their whizzing pops caught Repo off guard. The moment they bled smoke, the crowd boiled in frenzy.

What the...

Tear gas?

Through the haze, he could see troopers in riot gear advancing from all corners of the field, their rifles like pickaxes, flashlights like torches.

One of his guards fired a shot. Then another.

"No—no—*NO!*"

The crowd shrieked, bumping into each other, stampeding to disperse. Some fell into the fires. Others were trampled beneath boots.

He rushed to the shipping container.

Soon as the door rose, Trench was nowhere to be found.

The girl was seated on her throne in a trancelike state; her porcelain skin was aglow from golden light behind, casting an aura of sainthood.

Before he could fathom the reason behind his wife's absence, two officers climbed onto the stage, guns pointed, shouting for his surrender. He leapt off the stage, slipped out the robe and ran into the forest. Bullets whirred past his head. He pulled a pistol from out his boot and fired back, dodging in between trees. When his ammo ran out, he pulled his neck knife and hid. More shots rang out, bursting dirt about his feet. He began to sprint, crashing into wilderness, stumbling down an embankment. A round struck his back. Then another, the abdomen. Time stopped. He kept staggering downhill, his mind commanding the legs to move, but he couldn't be sure they were listening. Gravity barreled him to dirt.

30.

Lena was hyperventilating as she descended into the belly of the basin, crashing through bodies, trying to get where she told Perry to meet. The cloaked figure she'd seen earlier was now on stage, the speakers broadcasting his deep voice.

"Brothers. Sisters…"

Through the crowd she came across other faces she knew: Barb knelt before a bonfire, palms praising the sky, chanting undecipherable words. Lena pushed on through, determined, horrified. She saw Rayna up ahead, near the stage's front. As she squeezed through a pair of girthy truckers, loud wheezes and pops began to explode around her. Then smoke. She coughed, struggling to take in air. Her eyes began to burn. She pulled her shirt over her nose and charged forward through bodies clashing in delirium.

X-man lay in the bed of the moving truck, beneath the rear window, waiting for P-Stone's weapon to empty. Soon as he heard the first click, he lunged inside the cab, aiming the Glock at Stone's temple. P-Stone dodged the weapon and fought for control of it. A round fired, shattering the windshield. Pain surged in X's shoulder. The truck careened into the crowd, beginning to thump spectators. Noxious gas filled the air. The

Glock fell to the floorboard. P-Stone had X by the throat, no hands on the wheel. As he squeezed, leering at his reflection in X-man's shades, more flesh thumped across the Ford. He held the grip, leg fishing for the brake. When he finally looked out the webbed windshield, it was too late.

He growled, X-man limp in his fists.

The truck crashed into the stage's main generator, bursting into flame, prematurely setting off pyrotechnics that were to signal the end of days. Large mortar racks discharged explosion after explosion, the night sky raining fireworks in brilliant spectral hues. P-Stone was trapped, unconscious, the truck's cabin a writhing inferno. Before long, the Ford became a pyre, roasting both men alive.

"Mother, what's happening?"

The girl's words were met with silence. She remained on the throne, leering at what appeared to be a spiritual battle raging in the field.

Trench hid beneath the stage, trembling, holding her suitcase as if it were a writhing toddler. The scene unfolding in the field was horrendous. Police swarmed in gas masks. Tormented screams. She could see a vehicle charging toward the crowd. *P-Stone's truck.* Bodies began to thud off its hood—arms and legs akimbo. She thought fast. Without hesitation, she ran from under the flatbeds, jumping over bodies, gunning through the forest.

Her heart raced, paint dripping from her face. The wood was much darker than she'd remembered. Running, her foot snagged something, sending her crashing to the ground. She turned to see if any cops were in pursuit; instead, she was met by the corpse of her husband, bullet riddled and bloody, face still caked in grease. Fireworks tore into the night sky. She internalized her scream, launched up from the ground and continued on. Someone shouted, "Get her!" She didn't turn to see, sprinting as fast as her little black heart allowed.

Perry pushed Rayna through the horde, dodging police and revelers, back toward Dreamboat. Hopefully, Lena would be there already. The butt of a rifle kicked into his chest, sending him backwards. He went for his revolver, then realized the assaulter was a pig. Before the officer could level the barrel at him and force an arrest, Rayna had grabbed pepper spray from the guy's belt and unloaded it into his eyes. Perry, gasping for breath, ran toward Rayna; she slung his arm around her shoulders and guided him.

Fireworks began to explode, sending officers down to the floor, at first thinking they were being shot at.

Gatherers panicked in flight.

As they approached the RV, it was obvious Lena was nowhere in sight.

"They fucking shot him? Why?" Watanabe took the walkie-talkie from his lips, turning to Powell.

Powell grabbed the device. "Who the hell authorized that? What part of *taken alive* didn't your bozos understand?"

A fuzzy response with the officer's excuse was met by rolling eyes. Watanabe paced. Powell chucked the walkie-talkie. They'd head into the basin once things simmered down, needing to get a visual on their dead man for the report. Eighteen months of hard work and now their whole case was kaput. Reality sunk in. They leered at pandemonium in the field, emotionless.

Watanabe: "You hungry?"

"Starved."

"The wife packed me an extra sandwich."

"What kind?"

"Baloney, I think."

"On rye?"

"Like always."

"Well, what the hell are we standing here for then?"

They veered back to their surveillance van, chests out, chins high.

31.

As smoke cleared, Lena took inventory of her surroundings. There were several bodies on the ground, some writhing in agony, others still as stones. Rayna was no longer where she'd seen her before. She rushed toward the stage anyway, hoping to find Perry. Troopers shouted orders to each other; fireworks pounded. As she reached the first flatbed, a golden aura from within the stage's container commanded her attention. She squinted for clarity. Her chest heaved.

Could it be?

Struggling, she climbed onto the stage to confirm her disbelief.

How *could* this be?

She rushed toward the light but was tackled by two riot policemen. Her eyes did not waver, fixated on the girl seated on a sordid throne. Cops tried to contain her wiggling. A fire within helped her squirm loose, only to be tackled again by a third officer. Through screams and tears she called out to her baby girl, shoulder blade torqued for the clamping of a handcuff. She reached with an unshackled arm for her child, the shimmering dress—the end to their suffering.

An answer to all her...

But every cry went ignored, met by Tess' frozen stare, an empty vessel, devoid of humanity—lost to the gods.

32.

So, this was the end of days?

The girl adjusted on her throne, taking in the spectacle—a cacophony of torment and anguish. Mother and Father had said this would be her calling, a beacon to Babylon, Hand of Glory—Savior to the crestfallen. Lost souls rampaged the land, all being held down instead of ascending gloriously. Another round of mortars went off, sending sparkles among the trees. Her ears were ringing, deafened by every colossal *boom* echoing through the container.

She was alone now.

Mother and Father had been called home.

The ceremony must be nearing completion.

Bonfires raged as bodies continued to clash. Black archangels had stormed the field, capturing the last of a fallen legion by leveling weaponry. As promised, the girl began to recite her homily before this disposal of the wretched.

"Bestow thy blessings...of your infinite sins...unto me—"

A gnarled hand slapped the stage, then another, stifling the girl's oration. A woman pulled herself up as if crawling out a crypt. The girl gazed in wonder as the woman was trampled by archangels, her familiar face contorting in rage, beads bombing her cheekbones.

The poor soul was attempting to claw toward her.

The girl fixated on the soul's primal screams, yet she could not hear them (her eardrums filled with bells). Veins bulged up the soul's rosy neck and face: a boil about to burst. Never had the girl seen a being in such helpless agony. Then again, this realm was still so foreign.

But the screams.

Holy...

Mother never warned her about the dreadful screams.

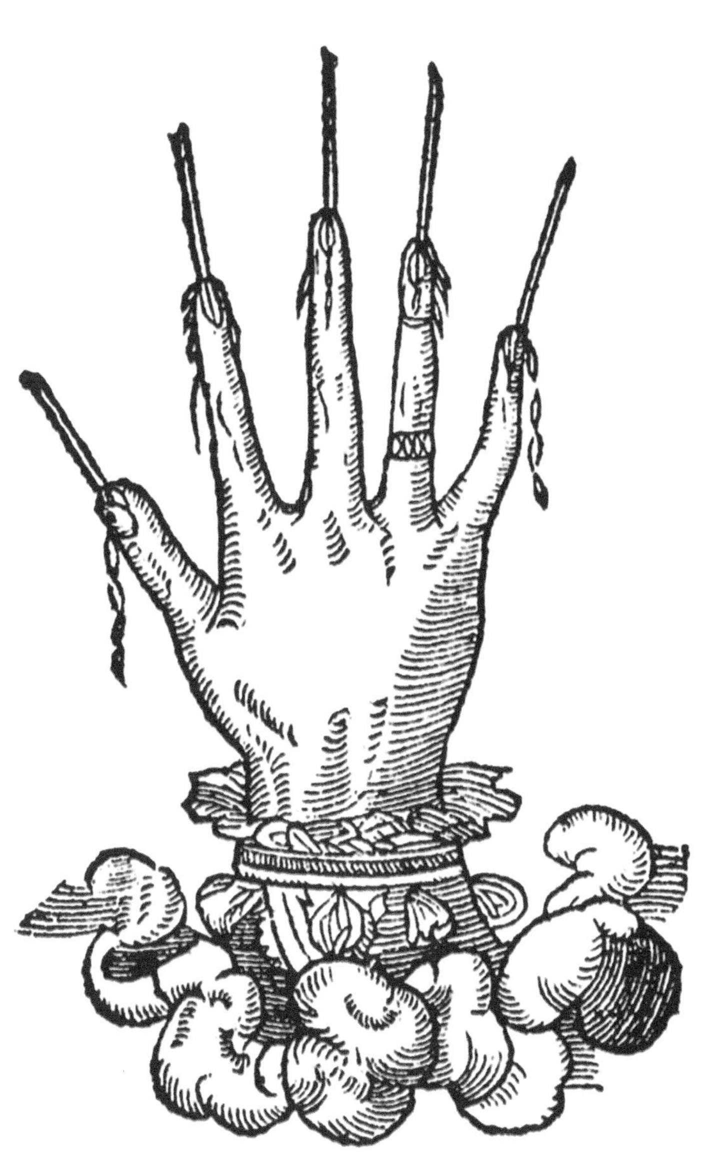

MONTHS LATER...

Perry lit his third smoke of the day, standing outside the 36 36 Club, taking in the morning sounds of Broadway surging to life. Long Beach had been fine without him, beach heads and burnouts holding the city up to its steady clip of easy living. He puffed through the heart of daybreak, watching a two-man film crew take exterior shots of the bar and its neighborhood. Life was a trip these days.

Dottie had beaten him into work again; her hair had changed from purple to mint. The regulars at their usual stools and familiar tunes out the juke helped ease him back home. At the pool tables, Clark, Ollie and Earl commiserated modernity; under the tube, Hildy and Mona nursed bloodys. Perry had been back for a while now, yet the whole journey with Lena felt like it ended yesterday. He climbed behind the bar, retrieved a dry towel and began his typical routine, dusting bottles, refilling olives.

Hildy tapped her glass. "'Nother go, Perr'."

He dumped the glass' contents and refilled ice. "How you over there, Mona?"

She blinked at dregs. "Still workin', hun."

He slid the bloody to Hildy. "Here you go, madam."

"Say, Perry, what are them boys filming out there again?"

"Episode of *Thin Air*. They're collecting B-roll—filler for the segment with my interview in a couple days."

A chipped tooth grin climbed Mona's face. "You excited to be on the TV again, Perr'?"

"Not after looking at myself in the mirror this mornin'."

Hildy: "Oh, hush. You've got a rugged masculinity—not many

folks can pull that off."

"That what you call it? Here, I thought I'd just pruned to hell."

The trio shared a chuckle.

Perry thought about what he'd say in the interview—what questions they'd ask. *Didn't matter.* The episode was about Tess and Lena after all. *One girl found, the other still lost in the breeze.* But that was a .500 batting average to be proud of.

The crew had him sit at a different spot on the *Bessie Mae*, not wanting to recreate the same marina shot as before, during Rochelle's episode. The sun blared, requiring the makeup guy to constantly step in and blot Perry's forehead between takes. This time he was speaking with a different "journalist"—a pretty blonde who looked like she still lived with her folks. She waited for an airplane to fly overhead before starting in again.

"At any time were you afraid for your life?"

"Well, the macho thing to say would be no. But that wouldn't be true. The way things unfolded—the madness of it all. Yeah. I was scared for my life more than once."

"Lena as well?"

"I can't speak for her and can't even fathom the experience she had compared to mine. We're all lucky to be alive—Lena, the luckiest of all, having been finally reunited with Tess."

"Have you spoken with her since that time?"

"Briefly, on the phone. She's doing well, considering. Her and Tess are up in the Bay Area getting specialized family treatment—psychiatric help for PTSD and other things. Needless to say, their situation is complicated, but I know, in each other's arms, they'll make it through this difficult time."

"Do you attribute any of the success in finding Tess Madadhi to the Federal Bureau of Investigation, specifically their probing into the criminal enterprise of Repo Helm by Agents Ken Watanabe and Bryson Powell?"

"No! And I seen their dumb faces all over the news and talk

shows. Can say with a hundred percent certainty that I've never seen the bastards in my goddamn life. If you ask me, they stepped in a pile of dog poo and claimed it to be roses." He jabbed a middle finger at the camera. "That's for them, if they're watching. You can blur that out, right?"

"It's not a problem. Now, what about your long-time friend and partner, Joe Delancey? How important was his contribution to the success in finding Tess?"

He cleared his throat, masking discomfort. "Without Joe up there on my daughter's case, we would've never gone into the Central Valley. To say he wasn't integral, or even worse, to paint him as some criminal like the local police have, would be a disservice to the man—a great man who held others' plight before his own. He was a..." He swallowed. "He *is* a hero. None of this would've come about without him."

The woman paused for Perry to collect himself.

"Are we almost done here, ma'am?"

"Just a few more questions."

He nodded. "Mind if I smoke?"

"Go right ahead."

He sparked a Red and leered at the marina, its calming sounds easing him back to focus.

She continued. "Will you be in attendance at the trial for Somerset Boyd, aka Trench?"

"I got a job here that I'd like to keep, so, no. They eventually nabbed her at the border with enough cash to build an army, am I right? With the harm she and her husband perpetrated on Tess, along with her trying to flee the country...That should be a case closed scenario. Mind you, I said, *should*. Ask me about what I think of our justice system, whenever you have a few hours to burn." He huffed.

"In that case, I'm sure you're satisfied with the deaths of Repo Helm and his accomplices?"

"Scum of the earth. I'd only be happier if it were me that pulled the trigger, but hey—you can't have it all in this life."

"I've heard rumors recently that Hollywood has come calling. Is there any truth to a movie about the events that took place in the works?"

"Don't know nothin' about that."

She flipped through a tablet with notes. "Um…have there been any new developments with your daughter's case…Rochelle Anne Quell?"

"I know her name, dammit!"

"Cut." She leaned over to him. "Sorry. It's just for the audience. We plan on tying Tess' episode in with a replay of Rochelle's on the same night. Viewers will be intrigued."

"Great."

"You look irritated. We can come back later, if you like."

He apologized for the outburst, wanting to continue, ready for this to all be over.

She made gestures to her crew. "We ready?"

Perry crushed his smoke in an ashtray.

"Perry, have there been any new leads in your daughter's case?"

"Not that I'm aware."

"Are you planning on another stint on the road to search for her? A lot of time has passed since her disappearance…"

He took a beat, pondering. "If there were to be a break that came—of course, I'd be out there in an instant. Right now, I'm in a good place. I feel her with me, I dunno how else to put it."

"Her spirit?"

"I didn't say that. There's hope—" He stumbled, realizing the words leaving him—almost as if Lena were speaking through him. "I still have hope for my daughter being alive."

"Before I let you go, there's one more thing we have for you. A letter." She handed it to him. "From Lena Madadhi."

The envelope had a Yorkie drawn by Tess. He opened it carefully.

"Would you mind reading it for us?"

He shook his head no, reflecting on Lena's pristine penmanship.

> *Dear Perry,*
> *Words cannot describe the joy in which I feel. A joy*
> *brought on by your courage and resiliency. Every*
> *night we pray for you...*

He wiped his eyes, folding the letter, unable to finish it before these strangers. He lit another smoke and asked permission to walk along the dock.

The woman obliged, ordering the crew to get a shot of him as he strolled.

He tranced on the water before bursting with emotion once the surge couldn't be contained.

The *Bessie Mae* motored out of port under the night sky, Perry standing tall at the wheel, crisp ocean air beating his clothes into submission. Harbor cruises had become his nightly routine nowadays. They weren't his idea at first either. They were Rayna's.

She came to Long Beach with him since she had no other place to go. Her days in that shabby back house were behind her. He moved every box filling the boat's hull into a dry storage used by the 36 36 Club. Most days, he'd get off work and she'd be grilling tilapia or snapper, monitoring a casserole in the tiny oven. There was an element of domesticity he hadn't been accustom since living in a house with his ex and Rochelle. They'd spend evenings cruising out past the breakwall, listening to seals sing, dropping in a few fishing lines over a sixer of suds. Color had returned to her face, and she put on a healthy ten pounds. He felt good helping get her on her feet. She warned him not to get used to her being around though. One night during supper, she'd said something witty, to which he replied, *Why don't we just...wait here for a little while...see what happens?* With her forced giggle and averting gaze, he knew. But her companionship, if only for a blink, was the perfect transition he needed in returning to the loneliness of being an old salty dog. The day she left, he gave her the keys to Dreamboat (with Lena's blessing) and his longest hug in years. She promised to be safe in her travels and to always keep in touch. She'd reached out to a friend from the Cali Gold who now lived in Albuquerque, working at a Wienerschnitzel. The girl's name was Devon. She gave Perry her new address. That was six weeks ago.

The nightly harbor cruises weren't exactly Rayna's idea—she'd thought of it only after he'd taken one with the other girl in his life these days: Becca. Needless to say, she was shattered when first learning of her father's grave condition. But after a few weeks, she was pieced back together once Joe pulled through. Strongest son of a bitch he ever knew. The cops were wrong about Joe trying to kill himself with fire and a bullet. Becca was certain. She was the last person to see him before the incident, vividly describing the night that a slender black man in wraparound sunglasses came to their defense, only to haul her father off into the streets. When Perry heard this, he knew exactly who the man was, although it turned out to be too late for X-man. Didn't help that Joe couldn't remember a damn thing either, these days engulfed in physical therapy, working on brain power, hearing and speech. His few burns suffered in the fire were the least of his maladies. But he'd eventually bounce back, his timetable set in years, a nice menacing scar about his jawbone forever broadcasting the story. Police took Perry's statement, but far as Becca knew, her father's case was still open.

They went out near Catalina Island during the first sail Perry had taken in years. Becca insisted on doing it at night, her dad being a night owl; Becca cradled Joe's frail arm the entire trip, careful of his comforts. Joe was gaunt and ghostly, a shell of what he once was—unable to hear most things or speak clearly. The long sail allowed Perry and Becca to become more acquainted. They exchanged lengthy tales of Joe's exploits—blackmailed politicians, outlaw biker brawls, double-crossed divorcees. Watching them laugh, Joe tried his hardest to grin. Although life these days was much slower for Joe Delancey, it was obvious to Perry that

Becca never held a breath of anger toward her dad's prior decisions; she said his actions were selfless, not selfish, and knew at a young age, after the passing of her mother, that she was smart enough to uphold the motel's day-to-day necessities. Now, she was grown and could add caring for her healing father to that list; the $150,000 stashed in his office helped ease the transition. After a few beers, she confided in Perry that her only wish was that she would've spoken to Joe more on their last phone call—to hear his voice reply when she thanked him for instilling his spirit into hers. That would have to wait a while longer, but the doctors held hope that it would happen. Perry promised her that it would too. In a strange way, he felt guilty for having heard this from Becca, words meant for his beloved friend, unable to hear them—words Perry could only dream he'd hear out of Rochelle one day.

But that's where he saw Rochelle: in his dreams, every night. Their happy place, away from the pain and longing that had been wedged between them.

A smile washed over his face as the sea became calm and quiet. He killed the engine to set sail. Hadn't planned on it, but now he was going to stay out here all night. Dottie would raise hell when he strolled in late, but that didn't matter. The night would be long and cold—but the stars were gold—and at dawn, he'd welcome hope into his bones once again.

ACKNOWLEDGMENTS

A novel's seed of thought only comes to blossom with the help of others to nurture it into a reality: I'd like to thank Down & Out Books for their continued confidence and support. My editor, Chris Rhatigan, who truly lifted this one into uncharted territory. JT Lindroos whose cover design nailed the vibe. To pals and early readers who provided motivation and inspiration along the way: Richard Lange, Jim Ruland, Greg Jay, Josh Pooley, CESL Buchanan, Faisal Kureshi, Mel Sanchez, Steve-O Brandon and Greg Mollin at Artifact Books. Special shoutouts to my Central Valley research offices: Clovis Book Barn, Rasputin Music and Tahoe Joe's (RIP). Home base, the LBC, a magical city for the imagination. To my parents, Bruce and Cindy, whose lofty education hopes for me materialized into this...Jigs and Trudy Jay, for always believing. Alicia Knight, the model of perseverance. My forever party crew: Jenny, Tallulah, Clyde and Studs. The three wise men: Dreamy, Ivan and Rod—great uncles who saw a kid in need of escape and provided endless comic books and monster movies; you are not forgotten. Finally, to Los Angeles: This smoggy heart beats for thee.

Photo Credit: Melinda Sanchez

NOLAN KNIGHT is the author of *The Neon Lights Are Veins* and *Beneath the Black Palms*, a fourth generation Angeleno and former staff writer for Los Angeles' Biggest Music Publication, the *L.A. Record*. His short fiction has been featured in various publications including *Akashic Books*, *Thuglit*, *Crimespree Magazine*, *Shotgun Honey*, *Tough* and *Needle*. He lives in Long Beach.